With
Twice
the
Love,
*Dessie
Mei*

JUSTINA CHEN

# With Twice the Love, Dessie Mei

KATHERINE TEGEN BOOKS
An Imprint of HarperCollins Publishers

Katherine Tegen Books is an imprint of HarperCollins Publishers.

With Twice the Love, Dessie Mei
Copyright © 2024 by Justina Chen
All rights reserved. Printed in the United States of America.
No part of this book may be used or reproduced in any manner whatsoever without written permission except in the case of brief quotations embodied in critical articles and reviews. For information address HarperCollins Children's Books, a division of HarperCollins Publishers, 195 Broadway, New York, NY 10007.
www.harpercollinschildrens.com

Library of Congress Control Number: 2023943321
ISBN 978-0-06-330652-3

Typography by Kathy H. Lam
24 25 26 27 28  LBC  5 4 3 2 1
First Edition

For Alex and Zoe,
my heart is your forever home

# Chapter 1

**My whole entire family has been lying to me.**

*This is your forever home*, my parents told two-year-old me when they brought me home from Hunan.

*We'll always protect you*, my big brother Jacob vowed as he carried me inside, me clinging to my baby blanket from the orphanage.

*We're not going anywhere*, my other big brother Ben promised as he bounced a stuffed baby bunny into my arms. And I smiled my first real smile.

That is the story my family tells me.

And I, Dessie Mei Breedlove, believed every single one of them and their promises, since we Breedloves keep our word.

Or so I thought.

Because with no warning—no warning at all—my parents yanked me from our forever home and moved us five hours away. Five hours away from my best friend since our Mommy-and-Me gym class. Five hours away from my two big brothers who are identical twins.

Gramps was a twin, too, but he always said that he and Grammy were the most important kind of twins: twin magnets. They found each other and never let go. That's what makes all of us so scared. After Gramps died last year, Grammy's memories started letting go. Fast. Like life was not worth remembering without Gramps. So we broke up our forever family: over the weekend, Mom, Dad, and I moved to Seattle to take care of Grammy while my brothers got to stay home to finish their senior year.

And me? I get to start sixth grade for a second time.

In a new middle school.

In the middle of the year.

It's January. By now, everyone has a friend group. By now, everyone has a best friend.

On my way to Grammy's kitchen, Owen, our black-haired, floppy-eared puppy, leaps on me: *Hello. Furry friend reporting for duty.* I stumble. Owen wags his tail, proud of himself.

Owen is a rejected service dog for good reason.

I kiss his little heart-shaped nose. And I report for duty, too: *Hello. Here to help Grammy remember.* I call out, "Good morning, Grammy!"

Even though we've been here since New Year's Eve, it is still shocking to see Grammy shrunken birdlike at the kitchen table. What's more shocking is how Grammy cocks her head like Owen when I ask our puppy to retrieve the ball and he flops down instead.

She doesn't remember me.

Grammy hasn't remembered me once in the last three

days. My heart starts beating in double time. I need Grammy to remember so she can move back home with us to our town that doesn't have many services for people with memory problems. Since that doesn't seem like it is happening anytime in the next couple of days, I need Grammy to share every last one of her many friend-making tips so I know how to make new friends in my new school.

With Owen busily crunching his kibble, I grab two mason jars of overnight oats from the fridge and set one gently down in front of Grammy, the other in front of me.

"Just the way you taught me: extra syrup means extra love, right?" I tell her with a huge smile. *Remember me, Grammy. Remember me now.*

Grammy just blinks.

She blinks like she doesn't even recognize herself as my grammy who makes friends with everyone, even the cranky post office lady who scares Dad. I don't even recognize Grammy, not in her baggy sweats. Her baggy gray sweats. Grammy used to greet every single day dressed like an exotic bird in paradise: jungle greens and juicy oranges. Scarlet reds and plummy purples. She never noticed, or cared, if Dad would blush and Mom would grimace and The Twins would walk approximately fifty feet behind whenever we went out with her and her clashing clothes in public.

I didn't care either. It meant more Grammy time for me.

I dump a big scoop of blueberries into her mason jar, which is not at all how Grammy taught me to make our favorite overnight oats. But blueberries, according to Mom,

3

help boost memory. I nibble my own overnight oats without blueberries because the last thing I want to remember is that I am starting a new school in thirty minutes.

Too soon, Mom stops me at the front door and fingers my loud scarf. She asks with a frown, "You sure you want to wear this?"

Of course I'm sure. I tighten my good-luck Grammy scarf, woven just for me. I tighten it again when Dad and I are in the car, idling in front of Marian Anderson Middle School, which is at least five times as big and ten times as grim as the building I shared with my brothers back home: their high school on the top floor, my middle school on the bottom.

Dad isn't turning off the ignition. He's not even looking at my new prison-turned–middle school. Instead, his head is bobbing in time to music only he can hear. He is a composer, mostly for video games. He says there's music in everything, even the harshest rainstorms, if you only listen. Maybe he's right. This morning, the rain sounds like a furious troll, drumming away on the roof. And bashing away in my gut.

"Dad," I say loudly.

I hate being late. The only thing worse than being the new kid at school is being the late kid at a new school where everyone stares as you walk in by yourself.

"Sorry, kiddo," Dad says, distracted. Then he grins his lopsided grin. "I'll go in with you."

What I want is for Jacob and Ben to go in with me. And Grammy to have her memory back. And all of us to be together in our forever home.

But I tell Dad okay, fine, he can come in with me if and only if he doesn't take a single picture. Not one. In three seconds flat, the rain soaks us. Even though I'm not late, everyone stares at me. And I stare at Dad because he just can't help himself. He snaps a photo of sopping wet me and does not notice the bunch of boys who walk past us calling out, "Hey, Donna!"

Donna? Why would they call me Donna?

"I promise you, you're going to make a ton of new friends," Dad says, now filming me like he is the official documentary filmmaker of my new life.

The problem is, I do not believe in promises, not anymore. Not when the soundtrack of my new life is a mournful dirge. Not when a redheaded boy with an explosion of freckles skids to a cartoon stop in his chunky skateboard sneakers. His eyes widen at me with astonishment. Or horror. Maybe both. He jerks back like a venomous snake is coiled around my neck instead of a handmade scarf.

"Hey, Donna, what are you wearing?" he demands like he knows me.

"Excuse me?" I ask.

What's with the Donna name-calling at this school? The soundtrack of my new life turns to a creepy track when that Donna-calling bully follows me into my classroom. I straighten my good-luck scarf. Before the door can close, he stares at someone in the class, then back at me, and stumbles like he's been punched. Hard. Unfortunately, he recovers fast, pointing at me and bellowing, "Hey, everyone, look! Donna Two Point Oh."

Hang on, is being called Donna an insult at Marian Anderson Middle School? An insult for the fashion-forward?

From the corner of my eye, I see a girl with shiny black hair in the front row. Unlike me, she is dressed in safe and sedate navy blue. She demands, exasperated, "What now, Max?"

"Look, it's your twin!" Max crows.

I hate it when people think all Asians look alike. We do not. Back in Chewuch, I was always the only Asian in my class. So this is the very first time this look-it's-your-twin "joke" has been aimed at me.

Since no one here seems like they're going to handle this bully, I do it myself.

"Hello," I say, hands on my hips, glaring at Max. "Just because we are Asian does not mean we are identical."

"Oh yeah?" Max says, grinning, as he jerks his head toward this Donna.

I prepare to blast him in round two. But then: I do a double take.

And another.

Because. The black-haired girl in the front row looks exactly like me.

# Chapter 2

This Donna girl and I don't look same-ish the way Ben and Jacob have the same-ish dirty-blond hair as Mom. And the same-ish lopsided smiles as Dad. This Donna girl and I look exactly alike, the way my twin brothers look exactly alike, right down to their same exact cowlick that curves a question mark over their same exact foreheads. She and I share the same exact high cheekbones and the same exact pointy chin. The same unruly wave poofs our black hair—or would, if mine weren't so soaked by the rain. We even have the same thick eyebrows hanging like storm clouds over the same stunned brown eyes.

Max looks back and forth at us like Donna and I are on display at the Woodland Park Zoo.

We are not.

Donna's mouth opens, then shuts, like she wants to snap something back at Max but can't.

Even though it is true and shocking that Donna and I look

alike, some things must be said and some records must be set straight.

A couple of weeks before (my first) middle school began, Mom called a Family Meeting. She was worried because back in Chewuch, there is no one who looks even somewhat same-ish as me except for a couple of tourists. All summer, our little town swells with tourists because our Main Street is straight out of the Wild West with its Wild West Saloon and Olde Fashioned Ice Cream Shoppe. Even more tourists flock to us in the winter when our Wild West turns into a wonderland of cross-country skiing.

So Mom had warned me, *Middle school is hell, especially for anyone who might be even a little different.* Ben had promised, *If anyone gives you a hard time, we'll take care of it.* And Jacob had instructed: *Do not let anyone bully you.* But Dad just grinned his lopsided grin and shook his moppy hair and said, *Middle school is the best! Plus, you grew up with two big brothers. You can handle anything.*

So I do.

"What," I say, looking straight at this Max guy, "are you twins with everyone who has red hair?"

"No," Max protests, blushing.

"Are you twins with everyone who has freckles?" I demand.

Max shakes his head wordlessly.

That taken care of, I say, "Exactly."

We grin at each other, Donna and me, and I notice that her desk is labeled with her full name: Donna Lee.

I repeat that name in my head. Donna Lee.

Donna Lee and Dessie Mei. Not exactly the same ring as Dessie and Sophie, my best friend since we were two. But Dessie and Donna sound like we could maybe, possibly fit together. Like we could maybe, possibly be friends, and not just because we look so much alike. Which I have to admit is highly weird. A little disturbing. And a lot embarrassing, because it is impossible to miss how everyone is staring at us. Staring and whispering: Donna Two Point Oh!

Thank you, Max.

Still. It is mysterious, us looking the same. How is this even possible? I side-glance at Donna. She side-glances at me. At the exact same time, we both tuck our hair behind our ears.

Since I'm not sure where to sit and our teacher is nowhere in sight, I stand awkwardly in the front close to Donna's desk. She whispers to me, "I always wanted to say that to Max."

Before I can answer, our social studies teacher, Mr. Guevara, saunters into the classroom. He is skinny with a scraggly, dark-brown beard that mostly covers his splotchy skin. The one empty desk at the back of the room is next to Max. Tragically, that is exactly where Mr. Guevara seats me. I speed-walk to my chair and plonk down, my eyes focused not on that bully, Max, but on Mr. Guevara, who perches on a metal stool like he's about to serenade us with an acoustic guitar. I'm almost surprised when he doesn't. With his cool musician vibe, Mr. Guevara would fit right in with my family's jam sessions.

"Everybody, let's give a warm Marian Anderson Middle School welcome to our newest sixth grader," Mr. Guevara booms, his voice bullfrog deep. He springs to his feet and drums his hands on his stool. To my horror, everyone starts drumming on their desks. Then Mr. Guevara does a double take, blinking at Donna, then me, then back at Donna.

*Please do not say anything, Mr. Guevara*, I plead in my head. I slide an anxious look at Donna and catch her sliding an anxious look over her shoulder at me. Even one little innocent comment will relaunch Max's snarking and everyone's staring.

At last, Mr. Guevara finishes his drum roll with an elaborate flourish that would impress my brothers, then flings one reddened hand toward me like he is the host of a Middle School from Hell game show, and thunders, "I present Dessie Mei Breedlove!" With that, Mr. Guevara thankfully returns to being a regular teacher and asks in a normal voice, "So, class, who's ready for our winter project?"

No one answers. Mr. Guevara clasps his hands to his chest like our silence is a dagger piercing him straight through the heart before he collapses against the whiteboard. Donna and I half smile in relief at each other before she faces the front.

"Class," our teacher tries again, his cheeks flushing pink with enthusiasm, "you better get excited. We are about to embark on the greatest project of all time."

I perk up. It's hard not to when Mr. Guevara bobs his head in the exact same way that Dad does when a new measure takes shape in his head. Then bounces on his toes like he's Grammy at Darn Good Yarn, bouncing, bouncing, bouncing like she was having a deep conversation with all those hand-dyed skeins, even patting them reassuringly like they were fussy babies.

Possibly, like me.

When I was adopted at two, the orphanage gave my family a note with my name, my birth date, and one and only one sentence: she is a vexatious child.

*Vexatious*: someone who is frustrating.

Unfortunately, I have not frustrated Max speechless because he aims a conspiratorial look at the skinny blond boy behind him, jerks his chin at my scarf, and mutters, "My eyes are bleeding."

Encouraged, his sidekick cups his ear and mumbles, "Eh? What'd you say? It's so loud I can't hear you."

Both of them snort-laugh.

Oh, really? Well, that settles it. My scarf stays on even though the heat from my cheeks makes me feel like I am personally responsible for climate change.

Our teacher fakes a bugle call while he unlocks the door for our principal, Mrs. Banerjee. I only recognize her because Mom showed me the principal's photo, along with all my teachers, to prepare me for a "smooth entry" into my new sixth grade. She should have showed me a photo of Max, the bully of Marian Anderson Middle School instead.

Mr. Guevara waves to the black-and-white photo projected onto the whiteboard: a regal black-haired woman in front of the Lincoln Memorial. The same memorial I studied with Sophie for our fourth-grade group project back home. His voice is awed: "The late, great Marian Anderson."

"Marian Anderson? Like, for our school?" Max asks without raising his hand, as if classroom rules do not apply to him.

"The one and the same." Mrs. Banerjee beams like Max has found a cure for cancer. He has not. "Our school's new namesake that the board voted on over the summer." She calls on Max's sidekick, who is waving his hand. "Yes, Lucas?"

"What was wrong with our old name anyway?" Lucas straightens his faded purple sweatshirt with SHERIDAN printed across the front and does the guy chin-lift at Max. "Right?"

"Because General Sheridan starved Native Americans to remove them from their own land," the boy in front of me answers sharply, spearing Lucas with a cold glare you would not expect from such warm brown eyes. He straightens his bright purple sweatshirt with MARIAN ANDERSON MIDDLE SCHOOL CHOIR splashed across the back. "And because of our music program."

"That's correct, Norman," Mrs. Banerjee responds, her heels clicking as she strides back and forth in front of the class. "We chose Marian Anderson because one, she used her voice to make history, and two, our award-winning a cappella choir honors her legacy."

A video plays grainy footage on the screen before us, as an old-timey announcer says, "Genius draws no color line." And then there is Marian Anderson. Her lips part, and it is as if an angel has descended. Her deep voice soaks into every nook of our classroom and seeps into every cranny of my soul. Dad says that music can transport us, ripping us straight out of our bodies. I have only experienced that when I listen to A2Z, and no one else.

Until now.

My heart swells, and I am soaring and—

A snicker ruins the moment. I thud back to earth as Max snorts to Lucas, "I can sing better."

"Then let's hear it," I mutter.

Somehow, in that miraculous way that teachers cannot hear bullies yet can hear everybody else, Mr. Guevara asks me, "Donna, do you have something to say?" He shakes his head before correcting himself. "I mean, Dessie."

Blushing, I mutter no. Then glower at Max and his minion, Lucas.

"The teachers and I agreed," says Mrs. Banerjee with a benevolent smile like she is giving us a present. Instead, she is giving us a project. "You, the sixth-grade class, have the honor of creating our new school logo."

"But I can't draw!" protests the skinny girl sitting next to Donna. She flips her thick auburn braids over one shoulder, then the other.

"Not to worry, Jacqueline. A professional designer will finesse the winning concept," answers Mrs. Banerjee, "for us to use for years and years and years."

I will not be here at Marian Anderson Middle School for years and years and years. I won't even be here in Seattle for another few weeks, if I can help it. Still, I glance at Donna, and I break into another sweat because she truly looks like my almost-twin. But how? How is that even possible?

With a determined smile and an even more determined bounce, Mr. Guevara announces, "I'll be teaming up with your English and art teachers on our next unit: Make Our Mark." Bounce. "Who are you? Who are we as a community?" Bounce, bounce. "And what logo best exemplifies Marian Anderson Middle School?"

"In one month, everyone," says Mrs. Banerjee, throwing her arms wide, "students, parents, teachers, and staff will be invited to vote on the winning design."

Mr. Guevara adds a particularly enthusiastic bounce. "This week, if you can, interview your grandparents. Your parents, your uncles, your aunts. Hunt for the story of who you are and where you're from. I cannot wait to see what you find."

That made one of us. Interviewing Mom and Dad is no problem, but how am I going to interview Grammy, who has lost so many of her memories?

I glance over at Donna, but she is taking notes. Lots of notes. Max catches my eye and covers his notebook like I am dying to know what he's writing. I am not.

What I really want to know—what I'm going to find out—is this: Who is Donna Lee? And why do we look so much alike?

# Chapter 3

**Mission Inquisition will begin as soon as I figure out a way** to ask Donna if she's adopted. The thing is, whenever I go out with my parents—grocery shopping, Mom's piano gigs, Dad's gaming conventions—people always ask them, not me, "Is she adopted?" As if it's any of their business. Which it is not.

As if I can't speak English. Which I can.

It feels like every sixth grader at Marian Anderson Middle School is clustered around me and Donna at our lunch table. Even the older students in the cafeteria are gaping at us. The only person not looking at me is Akshaya, who must be Donna's best friend because they're wearing matching BFF necklaces.

"I have never before seen anyone render Max speechless," says Jacqueline, the girl with two long braids down her back.

"Or put him in his place," adds Norman, as he flips a page in his graphic novel while chomping on an apple.

"Big deal," sniffs Akshaya before leaning over the table to peer at Norman's book. "Hey, the movie is way better."

"Never," Norman says with another bite of his apple.

While Akshaya is occupied debating with Norman, Donna aims a meaningful look at me and mutters, "I need to go to the bathroom."

I jump to my feet. "Me too." As we hustle out of the cafeteria, I ask, "Render?"

"That's Jacqueline of the big words, Max and Lucas's number two target when they aren't teasing Norman who knows everything. And now, well, you and your scarf."

I snort. "Too bad for them, I happen to love my scarf."

"Well, it definitely makes you stand out."

A school bathroom that reeks of chemical cleaners and what Mom calls "adolescent bodily odors" is not the place where I want to have a heart-to-heart conversation with anyone, much less anyone who looks like my maybe-twin. Worse, as soon as I'm in the bathroom, I realize, I need to go. Urgently. But I don't want Donna to hear me using the toilet. She glances at me, and I glance at her, and we both start laughing as if we know we're both thinking the exact same thing.

Maybe we *are* twins.

We slip into our own bathroom stalls, leaving an empty one between us.

One of us tinkles, then the other. One toilet flushes, then the other. One door opens, then the other. Four identical us-es are crowded in this bathroom, the two of us in front of the sinks, the two in the mirror staring back at us.

"Quadruplets," Donna says, nodding at our reflection.

My eyes widen as I lather my hands with soap. "That's what I was thinking!"

There is no question: we look alike.

Hope rises, then clogs my throat. Ever since I can remember, I've wanted a twin. Twins run in my family so much that everyone jokes that Breedlove means *breed twins*. Gramps was a twin. Dad's sister, Aunt Cindy, had twins. And everyone calls my brothers The Twins. Being a twin means never being alone in the world.

"So where did you come from?" Donna asks, rinsing her hands.

"The middle of Washington."

Donna shakes her hands dry. "I mean, before that?"

I know what she means. Shaking my own hands dry, I say softly, "Before that, I was adopted from China."

Donna gasps and turns to face me. "No way. Me too."

"Hunan," I tell her.

Another gasp. Another no way, me too.

She tells me her birthday: "February fifth. At least that's what the note from my orphanage said."

I gasp. "No way. Mine too."

Our stunned eyes meet in the mirror. Donna shares the name of her orphanage, but I shrug. I don't know the name of mine.

"My Gotcha Day is April twenty-fifth. How about you?" I ask hopefully.

"Oh." Her nose scrunches like she's smelled something rotten. "You mean Adoption Day, right? Mine's May seventh."

Even if we don't have the same Gotcha Day, could it still be possible that we're related? That somehow we might be sisters? That we might possibly be sister-twins?

No way, I think.

*Maybe*, whispers a still, small voice inside me. I wish, I hope, it is true. My body is overheating the way it does when I get excited. I tear off my scarf, then my favorite sweatshirt that I may or may not have borrowed permanently from Jacob. Donna gasps, pointing at my concert T-shirt. "A2Z!"

"You know them?" I say, surprised because up until six months ago, practically no one had heard of my favorite band. Not until their breakout song, "I Like Alike."

"Um, yeah. They're the best band." She shrieks. "Ever!"

I shriek back, "Ever in the entire history of music!"

"Ever in the entire history of humankind!"

"Ever in the entire history of the galaxy!"

We beam at each other, me and my maybe-twin, speaking in double time the way my brothers do with each other. Speaking like we are completing each other's thoughts before we've even finished thinking them. Speaking like no one else on earth knows us better.

The bell rings, blaring loud to scare unsuspecting students. It is successful. I jump, startled, and Donna laughs because she jumped, too.

She asks, "Jump scares in movies: yes or no?"

"Jump scares in books!"

Donna nods knowingly like she has a special collection of jump-scare books and a storm-reading flashlight by her bed, too. So I ask her. Guess what? She does.

"No way!" I scream.

Soon we're back in the hallway, with throngs of kids buzzing to class, totally and completely unaware of the miracle unfolding at Marian Anderson Middle School. I dig my phone out of my back pocket, hidden under my A2Z T-shirt. Dad is right: there are moments that must be commemorated on camera. First days of school. First places in track meets. First meeting of your maybe-twin.

I say, "We have to take a selfie."

Donna looks frozen for a minute. "Phones are against the rules during school."

I shrug. "We'll be fast."

So she leans in to me and I lean in to her. At the exact same moment, our cheeks rest against each other like we've taken selfies together dozens of times. Hundreds of times. I'm raising the phone high above us when I hear Mr. Guevara, "That isn't what I think I see, is it?"

Like the good photographer my father trained me to be, I get my picture a second before I tuck my phone back in my pocket. "See what?" I ask Mr. Guevara innocently.

"Good answer," he says, half smiling at me, then Donna. Then back at me. I can read his expression easily: *Whoa, you two really do look alike.*

As soon as he moves on, I turn to Donna, grinning. Until I see her face. She is ashen. Like a ghost has jump-scared her. "My grandmother will kill me if she knows I got in trouble."

"Don't worry, we didn't get in trouble," I assure her. "Besides, like my family always says, Make trouble now and ask for forgiveness later."

"True," Donna says, even though she looks dubious. Then she mumbles so softly I can barely hear her, "But that's not what my family says."

# Chapter 4

Otherworldly chanting rumbles from our silver station wagon. So deep and loud, the sounds echo in my body and throb in my bones. Everyone standing in the parking circle stares at our station wagon like it is a UFO direct from Planet Strange: the teachers, eighth graders, Donna. Akshaya. Max.

"Mongolian throat singing," Dad explains loudly over the rhythmic chants the second I yank the passenger door open. "Isn't it magnificent?"

I slam the door shut. Just as fast, I unwrap my blanket-scarf that feels dank from sweat. People-staring-at-me sweat. I fan myself with relief and mutter as I slouch down in my seat, "I thought we were walking home today."

The official plan was, the first week of school, either Mom or Dad will walk me home. After that, I just need to text both of them the second I set off from school. Grammy's house is a quick eight-minute walk from Marian Anderson. Mom timed it over the weekend. Twice. She could do the route in five minutes flat at her race pace, but no one except possibly a sleek jaguar moves at Mom's race pace. Then again, my entire body is vibrating with so much energy, I could fly home today. I have a maybe-twin!

Dad casts me a faraway look. Obviously, he was running too late to walk because the creative muse has swept him away. It still is. His head bobs slowly. "Just imagine mixing Mongolian throat singing with Gregorian chanting for an epic battle scene in *The Eight Banners*."

It's not unusual for Dad to collaborate with musicians from around the world: hip-hop mixed with Shanghai jazz bands. Sabar drummers from Senegal mixed with K-pop. I've been waiting two whole years for Dad to do a collab with A2Z. Even without A2Z creating music for the next version of *The Eight Banners*, I can spend hours with my parents listening to the soundtracks of games, which The Twins do not understand: *What do you mean, you just want to listen to the music and not play the game?*

But not today. Today, I turn down the music.

"Dad," I say, and then repeat myself because he is now rapping a beat on the steering wheel to the video game that he's scoring in his head. I wave my hand in front of his face. "Dad. Let's go."

He blinks at me and returns to earth. Better yet, he returns to driving, and we finally pull out of the parking circle.

"Dad, someone in my class looks just like me and she was adopted from Hunan and we have the same birthday," I tell him, waiting for him to go into excited no-way mode, too.

But Dad is silent.

"Dad, Donna really looks like me."

Silence. As in, there is zero excited energy from the driver's seat.

"Dad," I repeat louder. "I mean, she looks exactly like me. Exactly."

Finally, Dad's eyes bore into mine, but he looks confused.

I ask the question that crackles with hope: "What's the name of my orphanage?"

Dad says a name, and even I, who do not speak more than one word of Mandarin—*ni hao*, hello—even I know that his pronunciation could not possibly be right. Not even close. But as I repeat the name in my head, spelling it out in my mind, I am pretty sure that it is the same as Donna's orphanage.

"Why?" Dad asks.

Uncomfortable, I fidget with my backpack embroidered with the winged logo from *The Eight Banners* and ask, "Is it possible that maybe Donna . . . Maybe we're twins?"

"Twins?" Dad laughs at that. Not meanly like Max and Lucas would, but like I'm three and adorable and have brought home my first preschool disciplinary note, chastising me: *We bite apples, not our friends*. Dad shakes his head with a small smile. "I don't think so."

I wail, "Why not?"

But I have evidence: the selfie I took of me and Donna. I wriggle my phone out of the front pocket of my backpack and hold the screen in Dad's face as soon as we reach a stop sign.

Dad's eyebrows lift sky-high. He admits, "Whoa. You guys do look alike."

"I know, right? So it could be true, right? Donna and I could be twins."

"Honey," he says slowly, nudging the phone away from his face, "I know it would be incredible to find a birth sister—"

I hear the silent, hope-destroying "but" and interrupt, "You mean, a twin sister! We're both born on the same day!"

"But," he says, the word separating us like a wall as he pulls onto our street, "don't get your hopes up too fast. The chances of that being true are minuscule." Then my jokester dad returns. He shoots me his toothy grin. "I mean, people think Ryan Reynolds and I are dead ringers for each other all the time."

No one thinks that.

I turn the music back up. The thunderous chanting drowns out every other possible denial Dad might have.

# Chapter 5

It is astonishing that Grammy can sleep through the wailing of Mom's cello practice, but she does. Woeful notes weep from upstairs. Stubborn notes blare inside me: no matter what Dad says, I have a maybe-twin! But everything goes silent in my head the moment I spy Grammy's half-eaten overnight oats still on the kitchen table. Not a single one of the memory-enhancing blueberries has been touched.

This is a problem. Grammy hasn't recognized me yet.

Owen woofs in baleful agreement: this is a major problem.

So even though I want to interrupt Mom's cello practice and tell her this is a real emergency because my maybe-twin is on the loose at my new school, I head straight to the kitchen with Owen at my heels.

Mom says that food helps people remember because our brains shelve our memories of taste with our memories of experiences. So, what if Dad and I make all of Grammy's favorite foods to help her remember? What if we begin with her famous Ranger cookies that she used to bake once a week for Gramps, starting when he passed her first date test: he listened to her. Gramps really listened.

Max and his sidekick, Lucas, failed the first impression test.

But Donna? Meeting her was the opposite of a first impression. It was like a part of me hadn't just recognized her. It reached for her, jumping up and down: *I found you! I finally found you!*

I drape my scarf over a kitchen chair and ask Dad, "Hey, can we make Ranger cookies for Grammy?"

Dad checks his watch and frowns slightly. "Now?"

"Remember what Grammy used to say about Ranger cookies." I swallow at my words: *used* to say.

Dad swallows hard, too. His voice is a little thick when he quotes, "The trick to surviving life is a freezer full of Ranger cookie dough."

I open the freezer. It is empty of Ranger cookie dough. I tell him, "Grammy needs to survive her memory loss, and I need to survive sixth grade." Plus, I need sustenance to figure out what Donna and I are to each other.

Without another word, Dad starts foraging for ingredients: coconut, oatmeal, flour. Perfect. I will get Grammy to remember, then we'll all move home. But before we leave, I will solve the Donna puzzle: Who is she?

Who are we?

While I collect the measuring cups and mixing bowls, Dad preheats the oven to the perfect cookie-baking temperature. I assemble his workstation (the dry ingredients) and mine (the wet ingredients), side by side. We are an excellent cookie-making team, me and Dad. Soon, we're mixing the batter, rounding the dough into balls, and placing them in narrow lines to freeze on one cookie sheet, reserving a few dough balls to bake now on another. We have a one-cookie-per-human-per-day rule, except for Ranger cookies. Even Mom, who is a big believer in healthy eating, makes an exception for Ranger cookies. So eight cookie dough balls slide into the oven, two per human.

I pour four glasses of milk and wait. Three, two, one.

The scent of fresh Ranger cookies calls to Grammy just as Dad and I hoped. She rouses from her new bedroom on the main floor that we moved her to first thing over the weekend so she wouldn't have to risk the stairs anymore. As soon as he hears Grammy's shuffle-step, Dad leaps out of his chair, where he's jotting notes in his idea journal, and guides Grammy safely past the living room, where Owen is battling the great skeletal beast that is her old, abandoned loom.

Mom stumbles into the kitchen with the same dazed look Dad wears whenever he emerges from a couple of hours of composing. Like they are startled that the real world with ovens and cookies and uneaten oatmeal even exists. She sniffs the air and guesses hopefully, "Ranger cookies?"

"Mom," I blurt out, "there's a girl in my class who looks exactly like me. Donna could be my twin!"

Mom looks as confused as Grammy. Dad shakes his head fast at me: *Not now.*

Even in the best of times, Mom is not one for surprises. I sigh loudly. *Fine.*

Sitting next to Grammy, who is nibbling her cookie with neat little mouse bites, Dad says to her, "Do you remember when I was five and I'd just eaten three Ranger cookies, and Pops airplaned me and I threw up into his mouth?"

Grammy does not. The hopeful expression on Dad's face fades.

He tries again. "Mom, do you remember when I was in fourth grade and watched *The Exorcist* at a friend's house, and I was too scared to close my eyes at night? So for a week, you gave me a Ranger cookie to eat in bed while you read to me until I fell asleep?"

Grammy does not. The hope on Dad's face withers.

I notice Mom doesn't jump in with a scandalized *You watched what when you were how old?* Not even: *You didn't brush your teeth before falling asleep?* Instead, she asks, "Helen, do you remember baking Ranger cookies for our wedding? Hundreds of them?"

Blank stare.

Dad aims sad-puppy-dog eyes at me, pleading me to join in the remember game, but as much as I want Grammy to remember, I am uncomfortable because I do not know what to say. It's like all my memories of Grammy before dementia have been packed away and stowed on a shelf too high for me to reach. When I stay quiet, Dad collects the guitar from the corner of the living room. Back at the kitchen table, he strums a few notes. Then he begins Pachelbel's *Canon in D*. It's the wedding song that played when Grammy and Gramps walked down the aisle at their wedding almost fifty years ago. The same song that played when Mom walked down the aisle with Gramps at her wedding, since her own father had died when she was my age. The same song Dad plays Mom on their anniversary every year.

I'm worried we're going to be crushed because Grammy's face remains blank as a stranger's, but then her green eyes sharpen like she's facing Gramps at the altar. Like there is no one else who matters.

"My Eddie was so handsome," she says dreamily. "And an imp. What an imp." And then Grammy grins straight at me and says, "Just like you."

My heart soars, and I grin back at Grammy. Grammy who remembers me.

Maybe it's the music and Ranger cookies working together that jiggled her memory. Dad shoots a triumphant look at me. I might not be able to help with music, but what other recipes might help Grammy? We are going to find out.

Grammy gazes at me like she has missed me as much as I have missed her. Ben and Jacob used to fake-complain that I was Gramps's and Grammy's favorite, even though our grandparents took each of them on a special trip, any-where they wanted to go in America, when they turned twelve. Then Gramps died and Grammy lost her memory. So there is no way that she and I will ever be able to do the

Grandparent Trip when I turn twelve in a few weeks. I know that. She won't even be able to teach me how to weave after promising me she would when I was old enough.

There is so much I want to share with Grammy now. To ask her. The way I used to when she wove, her shuttle moving back and forth, back and forth on the loom. Our conversation moving back and forth, back and forth between us. What comes out of my mouth isn't a question about Donna. Or about our family heritage for the Make Our Mark project. Instead, I find myself asking, "Grammy, what do you do about mean kids at school?"

Beside me, I can feel Mom and Dad startle. No one ever dared to bother me at my old school because of The Twins.

Grammy is quiet for so long, I'm afraid I've lost her again. It is a weird thing to lose someone who is sitting right in front of you.

Then Grammy says, "There are some mean people who are mean all the way through to their very core. But most of the time, mean people are hurt people who hurt other people."

"But how can you tell the difference? Between mean people and hurt people?" I ask, because nothing—and I mean nothing—about Max and his sidekick looks like they are hurting.

"You can always tell by the company people keep," Grammy answers. "By their friends. By who shows up for them."

How does Grammy know this? Before I can ask her,

Grammy glances around the kitchen with eyes that are wide and scared. Then Grammy, my Grammy, glares. Not at Mom. Not at Dad. But at me and my good-luck Grammy-made scarf hanging over my chair. "Why do you have that scarf? It's important, that scarf. Did you steal it? Did you?"

It makes me want to weep, this accusation. Just like that, Grammy is gone again before she has even had more than a few morsels of her memory cookie.

Mongolian throat singing vibrates in the kitchen. Suds fling everywhere from Dad's energetic cleaning. As he always says, *A clean kitchen is a clear mind, and a clear mind is a creative mind.* To which Mom always says, *Really? Then what happened to your studio?*

Neither are teasing each other now, as if Grammy and her outburst have drained our world of hope.

"Hey, did you say earlier that there are people in your class who look like you?" Mom asks over the chanting when she sees that I'm worried.

"Donna doesn't just look like me," I say, setting the table with vivid orange place mats. "She looks exactly like me."

Mom's eyebrows arch up. I can tell she thinks I'm exaggerating. She brushes the cookie crumbs off the kitchen table into her palm. "See? Another great reason why we moved to Seattle. For now."

Frustrated, I dash to the front door where I dumped my backpack and rummage for my phone with its photographic proof when I overhear Mom muttering to Dad, "I knew we should have put Dessie in one of those Chinese adoptee summer camps. She thinks everyone Asian looks like her!"

I do not.

I hold out my phone to Mom, who is tossing the salad, but she doesn't take it. She doesn't even glance at it.

"Mom, look," I tell her.

She does not. Instead, Mom sighs like I am vexing her. Like I am a vexatious child.

Dad urges Mom softly, "You have to look at the picture."

Mom waves the salad tongs. Spinach drops onto the floor. Owen sniffs and snubs the green leaf. "Honey, doppelgangers are everywhere. People always mistake you for Ryan Reynolds."

Trust me, they do not.

I shove my phone in her face, the screen open to the picture of Donna and me.

Mom blinks. Slowly, suspiciously, she reaches for the phone like it is an invasive species infesting her paradise. Her eyes narrow as she studies the picture up close, me and Donna, cheek to cheek. The same nose that tips up ever so slightly. The same black hair with a hint of curl.

"Okay, maybe you do look a little alike," Mom concedes, placing my phone face down on the counter, then scooping up the fallen spinach leaf from the floor like it is radioactive.

"A lot alike," I insist. "Identical twins alike."

She tosses the spinach into the sink. "What are the chances, though?"

What I want to do is play the "remember when" game with my parents. As in: Remember when you said you'd help me find my birth parents when and if I ever wanted? I am pretty sure if I were to play that "remember when" game with them, they would fail.

The Mongolian chanting swells in the kitchen. And in my heart. It is a fiery war hymn. Battle music for the brave. The perfect soundtrack for a girl who will go to the ends of an unfriendly earth to find her lost twin.

# Chapter 6

Twins separated at birth.

Even if Mom would hate what I'm about to do, I'm going to prove that my maybe-twin is a possibility. A real possibility. My fingertips hover over the keyboard, and I glance at the door of Grammy's old craft room that's become my bedroom for now. No quick click of Mom's joy-killing footsteps down the hall. So I press enter, and Google spits out a list of articles and videos about identical twins who were separated by adoption in South Korea, then reunited in America. I can hear Mom's doubt: *Yes, but that's South Korea.*

Another glance at the door. Still no sound of impending parental invasion.

*Twins separated at birth in China*, I type into the search bar.

This time, Google spews out over two million results. There's even a documentary about twin baby girls who were left in a cardboard box and the adoptive parents who meet each other.

I want to thunder downstairs and chant—Mongolian-throat-singing style—*See? See! See.*

I want to tell Mom: Donna and I could be twins!

My phone rings, and my heart flutters. Is it Donna? Are we having a twin moment where she can sense what I'm feeling? Instead, it is my big brother Ben. The filter over his face has turned him into an enormous bunny complete with big teeth and even bigger ears. I bust out laughing. Somehow, Ben always knows what I need.

"Hey, Double Trouble," Ben says, using his special nickname for me. My middle name, Mei, doubled in Mandarin means little sister: mei-mei. From that, I became Double Trouble, but just to him. "How was your second first day of school?"

Wait, Double Trouble! Me and Donna. Donna and me. A shiver of excitement shoots down my spine. See, we were meant to be twins.

"I met a girl who looks like me. I mean, exactly like me," I tell Ben, hoping that he'll believe me, unlike Mom and Dad. "Identical twins alike. We even know what each other is thinking!"

"Sorry to disappoint, but that whole twin mind-reading thing isn't actually real."

"How about feeling what your twin's feeling even when you're miles apart?" I ask.

"Nope."

Because I don't want my heart to be demolished with

disappointment, I shrug like none of that matters. I half laugh. "What are the chances of finding a twin anyway, right?"

"I don't know about that," Ben says, losing the bunny filter. He scratches the side of his nose. "Weirder things can happen. I mean, what were the chances of Dad sitting next to a new game designer in the airport after he missed his flight, and Dad being Dad, was humming to himself?"

"And the designer wanted his humming to be the theme song, and her game became *The Eight Banners*. Okay, weird," I say, and it is as if my flighty hope settles down on solid ground. I rest against the twin bed that Grammy has decorated to double as a couch: full of colorful throw pillows. Big pillows. Small pillows. Most woven by her or her friends. A couple embroidered with affirmations: *Make good trouble. Keep moving forward.*

Keep moving forward. So I tell him, "I've been googling about twins separated by adoption."

"And?" he asks.

"It happens! Like, a lot more than you'd think! And one set of lost twins found each other when they were just walking across the same college."

"See? Weird things happen all the time."

Keep moving forward, I tell myself after we hang up. I should read all the articles about lost-and-found twins, watch all the videos, but I'm too nervous. What if Mom's right and Donna and I aren't twins after all? A2Z to the rescue! I turn on my favorite song and dance until I'm calm enough to text Donna: I'm from the same orphanage!

I wait. And wait. And wait. Two entire A2Z songs play. Still no answer. What if Donna has thought about it and doesn't believe that we're maybe-twins? Worse, what if she doesn't care?

It is an extremely hard thing, not knowing.

Sighing, I grab my backpack off the rug, pull out my computer, and finally turn to my homework: Who is my family?

Well, that's the problem right there, isn't it? I want Donna to be my family. I need her to be my sister-twin so badly it aches. But needing doesn't make it true. And aching won't change Mom's mind. It hadn't when I begged her to let me stay behind with The Twins in our forever home.

One documentary will not be nearly enough to convince Mom, who still to this day questions doctors after one kept misdiagnosing her dad's tumor until it was too late. So I start a brand-new folder on my computer and label it: Secret Sisters. Half an hour of research later, I stumble on a study that estimates up to fifteen hundred twins have been separated by adoption in China alone. I'm so absorbed in everything I'm reading about long-lost twins that I almost don't hear my phone ping. And ping. And ping.

*DONNA:* No way.
*DONNA:* No way!
*DONNA:* NO WAY! Same orphanage!
*ME:* Is it possible?
*DONNA:* Oh my gosh I hope so.
*ME:* We are maybe-twins!

*DONNA:* Maybe Yes Twins!

*DONNA:* I googled. A ton of twins in China have been separated through adoption. It really does happen!

*ME:* I know! I googled too!

*DONNA:* My parents think it might be possible but not to get my hopes up.

*ME:* My parents think it's impossible and not to get my hopes up.

*DONNA:* Why are adults such downers?

What I don't tell Donna is that Mom seems less than excited that I have a maybe-twin. And that makes me feel terrible. Like maybe I'm being disloyal to Mom for wanting a maybe-twin. As if Donna knows what I'm thinking, she sends me another text.

*DONNA:* I've always wanted a twin.

*ME:* So much me too.

*ME:* Even better, a sister-twin.

*DONNA:* So much me too.

*ME:* Hey can you come over tomorrow?

*DONNA:* I'll check but I'm usually only allowed to hang out on weekends.

*ME:* Check!

*DONNA:* You know what's weird? I felt like I knew you.

*ME:* So much me too! We have to be twins!

*DONNA:* The together for always twins!

*ME:* The always and forever twins!

Always and forever, that sounds like a Breedlove promise. One that I intend to keep.

Before bedtime, I perch my peacock blue idea journal on my knees and huddle under my blanket-scarf, it is so cold. Journaling is too high pressure to keep up every day. So instead, mine is filled with notes and scraps of ideas: Recipes for Dad and me to cook and help Grammy remember. Stories to tell The Twins. Questions to ask Grammy. Comebacks to a certain freckle-faced someone with red hair. I play with the ends of my scarf, cackling to myself as I write, when my best friend FaceTimes me.

"Sophie!" I cry out. Even though it is very obvious, I ask, "Are you wearing eye shadow?"

Sophie's stubby eyelashes flap like a severely injured butterfly. "And miracle-lengthening, tear-proof mascara." She frames her colorful face with her hands. "Plus, breathless-pink blusher. And damage-red lipstick. What do you think?"

I think Sophie does not need anything to make her look more beautiful and I say so. "You look better without makeup."

Which is true. But that is not what Sophie wants to hear. Her cheeks flush and not because of her breathless-pink blusher. And definitely not because she is pleased with my compliment. Her damage-red lips press together like I have damaged her feelings. She says tightly, "This is what all the other girls are wearing now."

"Not here," I tell her.

"Wait," she says sharply. She leans so close to the camera, all I see are her eyelashes lumbering under the weight of her miracle-lengthening mascara. "Please tell me that you did not wear The Scarf."

I tug the scarf tighter around my shoulders. "I did."

"I grew up with The Scarf. My eyes are used to The Scarf. No one in your new school is used to The Scarf."

I think about Max and his sidekick snickering about my scarf. I hear their muffled chortle. Why, why, why did we have to move?

"It's so weird, but I think I actually miss The Scarf." Sophie's tear-proof mascara does not look so very tear-proof as her eyes well up. "Why did you have to move?"

"I know, right?" My answering wail is automatic, but a part of me, a secret part of me, is giddy that we have moved. Because: I have found Donna, my maybe-sister.

"I didn't think it'd be so hard to make new friends," Sophie sniffs.

"Ditto."

She sighs. "What happened?"

I sigh back at her and say one doomy word. "Max."

She says one doomy word back to me. "Boys."

We grin at each other even though I kind of, sort of wonder why I've only mentioned Max and not Lucas. Clearing my throat, I tell her, "They are the same everywhere."

"Is he cute at least?" she asks.

"Eww," I say, because Max and his many freckles are the opposite of cute. "So something else even weirder happened."

Her lips quirk up. "Weirder than me wearing makeup?"

"So weird it will blow your mind, it's that weird." I tell her about Donna, my maybe-twin. Then I share the selfie with her.

"No fair! I've always wanted a twin!" Sophie squeals.

"I know, right?"

All hints of her tears disappear as she dissects this almost-twin situation with me. Under all her makeup, Sophie sounds like the Sophie I know and love. We could be lying side by side, gazing up at the wide night sky. Me trying to convince her that A2Z is the best band ever.

A treacherous thought passes my mind: I didn't even have to convince Donna about A2Z. She knew it was true.

"There is only one way to find out for sure if she's your twin," Sophie says, pausing dramatically. "A DNA test."

I gasp and tell her, "Sophie, you are brilliant."

"Yes, I am."

A DNA test would end my wondering. But what if the results prove that Donna and I aren't secret twins after all? I hug the Keep Moving Forward pillow hard to my stomach. No matter what I find out, no matter how it'll make me feel, I need to know.

There's just one problem: getting my mom to say yes.

Even my idea journal stays blank on that.

# Chapter 7

For twelve long minutes. I shiver out in the rain after Dad deposited me safe at school. Being cold and wet for twelve long minutes is a small price to pay to turn secret sisters into not-so-secret twins. At last, Donna slips out of her mom's white minivan, and I race to her through the sheets of rain.

I shove my sopping hair out of my eyes and announce to Donna, "We need to take a DNA test."

"DNA test!" Donna gasps and shoves her hair out of her eyes. too. "That's brilliant! I'll have to ask my parents, though."

My backpack suddenly feels a hundred pounds heavier. Without even asking, I can predict what Mom will say: a hope-flattening no.

I trudge beside Donna to first period, where it is clear that Mr. Guevara is not having a good Wednesday morning. There is no bounce in his step. His bony shoulders droop in defeat. He looks like he's spent back-to-back days in my kitchen trying and failing to get Grammy to remember. Or Mom to approve a DNA test.

I look at Donna. *What is up with Mr. Guevara?* She shrugs. I shrug back.

See? No matter what Ben says about mind-reading being a myth, we could be twins with our wordless conversations, Donna and me.

I just need to prove it.

Our art teacher, Ms. Lauchengco, breezes into Mr. Guevara's classroom in an outfit so vivid, Grammy would have given her a standing ovation. She is engulfed in a chunky sweater and bright green baggy pants the same color as my long-lost baby blanket that mysteriously "vanished" when I was eight, got sick, and threw up all over it. The stack of coffee table books Ms. Lauchengco is carrying is almost as high as the stack on Norman's desk. Hers teeters dangerously. Right before it topples, Max leaps to his feet like he is a superhero.

He is not.

(Although it might have been a tiny bit impressive how quickly Max moved to save the books.)

I adjust my eye-popping scarf, daring Max to give me a single snarky look when he walks down our aisle back to his seat.

Instead, that Max says a single snarky word: "Ouch."

As if my scarf has attacked him.

Ms. Lauchengco brushes her thick black hair over her shoulders, making her gold bracelets tinkle. "Who's ready to Make Our Mark for Marian Anderson Middle School?"

No one responds.

Bent over his notebook, Max scribbles something. I lean toward him, and as if he can feel my curiosity, that boy actually blocks my view with his shoulder. What is he up to?

Mr. Guevara musters a semi-bounce and taps the whiteboard. "Who are you?" he asks limply. "Who wants to share their family heritage?"

The first person brave enough to answer is Norman. "My moms think we're originally from Ghana, with a little Japanese ancestry."

Ms. Lauchengco holds up a book, pointing to circular shapes, a few filled with flowers, others with leaves and trees. "Some Japanese families have a family crest—their mark—called a *kamon*."

"According to my family genealogists," says Jacqueline, flicking one braid over her shoulder, "I'm primarily Irish."

"Some Irish families have a coat of arms to symbolize their family." Ms. Lauchengco opens another book, tapping an illustration of a shield with a ribbon floating underneath it. "And if the family had an official war cry, they'd sometimes include it in that ribbon."

"A war cry? I wish I were Irish," mutters Lucas, as he picks a scab of dried oatmeal off his gold sweatshirt with SHERIDAN stampeding across the chest.

"I'm half Mexican, some Native American, and all-American," says Gabriel, who must be the tallest boy in sixth grade.

"Some Native Americans carve totem poles that include symbols of their family," says Ms. Lauchengco, showing us a

44

photograph of an intricately carved totem pole that towers like it is touching the sky.

"Scottish on my dad's side, Irish on my mom's side. I even have our clan tartan." Max places his hands behind his head and kicks his legs straight out. "And my DNA says so. Homework done."

Donna and I look at each other again: DNA test!

"That's right. Scottish families have their own tartans," explains Ms. Lauchengco, showing us a book with different plaids. "The colors themselves can have meanings. Green for forests, blue for rivers."

Just how many kids in this class know their genealogy? Or have taken a DNA test?

That snarky snickering Max turns to me and asks, "How about you?"

His echo, Lucas, repeats, "Yeah, how about you?"

I glower at Max before I answer, "My family calls themselves a mutt mix of German, English, and other."

"You're not German or English," Lucas scoffs. "You're Chinese."

Well, duh. But the funny thing is, unless I catch myself in a mirror, I sometimes forget that I'm the lone black-haired girl in a sea of tall, blond, lopsided-smiling Breedloves. What does it even mean to be Chinese? I don't have a clue, not that I would ever admit that out loud.

"She could be part Laotian, Bhutanese, Nepalese, or Mongolian for all you know," Norman says, glowering at Lucas. "And besides, what are you?"

"I'm part Neanderthal," says Lucas, who smirks at Max, and they both snort-laugh. Lucas makes what he must think is a caveman sound. "I took a DNA test."

It's like we speak a secret twin language, because Donna nods firmly at me. I nod firmly back. Without a single word, I know what I have just promised: yes to a DNA test.

No matter what we discover.

No matter if Mom says no.

# Chapter 8

**Approximately one million years later, the last bell rings,** and Donna and I are finally standing outside in the parking circle, waiting for her family to drive us to my home. Our original plan was for me to go to Donna's, but Mom immediately said no like the Lees were the ultimate in stranger-danger. But after approximately fifty hours of begging, she finally relented and said that Donna could come over, which is what the moms agreed to last night. Donna and I aren't saying anything, just catching each other's eye and grinning like we have a secret.

We do.

Twins, my heart trills. Twiiiins.

Akshaya keeps giving us the side-eye, and I watch as Donna tries to make her feel included, telling her, "I can't wait for our sleepover next weekend." It'd be simple to invite Akshaya over now, especially when she hints at it: "Next weekend seems so far away." But I need time alone with Donna. We have Project DNA to plan.

"Amah's here," Donna says, squaring her shoulders after she waves goodbye to Akshaya.

Amah? An enormous black SUV with tinted windows swerves into the school's circular driveway before I can ask her what she means by Amah. I half expect Secret Service agents to burst out. Instead, a tiny old woman with silver-and-black curls and chunky red glasses is perched on top of a tuffet in the driver's seat. A tiny old woman who looks like she could be Donna's birth grandmother. I'm a little shocked. Maybe even a lot. It never occurred to me that Donna would have been adopted into an Asian family. I can almost hear the tiniest little crack form between us, because I've sometimes wondered what it would have been like to grow up with my birth family. Or even an Asian one. And Donna actually knows.

"Hey, Amah! Thanks for picking us up. Mom said to remind you that Lewis is at choir practice," Donna says.

"Amah?" I whisper to Donna.

"It's Grandma in Taiwanese."

"Chinese?" I double-check, thinking maybe I've misheard.

"Taiwanese," Amah corrects from the driver's seat, as she fusses with the windshield wipers. Her tone is sharp like I've made a terrible error. "It's different."

Donna murmurs urgently to me as I settle into the back seat next to her, "Buckle up fast."

"Why?" I ask, confused, as I reach for my seat belt.

Instead of explaining, Donna frowns at me as if I'm moving too slowly. Much, much too slowly. She mutters, "Hurry."

In front of us, Amah finally nods, finally satisfied with the speed of the windshield wipers and gives a sharp intake as she eyes me in the rearview mirror. Then she swivels around to stare at me like she has seen a ghost. Or a snake. Or the ghost of a snake.

Amah mutters something, fast and musical, in a language I don't understand.

Donna responds in English, "I know! Exactly alike, right?"

That I understand. I chime, "Exactly alike!"

As if on cue, Donna and I both break into the chorus of my favorite A2Z song: *"Alike, so alike / So it's all right / It's all good, even if we're up to no good, us two."* Our voices gather power. *"Alike! So alike!"*

We shoot each other an astonished look—one that Amah echoes with her uplifted eyebrows—and our giggles turn into breathless laughter.

I feel strangely at home in this SUV with this girl I have known for exactly two days.

That at-home feeling vanishes the moment Amah roars—and I mean roars—out of the parking circle. It is as if her right foot has never been acquainted with the brake, because we are blazing down the street.

Donna leans over to me, pats me on my arm, and whispers, "Don't worry. Amah just likes to drive a little fast."

A little? Dad drives fast, but this is stealth aircraft fast. This is McClaren fast. (Dad worked on a racing game once. I know my cars.)

This is *professional race car driver who wants to set the world record on fire* fast.

"In another life, Amah would have been a race car driver," Donna continues, like she's overheard my thoughts again. Unlike me, Donna does not appear fazed by Amah's speed queen driving. But I notice that her eyes dart over to my seat belt like she's making sure it is tight and secure around me. It is. I have checked three times in the last five seconds.

Amah corners hard around a turn. The SUV feels like it is tilting. Is Amah challenging the laws of physics? Is she defying death? Luckily, it is the dead of winter and the windows are rolled all the way up, so I and my scarf do not go flying out the car. Even so, I cling to the edge of my seat.

I'm especially grateful when Donna spits out of nowhere, "That Max!"

I echo her. "Yeah, that Max! And that Lucas! What's up with them?"

"Lucas just does whatever Max does. But more." She rolls her eyes. Her voice lowers, and she confides, "Lucas's mom died last year."

That, right there, is my biggest fear: one of my parents dying. Worse, both of them dying in a plane crash or car accident together, leaving me alone. Abandoning me.

Donna's hand slides over to cover mine, and she squeezes tight like she knows exactly what I'm thinking. Like she will never let me go.

I force the words out of my tight throat. "What about Max? What's his story?"

"My mom and Max's mom work together," Donna answers.

Amah corrects her from the front, "They own an architecture business together."

"But it's not just a business together. We camp together with our dads." Donna groans. "Every single summer since we were two."

I groan with her. Then I dare to let go of the seat to mimic Max with his hands behind his head and his legs kicked out in front of him like he owns our classroom. Like he is the overlord of Marian Anderson Middle School and maybe even the entire world. "Homework done."

Donna snorts. "That Max is only so full of himself because—"

Whatever she was going to say stays in the privacy of Donna's head, because Amah is shaking her own head at Donna in the rearview mirror.

"Because he's a mansplainer," I continue, gaining speed. "He's a mansplainer-in-training. No, he's a mansplainer-in-action."

Now Amah doesn't just shake her head at Donna but she death-glares. It is the death-glare of my mother when she disapproves of something I am doing. Or saying. But what is with Amah's death glare?

I hoot. "No, he's Mr. Know-It-All One Point Oh, right?"

Donna is silent, staring down at her backpack by her feet. In that silence, I catch the end of a news report on the radio: an elderly woman has been punched in the face in the International District.

That has got to be why Amah is upset, this terrible news story.

So I sit up straight and listen.

Nobody has been arrested, the news story continues. Amah's little hands grip the steering wheel. She tells us in a tight voice, "You can't trust everybody. You always have to keep watch. Always." As if to demonstrate how, Amah stares at me in the rearview mirror like she is watching my every move.

# Chapter 9

**A high-pitched note shrieks from inside my for-now home.**
Amah stares uneasily at Grammy's house like it is haunted.
Chords crash, ominous. Menacing. It's just Mom working on
a new song for Dad, but Amah wraps her arms around Donna
as if we are approaching a den of serial killers. I half expect
Amah to return to her deathtrap car once I unlock the sunny
yellow front door and she sees for herself that this is a perfectly normal home. But they both follow me inside, pausing
in the entry to kick off their shoes.

Amah's eyes drop to the dingy sneakers still on my feet.
She frowns slightly at me. "Where's your mommy?"

Like a police siren, two and only two notes screech from
upstairs, then stop. Screech, then stop. Perhaps this is not
exactly a perfectly normal home. I nod my chin to the stairs.
"She's busy practicing."

Rule number one in the House of Breedlove: no interrupting Mom when she is practicing, not unless someone
is bleeding. Even then, it better be a blood-gusher. So the

three of us stand there in the entry, me in my worn sneakers, Donna and her grandmother in their ankle socks. They gaze around, and it's as if I see our home clearly for the first time.

Grammy's home is what happens when a rainbow and a tornado fall in love and have a baby: color splotches everything. Hot-pink curtains lined with orange pom-poms edge the windows. On the scuffed dark wood floor, the watermelon rug lights up the space with its cheery reds, blushing pinks, and bright greens. Every piece of Grammy's hodgepodge furniture is draped with bold blankets—traffic-cone orange with cobalt blue, eggplant purple with tropical teal—all woven by her. Stationed at the front window is an enormous loom with her last, half-finished tapestry still lashed onto it. None of us know how to complete it, and not one of us has the heart to cut it off. Owen bounds over, barking in excitement before he circles back to do battle on our behalf with the big bad loom.

"Your mommy weaves?" Amah asks, studying the loom.

"No, my grandmother," I answer.

"Oh, she lives with you, too?" Amah asks with an approving smile.

"Well, until she needs an assisted living home." I shrug.

Amah's smile contracts into a frown. Maybe it's the clutter. I know that's what bothers Mom: *I can't breathe with all this stuff around!*

Over Owen's warning growls at the loom, I want to assure Donna and Amah that back in our forever home, everything has a place and there's a place for everything. Mom has her own proper music studio in our backyard. It is tiny and soundproofed, big enough for her cello and grand piano and a sedate beige armchair where she studies her sheet music. When I was little, I'd claim that cozy chair as my own while I listened to her practice and doodled ideas for Grammy. "You have excellent color sense," Grammy would always tell me, and she would always ask, "What should I weave next?"

I wish I could show Donna our real home.

I wish I could introduce her to my real grandmother.

A tiny part of me is relieved that Grammy hasn't emerged from her bedroom, because I am not sure which Grammy will show up: the Grammy who remembers me or the Grammy who scowls at me.

Amah inhales deeply and says, "What did your mommy cook?"

I sniff. Sourdough. "Dad's been baking." Which means he had a creative block that baking did not solve. Because: he's not here. Which means Dad must be on a mind-clearing run to woo the creative muse back to him.

With a tiny sigh, Amah glances at her watch and tells Donna that she'll be back in two hours. After Amah leaves, I take Donna on a tour, starting downstairs in the basement that houses Dad's temporary music studio along with his favorite instruments: sitars from India and erhus from China and guitars from Argentina on the back wall. A drum kit in the corner. A viola and a couple of violins, all safe in their cases. Black music stands spring up like a night garden. A bookcase is crammed with sheet music. On the wall, a huge screen, not for us to watch TV, but for Dad to watch a video game while he scores the music to the action.

"What do you play?" Donna asks me.

"A little piano." I grimace. "But not well."

"Me too!"

We beam at each other, and even in our silence, we continue our double-time conversation:

*We're so alike!*

*So alike, we have to be twins!*

Donna gestures at all the instruments surrounding us. "But if I could choose, I'd play guitar instead."

"I tried the guitar!" I waggle my fingers. "But these don't work on the strings."

"You're so lucky you got to choose," says Donna with a heavy sigh, gazing at Dad's fleet of instruments. "I have to play the piano."

"My brothers are the lucky ones!" I tell her with a dramatic groan. "They inherited our parents' musical skills."

*Inherited*. That word doesn't sit between us. It bridges us because our silent conversation continues with a shared look as if Donna knows exactly how I have sometimes felt. Like she was right there with me, after one of my not-so-stellar piano recitals when someone commented that I didn't play like a Breedlove. Mom's eyes had narrowed, and she said so fiercely it echoed in the performance hall, "Well, I married into the Breedloves, and if I play like a Breedlove so does my entire family." Yet sometimes—not often, but sometimes—it is painfully obvious that while I am a Breedlove, I do not have all the Breedlove qualities, including inherited musical ones.

Donna sighs. I sigh back.

I had no idea how much I have wanted to be understood, all of me. Even, and maybe especially, the non-Breedlove parts of me.

I clear my throat and continue, "So, Ben plays the drums and sax. Jacob, the viola. Mom, the piano and cello and some violin. And Dad plays basically everything."

"Everything?" Donna asks, her eyes widening.

"Everything. He can pick up almost any instrument and play it. Like that." I point at the didgeridoo, a long instrument from the Aboriginal people in Australia. "We go on sound safaris—"

"On what?"

"Sound safaris to hear different music," I explain as I lead her back upstairs and down the wide hall covered on each side with family photos of Grammy and Gramps. Dad and his sister growing up. Then Dad with Mom. The Twins. And me. "Before I was born, they went to Australia and Dad literally sat down and played that. No one could believe it."

"Lucky, you have the coolest family," Donna says as she follows me into my bedroom that is still stuffed with Grammy's weaving supplies. "And the coolest home."

"Really?" I'm astonished because what's truly cool is the entire bedroom wall my parents let me paper over from floor to ceiling with posters of A2Z in my forever home. What's cool in my forever home is the linden tree with heart-shaped leaves that juts out of the center courtyard like it is sheltering us. But here, I'm not allowed to repaint a single inch since we are prepping the home to sell for Grammy. Here, I am surrounded by a closet crammed with every possible color of yarn, Gramps's oil paintings of creepy old barns, and ancient posters framed in black.

Those handwritten posters captivate Donna. She stands in front of one: Do Not Be Silent. "What are all these?"

I shrug, then clear off a couple throw pillows from my bed. "Grammy's stuff. I don't know."

Donna breathes in deeply. "Your home smells so good."

"Food is my dad's love language," I tell her.

Donna grins. "Well, yeah, food is an Asian love language, right?"

I didn't know that, but I nod like I do. What I do know is that Dad says the Italian in him from Grammy's side believes that food is love. Whenever he says that, Mom looks at him like he's from a different planet. Food is fuel, she says. That's because all her meals are calibrated to make Mom a lean, mean music-making-and-marathon-running machine.

"I mean, the first thing my parents say to me in the morning is, Ja ban bae? Have you eaten rice yet? Like, that's the Taiwanese way of saying good morning to each other." Donna swallows hard like her throat is dry and looks at me expectantly. After a moment, she reaches down to her backpack, draws out her blue water bottle, and takes a sip. "It must be nice to have your dad's hobbies be baking and music."

I shake my head. "No, music is what they do, Mom and Dad. They make music for video games."

"Really? That's their job?" Donna looks confused.

"Yeah, Dad composed for *The Eight Banners*, and Mom played the theme song."

It's like Donna can't comprehend that. She blinks at the poster as if her eyes are dilated and everything is blurry. "Really?"

"Yeah, they're pursuing their passion. That's what I'm supposed to do, too."

"Not according to my parents." Donna delicately traces the letters on one poster, then another.

"Why not? It's your life."

Donna deepens her voice and says as if she has heard this a million times, "Donna, do you know how few dancers make it professionally? Do you know how little calligraphers make?"

"You do calligraphy?"

"Calligraphy is like dancing on paper! The loop de loops. The curlicues. I know it's totally weird, but I love calligraphy. It's okay, though. I'll keep dancing and lettering for fun. Just like my mom is an architect who does jewelry on the side."

"But why?" I ask. "Why does it have to be on the side?"

Donna cocks her head like this is the first time she's stopped to think about that. "Because," she says slowly, moving away from the wall of Grammy's posters, "my family says you have to be practical. Amah moved here from Taiwan with my grandfather, Agon, and nobody would rent them an apartment for the longest time. Like, nobody. Not even when the apartments had For Rent signs on them. And they didn't have friends or family to rely on either. But somehow, Agon still got his PhD and Amah worked as a tailor. And then when they finally retired and could rest, they moved all the way from Chicago to take care of me and my brother. And then Agon died before he could really have fun. So I kind of owe it to everyone to be practical, too."

If that were me, Dad would say, *Kiddo, you owe it to everyone to live your best life*. I ask, "Do you ever think about what life would have been like if you were adopted into a different family?"

"Or if we were adopted together?" Donna asks quietly.

Adopted together as twins.

The thought lodges in my throat. So does hope. And fear.

I swallow hard and drop to sit cross-legged on the floor. "Do you think your parents will let you take a DNA test?"

"I think so," Donna says, shrugging, as she slips down next to me on the rug, our backs against my bed. Our shoulders almost touch, we are sitting so close to each other. "They've always supported me on what Mom calls my adoptee journey."

That's what my parents said, too. Until Mom saw how similar Donna and I look. And then it was like she couldn't accept that I might have a family outside of ours.

"When do you think you'll ask them?" I run my fingers through the fuzzy carpet strands.

"Probably tonight. How about you?"

"Me too." My fist tightens on the shaggy rug. "Then we better be prepared." Unlike Donna, who doesn't look worried about talking to her parents, anxiety gurgles in my stomach. But information is power, Mom always says.

I grab my computer from my backpack and quickly google DNA tests. The first kind that pops up tests for everything: ancestry, potential medical problems, and relatives. It takes up to two whole months to get the full results.

"Two months! I can't wait two months!" Donna collapses on my bed. Then her eyes light up and she claps her hands together. "Hang on, can't we just test if we're sisters?" Even before she's finished asking the question, she's searching on her computer and says, "Ha! There are sibling tests." She scans the information. "The test can arrive overnight."

I read over her shoulder. "Each kit includes two tests."

She winds a strand of hair around her finger. "It's a hundred bucks."

"So fifty each," I say. "I have almost that much saved."

"And I can do extra chores."

"Results are ready in two days."

"Two days," she breathes.

We stare at each other wide-eyed. Forty-eight hours, and we could know for sure if we are sisters. Best of all, the fine print says that no parental consent is needed.

"It's too bad Gotcha Day is so far away. Then we could gotcha each other, too," I say, grinning.

"I actually don't celebrate Gotcha Day," Donna says, wrinkling her nose.

"What do you mean?" I ask. How could Donna not celebrate the day she was adopted? The day she left the orphanage?

Donna clutches a throw pillow to her stomach. "My parents and I talked with a couple of adults who've been adopted, too, and they said that they felt like Gotcha Day was disrespectful to our birth parents. For all we know, maybe our birth parents wanted to keep us but for some reason couldn't. Plus, we aren't puppies who've been adopted from a pound, right?" Her eyes slide uncertainly to me.

But I love my Gotcha Day, which my family has always celebrated. We always start the morning with pink-iced donuts and hot chocolate with extra whipped cream with pink sprinkles. For lunch, I always have my favorite ultra-gooey grilled cheese. If I'm at school, Dad makes a special delivery, fresh off the griddle. After a spaghetti dinner, I always get concert tickets from my parents, usually from some group Dad knows from work. I'd never once considered that anyone would not want to celebrate their Gotcha Day.

For the first time, silence stretches between us. It's as if all the moments that we do and do not celebrate divide us.

My stomach burbles with worry again. I change the subject fast, "Dogs or cats?"

As if Owen knows I'm voting for him, he bounds into my bedroom and leaps into Donna's lap like he recognizes her. Relieved, she laughs and cuddles him and says, "Dogs!"

"Me too!"

Donna asks, "Sweet or salty?"

"Both," I answer.

"Me too!"

We grin at each other. I could belt out the entire A2Z library of songs, I'm that grateful we're back in rhythm. How can Donna and I not be twins? Even Owen thinks so. He stretches over to lick my cheek, happy for us, too. I ask the biggest, most important question of all: "Favorite A2Z TikTok?"

Donna frowns. "I'm not allowed on TikTok." She brightens. "But my favorite song of all time is 'I Like Alike.'"

"Me too!" I leap off the bed. So does Donna. And Owen. Even if Donna's not allowed on the site, she knows all the dance moves. I play the music video. Giggling, we belt out the song and we dance every move. Owen gets in on the action, belting out a howl and wriggling his bottom. Wilder and wilder, we dance. Louder and louder, we sing as if we are making up for lost time.

Alike. So alike.

# Chapter 10

"Singing is a skill I need to a *choir*," Dad jokes from my doorway, pulling off his headphones. Sweat drips from his forehead and splotches his sweatshirt.

I groan and quit dancing. But it is the truth, especially when Dad croaks out the chorus. Singing is the only music that my dad cannot make, no matter how hard he tries, no matter how many lessons he takes: he wheezes tunelessly like a sick hippo.

"Make it stop," I plead. Then I get a whiff of him and gag. "Geez, Dad! You reek. Go take a shower." I cover my nose. "Like, now."

Donna looks at me, alarmed.

But Dad shrugs easily and says, "Yeah, I do smell. I smell good!" He actually steps into my bedroom, flapping his arms up and down.

Both Donna and I shriek and shrink away from Dad and his armpits of doom. I scream, "Dad, disgusting!"

Mom hovers outside my bedroom door, her eyes unfocused. She is wearing the I'm Still Practicing in My Head look that says her body may be here with us, but her spirit is in the realm of her piano.

"Is she okay?" Donna asks softly.

That's when Mom crash-lands on earth and stumbles into my for-now bedroom, her gaze planted on Donna. Mom's blue eyes widen like she cannot possibly believe what she is seeing, so astonished she's forgotten why she left her makeshift music studio upstairs: to tell me to keep it down while Grammy is resting. Finally, she gapes at Dad like she is drowning on land. He swivels in his running sneakers and steers her out of my room.

In the hall, I can hear Dad apologizing to Mom: "I completely forgot to tell you that she was coming over." Why can't Mom be thrilled that I've found my maybe-twin? At this point, I'd take her just accepting Donna, but she didn't even say hello to her. I make a quick excuse for Mom and tell Donna, "She's been practicing a new song."

"For *The Eight Banners*?" Donna's own eyes widen, mesmerized, when I nod

As Donna tells me that she's always wanted to play *The Eight Banners* since finding out it's based on her favorite Chinese myth about a weaver-fairy, I strain my ears to hear whatever my parents are saying, but all I make out is muttering, Mom stressing, Dad soothing.

If Donna thinks Mom's reaction is weird, she doesn't say

so. Instead, she glances at her phone, grimaces, and says, "I better do my homework before Amah gets here." She yanks her computer onto her lap like there is not a single moment to lose.

So I do the same.

Without looking at me, Donna asks uncertainly, "Do you always talk to your dad like that?"

"Like what?" I ask.

She nibbles on her lip, then changes the subject. "What does your last name mean?"

"I'm not sure," I say, but I can't help but think about Donna's first question. How did I talk to my dad? The way Ben and Jacob talk to him: normal.

Was there something wrong with that?

Donna sinks back against the wall of pillows on my bed and sighs, looking disgusted at her computer screen. "Did you know there are more than a hundred million people in the world with my last name?"

"Whoa," I say as I research my own last name on my computer. "What does Lee mean?"

"It says plum tree." Donna wrinkles her nose. "I don't even like plums. The skin is so sour."

"My dad makes a great plum tart. It would turn you into a plum believer."

"A plum believer." She looks skeptical but then sneaks a look at me. "If it's as good as his bread smells, then sign me up!"

"According to this, Breedlove might have been a nickname

for a popular person." I read from my screen. "Someone who could produce love."

"Popular! I bet you were popular at your old school."

Popular? Ben was popular because he played in a rock band that had gigs at all the parties. Jacob was popular because he could win almost every track event he's in. I'm not musical or athletic. "My old grade was too small to have anyone be popular."

"You'll be popular here just like Max."

I think of Max and how he snicker-scoffed at my Grammy-woven scarf. I hear Lucas's echoing snorts. If that's what it takes to be popular at Marian Anderson Middle School, count me out.

Too soon, the doorbell rings. Donna sighs. She collects her laptop and slides it into her backpack while grumbling, "Amah's always early. We're lucky she's only fifteen minutes early this time."

"But Mom hasn't played *The Eight Banners* for you yet," I protest.

Downstairs, I can hear Mom and Dad chatting with Amah. I slow down to eavesdrop at the same time Donna does.

Dad says, "It really is surprising how similar the girls look."

"The same," Amah corrects him. "They look the same. But how—"

Mom cuts in. "Well, the adoption agency never said anything about our Dessie having a sister. So this could just be pure coincidence. I read that we all have doppelgangers, a double who looks just like us."

I sigh. Enough with the doppelgangers. Mom must hear my frustrated sigh because she calls up to us, "Dessie, Donna's grandmother is here!"

When we join them, I notice Mom doesn't so much as even fake smile at Donna. She doesn't even look at her. I glare at Mom for ignoring her and catch Donna's Amah staring at me, her brow furrowed.

I wait for Donna to complain to her grandmother about being early, maybe even to glare at her, too, but she doesn't say anything except, "Amah! Thanks for picking me up!"

Amah notes the small keyboard in the living room and the black violin case next to it, and nods approvingly. "Dessie, you play."

"Um, not really," I answer, shaking my head.

"Oh." Amah tsks, disapproving.

"But Mom does," I say.

After some persuading, Mom sits down at the electronic keyboard, even though the music sounds better on the piano upstairs. She is perfectly still for one moment, and then her fingers parachute down to the keys.

The theme song from *The Eight Banners* swells, and every note transports me from this living room. From Grammy's home in Seattle. I am soaring in the cloud-kingdom with Peridot, the fairy who weaves spirit banners that grant their owners whatever they want. The theme song tells her ordeal—how humans trap her, forcing her to weave their wishes into reality. How she frees herself, time after time, slipping into the skies away from her captors. Always chasing hope. Always searching for her family.

And then: silence.

I blink and I'm back in the living room, my feet firm on the worn rug. Back to Donna, whose eyes sparkle like she's been dancing in her head. Back to Amah—Amah who looks luminous. Tears shine behind her oversized glasses. She whispers, "I feel like a little girl back in Taiwan."

Maybe Donna has it wrong. Maybe she can pursue her passion with her family's blessing. If only she would tell them what she wants.

Like a DNA test.

As if Donna knows what I'm thinking, she slides a look at me and nods firmly: tonight.

I nod back at her: tonight. We talk to our parents tonight.

Project Sister-Twin is on.

# Chapter 11

That night, for the first time since moving into Grammy's home, I am ready to help Mom and Dad with the Great Purge. In the next month, my parents will visit different assisted living homes, and we need to sort through all of Grammy's belongings: Throwing away what nobody will ever want. Giving away whatever we can. And keeping the most valuable mementos for Dad, his sister, The Twins, and me.

Tonight, we are tackling the basement storage, but I am tackling something much harder: figuring out a way to ask my parents to let me take the DNA test. Even if the website said "no parental consent needed," somehow it just doesn't feel right without their permission.

Owen refuses to set one paw in the storage closet. I do not blame him. In the long, spooky, cobwebby room are shelves and shelves (and shelves) of musty cardboard boxes and beat-up plastic bins, some neatly labeled: Christmas 1970– 1980. Kids' Ski Gear. Art Supplies. Others are mysteriously blank. Mom heaves a weary sigh as she eyes the rows of boxes on just one of the shelves we are clearing today. This does not bode well for Project Sister-Twin.

The Great Purge, as it turns out, is an extremely slow process because every item is a story. Or a question. Most of Dad's comments are versions of "Whoa! Did I ever tell you about the time . . . ?" And Mom's questions are "Huh, why would they have kept this?"

I do not have time for these stories and questions, not when it looks like it will take approximately five million years and an entire epoch to sort through everything in here. Especially not when all I want to do is confirm that Donna is my twin.

But Dad is on the hunt for anything that might remotely help Grammy remember. Especially pictures. Weeks before our move, we began assembling a photo album. Dad calls it "The Best Of" book—the best memories from Grammy's life collected into a single three-inch-thick memory book. Every night since we've been here, Dad sits next to Grammy and sets the album on his lap because the heavy album looks like it could crush her.

On top of a grimy shelf is a promising black portfolio. I lug it out to the sofas by Dad's computer setup. Inside the zippered portfolio are hand-lettered posters like the ones hanging up in my for-now bedroom.

## WE MARCH FOR FIRST-CLASS CITIZENSHIP NOW

## WE SHALL OVERCOME ONE DAY

And my personal favorite:

## MAKE SOME NOISE AND GET INTO GOOD TROUBLE

That is my kind of poster.

And my kind of opening for Project Sister-Twin.

"What are these?" I ask when Dad lumbers out of the storage with three medium-sized boxes.

"Those?" Dad frowns as he lowers the dusty boxes carefully to the ground. "Another piece of the Grammy puzzle I didn't know about. A couple of months ago, Aunt Cindy told me that your grandmother used to go on marches until her hip wore out. Early arthritis. So she had to stop marching when I was about five. I had no clue."

"I'm sorry, Dad," I say, and tap the top poster, its colors faded. "Is this why Grammy used to say, Make some noise? And Make trouble and ask forgiveness later?"

Dad looks stunned. "Yeah, maybe."

My hands twist together, I'm so nervous. But I tell myself, *Make some noise.* "That's why we want to do a DNA test, me and Donna. So we know about ourselves."

Mom rushes from the storage closet, her hair mussed, like she knows there's an idea for her to stamp out. "I don't know," she hedges, the way I knew she would.

"Mom," I start to huff, hands on my hips.

Dad blows dust off the top poster and gently cuts in, "It would be kind of cool if Dessie had a relative here."

A relative like a sister. A twin sister. I nod eagerly. "A DNA test would be an important piece of the Dessie Mei puzzle."

Dad half smiles at me. Mom does not. Instead, she asks, "Honey, how's it going at school, really?"

I flush. I know what Mom is asking: Who's the mean kid at school? Then she asks just that, "Who's the mean kid at school? Maybe I should talk to Mrs. Banerjee tomorrow."

"School's fine," I assure Mom and hold Dad's worried gaze. "Really."

That is the end of the DNA discussion. For now.

Even though I am still fuming at Mom, I try not to show it and ruin dinner because Dad is looking at Grammy so hopefully. So wistfully. The Great Purge must have revved up Dad's anxiety about getting Grammy to remember. So, at dinner, I try to help Dad and ask Grammy, "How did you meet Gramps?"

She looks up from her famous garlic mashed potatoes that Dad and I tried to replicate, but instead we have created failure mashed potatoes that are more clumpy than creamy.

"Gramps," I prompt.

"Eddie. How did you meet Eddie?" Dad clarifies. He glops another spoonful onto Grammy's uneaten mountain of chunky potatoes. *Eat and remember. Please, eat and remember.*

"Eddie!" Grammy gets a huge smile like she is reliving the moment. "In sixth grade."

Excuse me, sixth grade?

As in: my grade?

Mom and I meet each other's eyes while Dad waggles his eyebrows at me.

I cannot even imagine—no, I do not even want to imagine—meeting my future husband in my middle school either here or back home. Not when my grade is filled with boys like Max. Max, who slings his head back when he snickers and brays.

"We were meant to be." Grammy sighs like she is swooning. Grammy, swooning! "I don't think I could have fallen in love with Eddie more than at the march."

"What march?" I ask, leaning toward Grammy.

"Eddie is a Quaker, you know," she answers as if that explains everything.

I shake my head and look at Dad, who tells me in a low voice, "Quakers are Christians who played a huge role in abolishing slavery and demanding equal rights for women." Dad clasps Grammy's hand. "Mom. Which march made you fall in love with Eddie?"

Grammy continues like she hasn't heard Dad. "I thought, well, maybe I could show my support and march in back of everyone. And there he was, too, so tall and so skinny, he stood out." She chuckles. "We both did. Two peas in a marching pod."

It's hard to picture Gramps marching at a protest, not when the last memory I have of him is sickly skinny and stuck in bed. At the end, getting up to go to the bathroom for Gramps might as well have been a triathlon and climbing the stairs like scaling Mount Rainier. If it's hard to remember Gramps walking on his own, it's impossible to imagine Grammy shouting and carrying one of the signs in the art portfolio or on my bedroom wall.

"Were you scared at the march?" I ask.

Grammy is back to confused. "What march?"

That's what I want to know. I prompt her, "Gramps. Eddie and your march."

"Eddie? Where's Eddie?" Then Grammy gets . . . mean. "Why are you asking me all these questions?" she demands, suspicious, like I'm trying to steal something from her. Like I'm the one who stole her memories. She scowls and growls at me, "What did you do to Eddie?"

The Grammy I know doesn't scowl. The Grammy I love does not growl. It's scary, her acting mean—as if an alien is occupying my grammy. If mean people are hurt people, then maybe losing your memories is as painful as breaking your bones. Maybe lost memories are no different from an amputated limb you think you can feel but is no longer there.

Mom slips her arm around me and tugs me out of the dining room and downstairs to the storage closet of spiderwebs. She tells me, "It's okay." Upstairs, I hear Dad comforting Grammy with the exact same reassurance, "It's okay."

But Grammy losing herself is no more okay than me losing a maybe-twin.

After Grammy is settled back in her bedroom, Dad thumps down the basement stairs with a plate of comfort cookies, ginger molasses this time. He shakes his head. "I've never heard that story about the march."

Mom slides her arm around Dad's waist and says, "Grammy is a constant surprise, isn't she?"

"Yeah, I didn't know she and Gramps met in sixth grade," I say, which is still a weird and uncomfortable concept.

"They did," Dad says, "but meeting and falling in love are like two entirely different songs on the same playlist."

Not on any playlist of mine, thank you.

I tell my parents, "It scares me that Grammy is losing her memory. She can't even remember her activism, and that seems like a huge part of who she is. I really want to do a DNA test to know everything I already don't remember. Like whether I have a sister."

Mom sighs heavily, and that says it all: in your dreams.

"I can pay for it," I tell Mom.

Even though I know Mom is about to have her post-dinner surge of energy to clean or organize or research any moment now, she fake-yawns and says tiredly, "We can talk about this later."

Later means never.

I shoot back, "But it's my money. And Donna's mom—"

Dad clears his throat and shakes his head at me in warning.

Too late. I'm already finishing my thought, "She's okay with it."

Which may or may not be true, but it's clearly the wrong thing to say to Mom. Her mouth flattens into a grim line, and she sprints up the stairs like she's in a race that she didn't know she was in. Like she can't stand to be breathing the same oxygen as me. It panics me, Mom running from me.

My heart is banging so hard like it wants to leave me, too. But then Dad hugs me and promises, "I'll talk to her. She'll come around."

Try all he wants, but we both know that once Mom has made up her mind, the decision is final.

Then again, the same is true for me.

# Chapter 12

Some plans need to be plotted face-to-face. Before I can utter a single word on FaceTime later that night, though, Donna takes one look at me and sighs. "Your parents, too?"

"My parents, too." I sigh back at her. "So how can we convince them to let us take the test?"

Donna blinks, surprised. "Actually, mine are totally open to it. Mom just wants to talk to your parents first. But your parents won't let you?"

I think back to Mom bolting up the stairs like the house was on fire. How she didn't look back at me, not once. I shudder. It was almost like Mom thought I was betraying her or something, and that makes me panic all over again. Being left by a second mother just might be a fate worse than death. There's no way I can ask Mom about the DNA test again.

"Maybe your parents could give me one of the tests?" I ask hopefully. "I mean, each kit comes with two."

"Not without your parents' permission."

"Fine. We need to get the DNA test ourselves," I say, expecting Donna to nod eagerly back at me. I remind her, "No parental consent necessary."

Instead of agreeing with me, her lips press together and her forehead furrows. Donna looks like Amah: disapproving. And like Mom: disappointed. "No way. I can't get in trouble."

"But we're supposed to make trouble."

"Maybe you are, but not me."

"Why?" I wail.

"I . . ." Donna frowns. "It's the whole respect your elders thing, right?"

"We're supposed to challenge authority," I argue, because that's what I've always been told.

"Maybe in your family," she says uneasily. I'm about to protest, but Donna's eyes drop and she twists her hair around her finger like she's gathering the courage to tell me a secret. A secret that only a maybe-twin who's been adopted, too, could understand. So I stay quiet until she finally confesses, "It's just that my parents couldn't have kids. That's what all the doctors told my mom. And then surprise, surprise, a month before they adopted me, Mom found out she was pregnant with my brother. So I know it's stupid, but sometimes I feel like I have to be perfect so they don't regret adopting me."

Her eyes lift to mine, and I understand her desperation perfectly because it is my desperation exactly: never regret adopting me.

"Okay, but what if we got the test kit before our parents

talk? What if we took the test before my mom could officially say no?" I brainstorm. The ideas are fireworks, lighting up possibilities in my head. "Then, technically, you wouldn't be disobeying your parents, who pretty much approved, and I'm not disobeying mine."

"Oh," Donna says, then slowly nods. "That might work. But how are we going to get a kit? I don't have a credit card."

I don't either. "I'll figure something out," I promise.

"My family's Lunar New Year party is on Saturday night," Donna says, brightening. "You should come. You have to come. We can take the tests there if we get the kit in time."

We don't celebrate the Lunar New Year because the day has never really been important to my family, but I don't tell Donna that. Not a single thing can separate us. Not now. Not ever. That's the same reason why I've never told my parents that I kind of, sort of do want to celebrate Lunar New Year. And that I wonder how my birth family celebrates. And whether they think about me when they do.

My heart swells with excitement. This year, I'll finally get to celebrate Lunar New Year for the first time with Donna. I grin and say, "Good idea!"

Donna sings our favorite A2Z song: "'It's all good, even if we're up to no good.'"

I chime in to sing the last verse with her: "'Even if we're up to no good, us two.'" We giggle, and I say, "We could be our own band. The Lost Twins."

She says, "The Lost and Found Twins."

"The Secret Sisters!"

Donna blares, "The Not-So-Secret Sisters."

"The In-Your-Face Sisters!"

I wait for Donna to keep going, adding to our band names. Instead, I hear Amah in the background. Donna blurts out, "I'm not supposed to be on my phone on a school night."

With that, she hangs up before I can even say goodbye.

Ben, I text under the covers in bed after midnight. The comforter is so thick and heavy, I can barely breathe. That weight is nothing compared to my smothering anxiety that's kept me wide awake. I need the DNA test kit before Saturday night.

I clench my silent phone tighter in my hand.

Ben, I text again, willing him to answer. Ben. Ben. BEN.

Finally, after approximately fifty-seven texts, a sign of grumpy big brother life.

> *BEN:* Double Trouble aren't you supposed to be asleep?
> *ME:* I know what I want for Gotcha Day!
> *BEN:* I already got your present.

Let me guess. Ever since he gave me my first stuffed bunny, growing my collection has been both a tradition and responsibility Ben takes seriously. Bunny slippers. Bunny stickers. Bunny pins. Bunny posters. One of my all-time favorite T-shirts featuring a chubby bunny lying on her stomach over the words, *I don't carrot all.* And once, a real living, breathing bunny that Mom made him return to our neighbors because she didn't want a house rabbit even if I did.

I hope Mom won't make him return this year's birthday present.

> *BEN:* OK what do you want that's so important you're interrupting my beauty sleep and stunting your growth?
> *ME:* A DNA test!

Instead of texting, Ben video calls. His eyes narrow suspiciously at me, not one bit drowsy even though I've woken him up. He looks so much like Mom when she is sniffing out trouble that my stomach aches. "Why aren't you asking Mom and Dad?"

I hunch over my knees and whisper, "Mom doesn't want me to have a sister."

"Nah," Ben says, and scratches his neck, "she's probably worried that you wish you were in Donna's family."

"But you guys are my family. I don't want any other family," I say, yet there it is: a little wistful twinge smack in the middle of my heart that I get whenever I think about my birth family. Who are they? What are they doing? Do they miss me? "So can you get me the DNA kit? Please?"

"I don't know," he says uneasily.

"I'll pay you back," I tell him. "If I had a debit card, I'd get it myself."

"Mom will kill me."

"What if this were happening to you? What if you were the adopted one and you were separated from your twin? What if you met Jacob out of the blue? Wouldn't you want to know for sure if you were twins? No matter what?"

A long pause. "Probably."

"You mean, one hundred percent yes. Just think about everything you would have missed out on with Jacob. Wouldn't you want to make up all that lost time as fast as you could?" I shoot back. As soon as I see his barely perceptible nod, triumph wings through me. "You know what Mom and Dad always say, right?"

At the same time, we both chant, "Make trouble now and ask for forgiveness later."

I continue, "This is trouble worth getting into."

"Fine," Ben says.

"So you'll order the kit? Now? I need it by Saturday night."

"Fine. I'll express ship it." He sighs heavily, then points a finger at me. "But you'll be the one who's asking for forgiveness when Mom finds out."

# Chapter 13

The alarm blares, the shrill sound stabbing my eardrums. But it's not my clock.

It's Mom, downstairs. "And now she wants a DNA test?"

Mom's radar-detection for lies is excellent, but not so excellent that she's already found out that Ben's ordered me a kit, is it? I sit up quickly, the comforter falling off my shoulders, and strain to listen. I can't make out another word, so I creep to my bedroom door and crack it open.

"We let her down," Mom is saying, her voice tight. "We should have introduced her to her culture earlier, the way I said. Plopped her into Chinese school."

Dad asks, "What Chinese school in the middle of nowhere, Washington?"

Back in our forever home, my parents rarely argued. But now, their chords clash and clang like they're playing two different songs at once.

"She's going to wish she'd been adopted by a different family," Mom cries.

"How? We're her family. We're good parents. It'll be twice the love, honey," Dad responds quickly, but not quickly enough.

"That's easy for you to say!" Mom snaps. A cabinet door bangs shut. "At the orphanage, she practically leaped into your arms. She'd only take a bottle from you. Her first steps were to you."

"This isn't easy for me either. I'm not sure how I'm going to feel when I first see her with Donna's dad."

"Yeah." Mom's sadness weaves its way up to me and cements me at my door.

Ben was right about the source of her worry, but I never even considered that me finding Donna would be an issue for Dad. Dad, who supports me and my every idea. I swallow hard, but the guilt stuck in my throat doesn't budge. Everything in me wants to reassure my parents that nothing and no one is taking me from them. So even though I usually get dressed before breakfast, I race down the stairs in my pajamas, announcing, "I'm starving."

"Good thing my famous egg bake is coming out of the oven in thirty seconds," Dad says, already grinning in my direction as I round the corner into the kitchen that smells of cheesy-eggy goodness.

At the kitchen island, Mom is setting out two large thermoses, one filled with steaming hot coffee for Dad to take down to his music studio, and the other filled with Earl Grey tea for her to take upstairs to hers. She says brightly out of nowhere, "So we were thinking that it might be fun for you to go to Chinese school."

Fun? Chinese school? I stop filling my glass with water from the fridge to stare at her. "What?"

"It'd be good for you to get to know your birth culture," Mom says, smiling at me. "Learn your birth language."

My breath catches—oh, no—because Mom is wearing The Look. The You Are Going to Love My Big Idea look. The look that says, *Just wait until I turn everyone's life upside down.*

Like Project Secret Resettlement.

My culture is not going to become one of Mom's projects that she has researched and Dad will orchestrate the same way they did our move to Seattle. All without warning me.

So I blurt out, "Donna invited me over to celebrate Lunar New Year."

"Oh." Mom frowns as she tightens the lid on the thermos like she doesn't intend for it to be opened ever again. "I'm so proud of you for making a new friend."

New friend? It is irritating that Mom refuses to acknowledge that Donna could be my new sister. This only confirms that getting the DNA kit on my own—with Ben's help—was the absolute right thing to do.

The only thing to do.

The thunderous boom of a taiko drum startles me. Then, deep chanting in dragon language fills the kitchen. Dad's switched on the theme song from *The Elder Scrolls*. Seeing a symphony perform this score live with my family made me understand what Dad means by musical landscape. Music is so much more than the notes in a song, but the emotions you feel and the images you see while listening. It's as if Dad is trying to remind me of the most important landscape: Our family. Our history. Our togetherness.

He scoops the egg bake muffins on three plates and asks, "Do you want to go to Donna's party?"

I nod and repeat Mom's magic words: "It'll be good for me to know my culture."

That wins Mom's reluctant approval even if it looks like it hurts her to say, "Absolutely." Then she gets The Look again. "I can do some research on Lunar New Year. Knowledge is power."

"That's a great idea, honey," Dad says enthusiastically, squeezing Mom on the shoulder.

Before I know it, Mom will finagle herself and Dad an invitation to the party. Then it'll be goodbye DNA testing.

"Geez, guys, it's just a party," I say with an irate huff that stills Mom's fingers on the keyboard and shuts down Dad's grin but not the nervous guilt strumming inside me. That plays loud and strong.

# Chapter 14

"We got the test!" I whoop to Donna outside in the rain before school begins.

"No way!" Donna cries, jumping up and down.

I break into one of my all-time favorite A2Z signature dance moves: a spiraling kick. Neither of us cares that we are splashing ourselves with rainwater.

Nothing—and I mean nothing—can ruin this day, not the way Donna and I are two peas in a dancing-spiraling pod of twins. Twins!

And we are about to prove it.

Giggling as we walk to math together, Donna is gripping a binder tight to her chest. Photos of girls our age are collaged all over the cover. Who are these girls surrounding Donna with their glossy black hair, some tall and thin, others shorter with full, round cheeks? So I ask.

Donna says, "Oh, these are my Hunan sisters."

"Your sisters?" I echo, shocked, as my soggy sneakers squeak down the hall. I thought I was her only maybe-sister.

"Yeah, all the girls who were adopted at the same time as me. How many do you have?"

"I don't know."

Donna looks at me curiously. "You didn't stay in touch with your adoption group?"

I shake my head. Were we supposed to? How much have I missed out on? Somehow, it feels colder inside the school than outside. Even with my arms wrapped tight around myself, I shiver.

"Oh, we get together once a summer," Donna says, then adds, "but it's been getting a little weird, if you know what I mean."

"No, how come?"

Donna tilts her head the way she does when she's thinking hard. "Everyone else was adopted into white families, and a couple of their parents are like, you will know your culture!"

Not my parents.

"So, some of them go to these Chinese heritage camps for adoptees in the summer, and I'm the only one who goes to a Taiwanese American summer camp instead."

I admit, "I don't even know the difference."

"Okay, here's how my parents explained it to me. China and Taiwan are different: different culture, different countries. Taiwanese is even a different language from Mandarin. And even if China doesn't recognize Taiwan as an independent country, Taiwan is its own island and a democracy. That's what my family thinks. So, Taiwanese camp for me, but at least it's fun, right?"

"But we're from China," I point out in front of math class. A small voice whispers, *What's Amah going to think about Mom threatening to pop me into Chinese school to learn Mandarin?*

"I know." Donna's eyes dart to mine and her voice lowers as kids maneuver around us to go inside. "Sometimes I worry Amah might hold that against me. You know, I have to be all rah-rah, go, Taiwan. All. The. Time."

I whisper, too. "I wonder if me having Hunan sisters might have freaked my mom out? Like, rah-rah, go, Breedloves."

The bell rings. We slip inside math. When Akshaya gives me a dirty look as Donna and I walk into class together, I know how she feels: blindsided by an unknown sister.

Dad plucks his AirPods out as soon as he sees me after school, and the ethereal music from *Ori and the Blind Forest* pours from his phone from where he's standing, hunched in the light drizzle. This sweeping theme song is Dad's go-to when he's wrestling with a decision. That decision usually has to do with having a tough conversation.

Did Ben blab about the DNA test?

My heart stops. I force my feet down the concrete steps to him. Did the DNA kit arrive while I was at school?

Did Mom open the package even though the box was addressed to me?

That I could believe. As fast as I want to power-walk home to check on the kit, Dad keeps his pace slow and steady on the sidewalk like he wants to anchor me in this moment with him.

"Kiddo," Dad says, hands shoved in the front pockets of his jeans. "Both your mom and I know how important it is for you to discover as much about yourself as possible."

The orchestral music swells from Dad's phone, and I remember: Ori, an adorable guardian spirit, was an orphan. All Ori wanted was to restore its home. That's what I want, too. Restore my home, and my home could be Donna. My home could have been with my own Hunan sisters for all these last years. Maybe then I'd know more about my own culture.

"Then why won't Mom let me find out whether Donna is really my twin?" I glower at him.

"Your mom just needs time."

But I don't have time. I swipe my rain-dampened hair out of my face. "I've been alone for almost twelve years. Isn't that enough time?"

Dad flinches, then sidesteps a squiggly worm. His voice is low, his eyes focused on me when he says, "You've had us."

"It's not the same, Dad! We didn't keep in touch with my Hunan sisters."

"We tried, but not everyone had the money for a reunion. I know we should have tried harder."

I can feel Dad's hurt. Why can't my parents understand how important it is to me to find someone in the world who is mine? We walk the rest of the way without saying anything until we pass the bus stop near our for-now home.

"Okay, that went sideways. Let's rewind." Dad makes what he must think is a rewinding noise. "Hey, kiddo! How was school?"

I mutter, "Math sucked."

He quips, "Dear Math, grow up and solve your own problems."

He is so corny, my dad. I can't help but crack a smile, which only invites him to share another dad joke: "What did the zero say to the eight?"

I fake-sigh even though I am grateful that Dad is trying to make things normal between us. "What?"

"That belt looks awesome on you."

"Dad."

By the front door, sitting right on top of the doormat with our name—The Breedloves—is a small brown box. I lunge for it, but Dad is faster. The package looks so tiny in his large hands. He flips it over to read the label and immediately holds it out to me. "It's for you."

I grab the box and hold it tight to my chest. This is my moment to come clean to Dad. To tell him what's inside: My heart. My hope.

My secret.

Just then, my phone pings, and I dig it out of my back pocket. It is Donna in what has got to be a twin moment. She sends me the one and only message that would keep me from telling Dad the truth this very second: Knowing if we're sisters is worth everything.

It is.

# Chapter 15

"I'm not wearing that." I grimace at the new "outfit" Mom has laid out on my bed: red sweater, red skirt, red socks. It's almost six on Saturday, and we are running late and I have a twin sister to confirm. I say flatly, "Mom. I'm going to look like a Twizzler."

"What's wrong with that?" Dad asks, lifting his phone to commemorate family history and personal humiliation. "We all wore matching red onesies for our Christmas picture last year. Hey, I bet you could still fit into yours."

"Dad."

"But you need to wear both new clothes and red to Lunar New Year," Mom protests. "It means good luck and happiness."

"Mom."

Mom looks so crestfallen I agree to the new red sweater and new red socks. But I draw the line at the red skirt and wear my favorite black leggings with zippered pockets instead. After I throw on my New Year outfit, I triple-check the DNA test I've stashed in my new tote bag, silkscreened with white rabbits, a full moon, and pink and red peonies.

Donna's condo in downtown Seattle is in a high-rise building that towers over Pike Place Market. Rain thrashes from the sky like it's determined to cancel all celebrations tonight. Obviously, the rain hasn't met Donna. She waves both arms at me from inside the lobby. Like she is flagging me down and doesn't want me to run away.

Before I leave the car, Mom says, "Remember the flowers." She thrusts the bouquet of white roses I've forgotten in the back seat into my arms. It's like my brain can only hold one thought: Donna and I are going to do our DNA tests tonight. As soon as I shut the passenger door, Mom rolls down my window and calls after me, "Have a great time! Be a good guest! Take a no-thank-you bite of everything!"

The heavy rain and Mom's etiquette reminders chase me to the lobby, covered floor to ceiling in white marble, where Donna is waiting for me. She throws her arms tight around me, even though I'm dripping with rain from the short sprint to her. Some of my tension releases.

"Do you have the tests?" she asks.

I pat my tote bag. "Got 'em."

Even more tension disappears when Donna grabs my hand. Sister-twin! The last bit vanishes when I notice she's wearing a same-ish red sweater and same-ish black leggings as me. But once in the elevator, her eyes fall uneasily on the flowers wrapped in craft paper and tied with a mossy green ribbon and says, "Oh, they're white."

"What's wrong with white?" I ask.

The elevator dings at the thirty-third floor, and Donna shakes her head. "Never mind, it's nothing."

This is the first time I've ever been so high up in a building except for the Space Needle. The long hall is filled with unfamiliar scents. Unfamiliar, but they tug at me. Like when I smell coconut and think of Sophie, who loves coconut macaroon cookies. Or when I get a whiff of grilled cheese and miss Jacob and Ben and their grilled-cheese-eating contests. (Jacob holds the record at ten grilled cheese sandwiches in a single sitting.)

Donna hears me inhale deeply, like I'm trying to stash these new fragrances in the part of my brain that stores memories, and says, "You better be hungry. My parents have been cooking nonstop."

When we reach the end of the hall, Donna can barely open the dark wood double doors covered with squares of red paper in a diamond shape.

"What are those?" I ask, nodding at the decorations.

"What, those? Fu characters," Donna says.

I shrug. *I have no clue what you're talking about.*

She taps one of the gold characters. "This, fu, means good luck. You hang it upside down on New Year's so your luck doesn't run out."

What if luck doesn't want to let me in? A pile of shoes barricades the entrance. Rain boots. Black heels. Brown loafers. Donna shoves the door and wedges through the sliver of an opening. I follow. She kicks off her white sneakers and waits for me to do the same. I feel uncomfortable. In both my for-now home and my forever home, we wear shoes inside. Dad even has special indoor sneakers for his worn-out knees that creak from running so many miles. I'm glad for my new red socks so I don't pad barefoot after Donna to the kitchen, where a bunch of adults are gathered. Everyone is wearing socks or slippers. Everyone is inhaling the savory scents bubbling from the stovetop and seeping from the oven.

Everyone has black hair. Brown eyes.

I have never been around so many Asian people before.

"Hey, kiddos! You must be Dessie," says Mr. Lee heartily, lifting his phone to snap a picture of me and Donna, just like my dad.

"These are from my mom," I say, holding out the white roses.

Behind Donna's dad, Amah gives a sharp intake of breath like she's horrified. Or afraid.

What? What did I do? I look at Donna, who whispers to me, "White means death."

Death?

"That's just superstition," Mr. Lee says easily, already reaching up to the topmost shelf for a glass vase.

Donna's mom takes the roses from me even though the petals are deathly white. She pushes back her long sleek hair with a hand weighed down with three chunky gold rings and inhales the flowers deeply with a satisfied *mmm*. Hugging me, she says, "These are gorgeous and super thoughtful."

Donna beams at her mom. "Isn't she?"

"You're right. Just like you." Her mom kisses the top of Donna's head, then tugs me into a hug and kisses me on the top of mine.

That's when I notice that Donna hasn't just unintentionally twinned with me. She and her mom are intentionally twinning with their identical red hoodie sweaters on top of identical shiny black moto leggings. Something I would never in a billion years do with Mom.

If Mom hated the idea of me twinning with Donna, she would absolutely detest the sight of the three of us tripleting together.

With Mom's coaching and Dad's support, I've been practicing saying "happy New Year" in Mandarin. Because I'm so embarrassed about my pronunciation, I even rehearsed on Owen, telling my dog, "Xīn Nián Kuài Lè"! But before I can muster my courage to wish Amah a happy new year, she says, "Sin Ni Khòai Lok!"

I blink, confused.

Amah blinks, expectant.

"That's happy New Year," Donna translates for me under her breath. Amah's pronunciation is not at all what Mom and I had studied on Duolingo. When I frown, Donna mutters, "Remember? Taiwanese is different."

I should have remembered. No, I should have learned how to say it in Taiwanese, because Amah's face looks sour. She demands in a curt voice, "Why do you have a bag with the harvest moon?"

"Harvest moon?" I repeat.

"The Moon Festival," she says, eyes narrowing at me.

Moon Festival? I flush and wish I could hide my tote bag with the bunnies looking at the full moon. My flush deepens into a blush. One more holiday I've never celebrated. Donna's lips are tight like she's mad at Amah, but she doesn't say anything.

Donna's mom adjusts the oversized gold medallion dangling from her long necklace, then beams at me. "It's a beautiful bag. You'll have to let me know where you got it, so I can get one for Donna. And please call us Uncle Carl and Auntie Susie. I think you already met Amah."

Auntie? Uncle? Amah? Even without the DNA test, the Lees are treating me like family. At least Donna's parents do. Amah is setting the vase in the farthest corner of the kitchen, like she does not want the death flowers polluting this party. Donna spears a chubby meatball on a toothpick and hands it to me before helping herself to one, then steers us out of the kitchen.

"Don't worry about Amah," she says as she chews. "She's just mad that my brother and I aren't fluent in Taiwanese."

The doorbell rings. Who walks in like this is his home but the be-freckled, redheaded bully of Marian Anderson Middle School.

# Chapter 16

"What's Max doing here?" I hiss at Donna.

Donna groans. "Remember? Our moms work together and we have to"—she makes bunny ears with her fingers—"'share our culture' with him. Like this is a field trip, right?"

But it is. For me.

I don't recognize the tasty smells wafting all around me. I have brought white flowers of death. I am carrying a tote bag that celebrates the Moon Festival, not Lunar New Year.

We may speak the same language, but I don't seem to understand anything.

Meanwhile, Max is kicking off his skateboard sneakers like he's been here a billion times before. He doesn't just hold a bouquet of pink and red tulips. He makes a beeline with them to the kitchen where Amah fusses over his flowers of life and feeds him a fat meatball. He is greeted like real family. Amah even coos at him, "Guai-guai."

I look at Donna for a translation. She says, "He's obedient."

Obedient? Max? I scoff. "Is that a good thing?"

"It's a compliment." Donna tilts her head, thinking. "Yeah, it's like, he's respectful."

And I am not? I think about Amah's scowls of disapproval whenever I seem to open my mouth. But if Donna is my sister-twin, then I need Amah to at least accept me. I want more than that, though. I want her to like me.

A flurry of activity bursts in the kitchen, and soon, all the adults are lugging platters of food one by one to the dining room. We all hustle to the long dining table covered with more food than I've ever seen for Thanksgiving. And Christmas. Maybe combined.

The kids, including Donna's younger brother and two cousins, take a seat at one end of the table, the adults on the other. Red paper place mats ring the entire table, each featuring twelve animals. I've seen similar ones when I was little, and we ate in the International District with my grandparents. But this red place mat looks like a piece of modern art: the year sits inside a bold black square and each cute animal strikes a martial arts pose. I ask Donna if I can bring one home to show Mom.

"Sure," Donna says. "Max and his mom designed them."

"Max?" I ask, astonished.

"Yeah, he drew the animals."

My mouth drops open.

Max is listening. He doesn't even try to pretend that he's not eavesdropping on us. He asks like he's an important part of our conversation, "So, what animal are you?"

"Monkey," I say fast because Dad used to call me his "little monkey."

"Are you sure about that?" Donna's eyes cut to her younger cousins, who are squabbling over their chopstick holders. "They're monkeys."

"Yeah, I used to climb out of my crib and my dad would find me asleep on the floor."

Max throws his head back and laughs so hard, his face turns crimson. Worse, Donna laughs, too. What did I say wrong this time?

"No, what Chinese zodiac animal are you? But maybe you *are* a monkey." Max snickers and reads out loud, "'Monkeys love to have fun. They may be wise and inventive, but they have no self-control.'" He stares at me meaningfully. "'They can be impatient, egotistical, and crafty.'"

After living with two big brothers, I have learned one thing: I'm not going to let this Max guy quiet me. Still, I flush. Sophie and I would get into trouble all the time for laughing in class. Was that fun-loving and crafty with no self-control? Did I tell Mom not to research Lunar New Year because I'm impatient? Was I worried about Donna having Hunan sisters because I'm egotistical?

"Your animal sign is based on your birth year." Donna points to herself and Max. "We're rabbits. So you've got to be a rabbit, too."

"Yeah, a cute little bunny," Max says like he is making fun of her. Or me. But it comes out like he is telling the truth.

Like he thinks she's cute. Or I am. He flushes red. Almost as red as the paper place settings.

"I'd be happy to be a rabbit," I say loudly and skim the description of the rabbit: *kind-hearted and cheerful, a rabbit makes many friends*. That does not sound like me, the vexatious child of my orphanage. "That sounds like you," I tell Donna.

Donna says loyally, "It sounds like you, too."

Max shakes his head like he knows I'm a rabbit impostor. A Lunar New Year impostor.

"I know more than you do about all this stuff," he scoffs.

Before I can answer—what can I say? Max is right—Amah finally takes her seat, smiling and nodding at everyone. Including me. That seems to be the signal for the feast to begin because, with a whirlwind of serving spoons and forks, everyone begins dishing up the food, one platter after another winging around the table. Like large moons circling this solar system of family and friends.

At Amah's urging, Donna scoops some sweet-and-sour shrimp onto my plate, but her grandmother is dissatisfied with the ones Donna has chosen for me. She points at the biggest and fattest shrimp.

"You're our special guest," Donna explains as she sets that big, fat shrimp next to a sliver of sliced chicken on my plate. "You get the best."

So I help myself to another plump shrimp. I look up and find Amah glowering at me. She's so focused on me that she doesn't see Donna placing the smallest, skimpiest shrimp on Max's plate.

Soon, everyone's plate is heaped with food, and I start to worry about using chopsticks. Except for the serving forks, there are no other forks on this table. We have chopsticks at home, but the last time we used them was at my tenth birthday party for a game where we moved tiny marshmallows from one bowl to another. I did not win.

I can feel Max watching me, almost daring me to pick up my chopsticks. I notice that he doesn't have any problem using his. He expertly shovels long noodles into his mouth like he is a champion user of chopsticks.

Max Morrison would win the marshmallow game.

"Do you need a fork?" he asks, too loudly.

"No, I do not, Max," I say confidently. But maybe I do because I do not lift a single morsel of food to my lips. Max smirks, and I blush even harder.

I study my plate for a bite bigger than a mini marshmallow. The plump shrimp look too slippery. The sticky rice is dotted with mushrooms and tiny dried shrimp. Tiny dried shrimp with tiny dried eyes in tiny dried heads. I probe what looks like a vegetable impersonating a lizard, all lumpy and bumpy and green on the outside. Each thick slice is mounded with minced pork.

"I wouldn't eat that if I were you," Donna warns with a small shudder. "Bitter melon."

Which sounds like a dare to me.

The bitter melon is big. Big enough for me to grip with the chopsticks. Big enough it won't slip free if I press tight. Back at home, Mom says to cut everything into polite bite-sized pieces. But I do not have a knife. Donna catches me watching her, and she easily lifts her shrimp up to her lips. One neat bite. Then two.

How hard can that be? I pin the bitter melon between my chopsticks. It slips. So I stab the bitter melon with my chopsticks. I lift the bitter melon skewer to my lips. I take a big bite. Instantly, my mouth is filled with bitterness. So much bitterness, it fuzzes my teeth. And coats my tongue. The rest of the bitter melon (thankfully) falls off my chopsticks and splats on the noodles.

Max snickers. Even though he doesn't say anything, I can hear him clearly: *I can even use chopsticks better than you.* Amah stops in the middle of her sentence about how scary it is to walk outside with all the attacks on elders in the community. Her lips purse like she agrees with Max.

As I gulp an entire cup of water, Auntie Susie stands. "Thanks to everyone for being here tonight," she says, holding her glass of red wine. "Lunar New Year is so special because it's about family coming together and new beginnings. I just wanted to say a special thanks to Carl for always bringing our family together. There is nothing—nothing—more important than family."

Uncle Carl translates into Taiwanese, each syllable as unfamiliar as every bite of this feast. A wave of excitement washes over me. This holiday is a day of celebrating family.

Family like a maybe-twin, confirmed with DNA. An angry squeak as Max shoves his chair back silences all the conversations around the table and in my head. Max's face is fiery red, but not lucky New Year red. Not laughing so hard you cry red. Not even dying of embarrassment red.

This is the furious red of remembering you are leaving your forever home and your forever friend and your forever life.

Max jerks to his feet. His curly-haired mother follows him out of the dining room with a faint, "Max!"

That's when I realize that Max's father is not here, celebrating with his family.

"His parents are getting divorced," Donna whispers to me.

Maybe no family is perfectly whole.

Maybe every family is a little fractured from pieces that have gone missing: Dads. Grandpas who are soulmates. Grammies and their memories. Sister-twins who were separated at adoption.

Donna sends a look to me. I send a look back to her.

It is time for Project Sister-Twin.

# Chapter 17

Just as we are about to make our break from the table, Amah beckons Auntie Susie to collect something from the kitchen. Auntie Susie returns with little red envelopes that Amah hands out to Donna, her brother, and her two cousins. And me. Max's, she rests next to his half-eaten dinner.

"Ang bao. Red envelopes," Donna explains to me. "There's money inside."

No one opens their ang bao. So I don't either.

What no one expects are the bright red safety alarms with flashing lights and screeching sirens that Auntie Susie hands to each of us. She says, "To put in your pocket. With more Asian people getting hurt—"

"Aiyo," Amah says, fanning herself. "The world is getting so mean."

"Not the whole world," says Donna, who weaves her arm around her mom's waist, and for a moment they stand, leaning into each other. It is hard to imagine the two of them getting into fights.

Max's mom returns to the table alone. His abandoned dinner looks all wrong. As much as I hate to admit it, the circle around the table is broken without him. So I take his red envelope and search for Max, even though Donna tells me to leave him alone. But maybe that's the problem: it is a terrible thing to be left.

We find Max in the living room, sitting in the corner, immersed in a game on his phone. When we draw close, Max barks, "What?"

His question jumps on us, shoving us away. Out of the living room. Out of this party. His eyes narrow, and his mouth puckers like he's eaten an entire platter of bitter melon.

Maybe being left can leave us bitter.

Even though Donna huffs and says, "Fine!" like she's about to leave, I stay.

Because I stay, so does Donna. I stay and hand Max his red envelope. He sets down his phone and accepts the envelope with two hands. That's when I notice that Max Morrison is playing *The Eight Banners*.

"My mom played the piano in the theme song," I tell him.

Max forgets to be mad. Instead, he looks amazed. "She did?"

Donna nods. "She did! I heard her!"

"You did?" Max asks, looking jealous.

I don't mention that my dad composed the theme song. Not when Max's dad is missing tonight.

Maybe Max's dad is missing most of the time. There is a lot I don't know.

"You can come over someday, and she can play it for you," I offer, because Lunar New Year isn't just about family. It's about new beginnings, too.

The best new beginning can't happen soon enough. As soon as Max leaves the party with his mom, Donna looks at me and says, "Let's go, maybe-twin."

The only non-pink and non-white item in Donna's enormous pink-and-white bedroom is a piece of red fabric, folded carefully on top of a fluffy white throw pillow. I draw closer to the cloth: it is crocheted. Rippling stitches dance from top to bottom. I know those rippling stitches. They skipped down my long-lost baby blanket, too.

"That's from the orphanage," says Donna, drawing to my side.

"I had one, too. Same pattern." We stare at each other—another sign that we have to take the DNA test. "But mine was green."

"What color green?" Donna asks, pointing to the sheets of paper tacked above her desk. One is covered with green color swatches, their names written in her swirling calligraphy. I study the colors: not forest green. Not leafy green.

"This one." I tap a color and read its name. "Jade green."

"Jade is precious," Donna says, touching my arm. "It stands for strength and luck and great ideas. Mine is good luck red. Do you think the orphanage was sending us a message?"

"A message, like, hey, good luck with life?" I ask, nose wrinkling because that seems so cold.

"No, like, let us wrap you up in good luck."

"So you can find your sister."

Our smiles wobble. Now that it's finally time to take the DNA test, I'm scared as I follow Donna to the bathroom.

Her bathroom could be a celebrity's dressing room: light pink cabinets with gold fixtures. A mirror that stretches from one end of the bathroom to the other. The heated floor lined with tiny white tiles. It is so big, she even has a pink pouf at a vanity table. There's no makeup on the counter. Just a framed photo of A2Z.

Donna with A2Z.

"No way," I say, grabbing the bedazzled frame and holding it up to my eyes. "No. Way."

"Definitely no way," Donna answers, laughing. "Max's mom needed to learn Photoshop."

"Whoa. This looks so real." Just the way that Donna and I look like real twins. I swallow hard.

Donna swallows hard, too. It is time to prove once and for all that we are sisters. No more detours and delays. It feels dangerous what we're about to do. As if she senses that, too, Donna pads over to lock the bathroom door. I laugh nervously because she is tiptoeing like a not-so-stealthy superspy. She nervous-laughs, too.

"Ready?" I ask, digging the box containing our two DNA tests out of my tote bag. My hand trembles as I set the package on the marble countertop.

"Ready," answers Donna with a firm nod.

When neither of us makes a move for it, we giggle. At the

same time. And exactly alike. That gives me the courage to rip the plastic wrapper off. And it gives Donna the bravery to shake all the contents out: the instructions. The cotton swabs in individual packages, one swab for each side of our cheeks, two swabs for each sister.

Sister!

With a trembling hand, I give her one swab, then hold up mine like it is a banner straight out of Dad's video game.

"Three," Donna says, her fingers wrapped delicately around her swab.

"Two," I say, my fingers wound tight around mine.

"One," we count together and open our mouths, brushing the swabs against our inside cheeks, one side, then a fresh swab on the other. Her eyes water from trying to control her laughter. Or her tears. Mine do, too. It is emotional, this swabbing. Are we or aren't we sisters?

"Two business days before we know for sure," Donna says, staring down at her cotton swabs that are hopefully swimming with the exact replica of my DNA.

"So maybe Tuesday. Or Wednesday," I say.

It is as if the universe is handing us a sign—Sisters, get ready to celebrate!—because right after we seal our swabs into plastic sleeves, our phones alert at the very same time.

"No way!" we both cry out when we check our phones. Our voices scale the exact same notes of excitement. "No! Way!" Then we are jumping up and down, holding each other by our forearms.

I scream, "A2Z is coming!"

Donna screams back at me, "To Seattle!"

I grab the photoshopped picture of Donna with A2Z and kiss it. My lips make contact with the cool glass, and I make a huge smacking sound: *mwah!*

Donna snatches the frame from me and does the same: *mwah!*

"We need tickets," I say seriously. My eyes widen. "Tickets would be the best birthday present ever in the entire history of humankind."

"They would be the best birthday present in the entire history of twin-kind."

I jump up and down. "They would be the best birthday present in the entire history of sister-twin-kind!"

"They would," Donna says, grabbing my hands to jump up and down with me. "They really, really would."

Actually, tickets would make the perfect Gotcha Day present, since my parents usually give me concert tickets, but I do not say that to my no-Gotcha-Day maybe-twin.

"Yes to birthday tickets." Donna pirouettes, once, twice, but she bumps into me and the walls. So she unlocks her bathroom door and sashays into her bedroom. Then Donna sighs. "I'm going to need good luck to go to the A2Z concert. My family kind of thinks concerts are dangerous."

"Really?" I ask, surprised, because in my family, music is life. Summers mean toting picnic baskets to outdoor concerts, laying out feasts of a homemade spread on blankets, and listening to great music while we gorge and feel the setting sun on our faces. I tell her, "We will have so much fun together at the A2Z concert." To prove it, I belt out our favorite song, but because I know I sing like a mournful cow, I pull up TikTok to help me carry the tune.

Honestly, Donna does not sound much better than me.

It doesn't matter that we sound like a herd of yodeling cows. We are dancing and laughing and yodeling when Amah walks into Donna's bedroom without knocking. Or maybe she did knock, but we didn't hear it above ourselves.

Hastily, Donna flips my phone over on her white comforter. Too late.

Amah frowns, staring at my phone like the forbidden Tik-Tok reel is seared onto her eyeballs.

It feels like a thousand gallons of ice-cold water douse me on my head when Amah points to the bedroom door like she can't wait to get rid of me. "Dessie. Your mommy is here."

# Chapter 18

**The Great Purge has been in overdrive while I've been gone.**
Overstuffed plastic bags headed to Goodwill tomorrow morning are piled so high in the back of the station wagon, I'm not sure how Dad can be driving safely. Mom doesn't issue a single warning for him to check his blind spots when we pull away from the curb into the traffic either. She's too busy watching Donna and her mom walk back inside their condo building, their heads bent together as they laugh over something.

"So, how was it? The party?" Dad asks right when Owen leaps off Grammy's lap and into mine, his tail wagging like rapid-fast windshield wipers, he's so happy to see me.

How was my first Lunar New Year celebration? Sweet and sour. Bitter and salty. I've never been with so many Asian and Asian American people before. Or tasted half of those dishes before.

Or taken a DNA test before.

Different, I decide. But different can be good. I say so, even though I can remember Amah's glowers.

"Auntie Susie packed us a bunch of leftovers," I say, as I guard the big bag that Donna's mom pushed on me as she said goodbye, but Owen's already stretching over my lap to sniff the containers.

"Auntie Susie?" Mom repeats tightly.

"She gave us all red envelopes and these alarms," I say, passing the red personal safety device up to Mom in the front seat.

Mom flips the alarm in her hand before handing it back to me. "That's a weird party favor."

"Not really. They're worried that Asian people have been beaten up lately."

"Well, you don't need to worry about that," she shoots back.

*Tell that to Donna's family*, I think. *And take a good look at me while you're at it*, I think, looking hard at my wavy black hair and brown eyes in the rearview mirror.

"Hey, kiddo, do you have room for a milkshake and fries?" Dad asks, and I notice that Mom doesn't mention anything about the perils of eating late at night or the horrors of junk food.

Even if I were stuffed (which I am not because: chopsticks), I want the last thing I taste tonight to remind me of my family and my forever home. "Yes!"

"Tell us everything about the party so we can celebrate next year," Mom says, looking straight ahead.

I hear Max's laughter because I didn't even know my zodiac animal. Or how to use chopsticks. What else do I not know?

"How about we learn about the next big holiday? The Moon Festival, so we're ready to celebrate that one?" I ask, toying with my wrong tote bag.

"Okay," Mom agrees with an enormous grin that looks a little too enormous.

"Sounds like a plan," says Dad as we pull into Burger Master.

No, I tell myself, it sounds like a promise. Even if I don't say that aloud.

Even if Mom is over-smiling and Dad is squeezing her hand.

A news report catches Grammy's ear and she says, "Turn it up, please."

Another elderly man has been attacked in the International District. See? I want to say. Maybe Donna's family is right to be worried.

"Who on earth would punch an old man?" Mom cries like she wants to hunt down the attacker herself.

"Someone cowardly," Dad says.

"We need to march," Grammy mutters next to me.

# Chapter 19

When I wake up, my stomach hurts from overeating. It's as if the late-night burger is battling the bitter melon, and I am the one losing. I roll over onto my stomach, hoping the pressure will help, and overhear my parents in the kitchen, fighting again.

My stomach hurts even more, especially when I think about the next part of the Make Our Mark project: What does your family name mean?

Breedlove translates to producing love. But Mom is rumbling downstairs, louder than ever. It makes me worried. I've already lost my first family. I don't want to lose my forever family, too.

So, I sidetrack from starting my school project and research the Moon Festival on my phone instead. As if Owen knows that I could use a good snuggle, he noses my bedroom door open and leaps onto me. With Owen tucked close to my side, breathing noisily, I read that for three

thousand years, the fullest, fattest moon has been celebrated with lanterns and mooncakes to give thanks for the
harvest. Like Lunar New Year, this holiday brings families
back together.

"What if we lose her?" Mom says downstairs, her tone
short and sharp.

"We're not going to lose her. She's ours. She's a part of
us," Dad reassures Mom in his boisterous voice. I smell waffles and imagine him wearing the chef's toque hat that Ben,
Jacob, and I gave to him on Father's Day a few years ago. But
then I remember: the toque hat stayed back in our forever
home. He continues, "And we're a part of her."

"What if she wishes she were in Donna's family?"

"We're her family."

Mom has nothing to worry about. I think about Amah and
her frowns whenever she looked at me at the Lunar New
Year party. Even if Donna is my twin, there is no chance that
I would ever be invited to join her family.

"We're her parents," Dad says firmly. "You're Dessie's
mother. We'll plan a blowout birthday and Gotcha Day for
her this year. A Gotcha Day of all Gotcha Days."

Mom cries, "You aren't listening to me!"

I do not like being the cause of anyone's arguments, especially my parents' now, any more than I like people talking
about me behind my back. So, I slip Owen's sleepy head off
my shoulder and onto my pillow, swing my legs off my bed,
and tiptoe to the door. Sometimes I want to tell Dad that his

ho-ho-ho happy voice is off-tune. That sometimes an energetic pep talk is the exact opposite of what someone wants to hear. Sometimes, all we want is a quiet sigh and a heavy "that sucks" as someone sits beside us.

Like Sophie when I told her I was moving.

Like Mom right now, as if me finding Donna has physically hurt her. Her voice rises. "How can you say that? Can you read the future? And look at your mom. We're losing her and she's still here."

I force myself to move off the top step and tromp heavily down the stairs so my parents know that I'm up and about. That I can hear them and their every word.

It may be Waffle Sunday like always, but there are two tragic differences. The Twins aren't here.

And Dad is experimenting.

"Kiddo, you're up!" Dad taps the new recipe on the kitchen island. "These are supposed to be the Best Ever Waffles. And they need a second taste tester."

Yes, because the first taste tester looks like these are the Worst Ever Waffles and she's about to cry. Mom sniffles. I do not want my mom to worry about me since she's dealing with so much already between Grammy, downsizing this home, and learning her new music.

"Why aren't we having the normal ones?" I ask as I sit next to Mom at the kitchen table.

"Because new is good," Dad says firmly.

Mom and her puffy red eyes look like old is better. So I say that: "But sometimes old is better."

Mom nods and nods and nods. "Yes, sometimes you just want tried-and-true."

I know Mom isn't just talking about tried-and-true waffles. I know she's talking about our tried-and-true family. Our family with Ben and Jacob, who are five hours away. Our family with me—and me alone—as the little mei-mei sister. I think about Mom and Dad, who've been fighting since they decided to move to Seattle. I think about the DNA kit, all packaged up and ready to mail, hiding in my tote bag upstairs.

How do I stitch our fractured family back together when Project Sister-Twin is tearing us apart?

Mooncakes are the answer.

After the saddest Waffle Sunday in the entire history of the Breedlove family, I return to my room. I discover that every little thing about these Moon Festival delicacies has a meaning. Their circular shape means wholeness and completeness. My family needs to be whole and complete again. The salted egg yolk inside a mooncake symbolizes the full moon. My family needs to be full of love again.

Mooncakes are given to friends and family as presents in places like China and Taiwan. Maybe even to Amahs who do not look like they want their family to expand. Maybe even to Moms who are afraid of their family changing.

An idea forms. I jump out of bed.

There is no time to lose. I must become an expert mooncake maker. I will gift love to my world. Which admittedly might be a challenge, considering that I have never seen or eaten a mooncake before in my life. I have no idea what red bean or lotus seed fillings look like or taste like. Or, for that matter, salty egg yolk.

"Dad," I announce in the spotless kitchen where Dad, my baking buddy, is taking a creativity break. He's poring over one of Grammy's hundred or so cookbooks that we've been bookmarking to re-create her favorites and unfreeze her memory.

He is not the only Breedlove who believes in the power of good food. That is what I'm counting on.

Dad looks up from the stained page with a dazed expression. "Hey, kiddo."

"Dad," I repeat, because this is an important announcement, and I want to make sure he is paying full attention instead of hearing a new beat or capturing a new melody as I speak. "Dad. We have eight months to become experts at making mooncakes."

I show him the recipe. It is long. Three pages long.

"Kiddo, I love me a good culinary challenge, but I've never even tasted a mooncake," Dad says as he scans the long recipe. And then flips through all three pages again.

I counter, "Macarons take approximately a billion finicky hours to make. And you learned how to make them until they're better than a Parisian bakery. That's what Mom said. And just this morning you said that new is good."

"True, all true. But maybe we should buy a couple of mooncakes first, so we know what they're supposed to taste like. And if we even like them."

I already thought of that. "You can only get mooncakes during Moon Festival time. But Donna can be our taste tester. She knows what mooncakes taste like."

Dad is reading the second step of the recipe. "Golden syrup should be made up to a year before you make the mooncake skin."

"See? We're already behind!" I tell him.

"Why does it need a whole year?"

I cite my research: "For the syrup to get more fragrant and flavorful."

"Like friends, the syrup gets better with age?"

Mom pops into the kitchen with her empty mug for her afternoon ginger turmeric tea. "What gets better with age?"

Dad grins at her. "You do."

"Bleah," I say, pretend-grimacing. Usually it makes me want to throw up, their smoochiness, but now it's a welcome reminder of how they used to be. How maybe they can still be: nauseatingly playful. The mooncakes will be just the thing to bring them and all of us together.

Maybe even Amah.

I squash the image of my brothers in college somewhere during this year's Moon Festival. I stomp on the thought that Ben and Jacob probably won't even return home to celebrate with us, whether here or in our forever home, because we've never celebrated the harvest moon together before.

None of that matters. If I can't have my family in the home where we used to live, then I want my family back to how we used to be.

I tap the recipe. "This is important to me." So is the DNA test hidden upstairs. Stitching my family back together is as important as knowing whether Donna is my twin.

With a grin, Dad says, "You know how we Breedloves love a good project. Project Mooncakes is officially on. How about I get the ingredients tomorrow?"

While I'm on a roll, I ask my parents—please, please, please—for a ticket to the A2Z concert as my birthday present and Gotcha Day present and Christmas present combined.

Mom sighs. "You're pushing it, kid."

Dad winks at me, and Mom half smiles at me. That wink and half smile mean one thing: yes.

Screaming, I rush to my bedroom, their laughter trailing me. My hands are even shakier than they were swabbing for the DNA test, but somehow I manage to text both Donna and Sophie.

*ME:* Guess what?!
*DONNA:* What?!

*ME:* Guess what?!
*SOPHIE:* What?!

*ME:* Guess who might be going to an A2Z concert together?

**DONNA:** No way!!

**ME:** Guess who might be going to an A2Z concert with her new maybe-sister?
**SOPHIE:** No fair.

# Chapter 20

The post office is four blocks in the opposite direction from school. Four long, never-ending blocks. My backpack beats out a rhythm, thumping against me, as I run: *almost there, almost twin*. No matter how much I played and replayed this detour in my head, I have made one rookie mistake after another on the first morning my parents allowed me to walk to school on my own: I didn't account for all the cars clogging up the streets. And I didn't account for waiting so long at every crosswalk.

I sigh, tapping my foot at the red light. *Almost there, almost twin*, I chant in my head, as I check my phone again. Four minutes before school starts, but I cannot miss the morning pickup of mail.

The stoplight thankfully changes. Finally—miracles!—up ahead, the blue drop box in front of the brick-faced post office. With huge panting breaths, I race down the rest of the block until I am standing in front of the banged-up mailbox. The way I had rehearsed this moment in my head, I kiss the DNA kit for good luck before I send it off. In my head, I record myself dropping the package down the mail chute. Me crowing, *Two days before sisterhood is confirmed*! Me sending that video to Donna. Instead, I am sweaty, out of breath, and out of time.

Three minutes before school starts. Just my luck, who do I see inching past the mailbox right as I pop the package inside? Who is the last person I want to see that I am late for school?

Yes, Amah.

Of course, Amah.

On her way home after dropping Donna off. On time. At school.

I groan, hoping Donna's grandmother doesn't see me. Who am I kidding? I can feel the scorching heat of her disapproving glare in every particle of DNA in my body. Including every particle of secret DNA now in the blue mailbox.

Two minutes before school starts. I feel like I'm doing a perp walk in Mom's favorite crime series as I sprint head down past Amah's SUV: disobedient.

Guilty as charged.


"Two hundred and fifty million years ago," my science teacher, Mrs. Pinero, is intoning in a creepy voice like she is the voiceover of a horror film. I knock on the classroom's locked door, shifting my weight uncomfortably from side to side while she slowly walks over to let me in. Every eyeball is on me as I slink over to my seat, and Mrs. Pinero continues as if I haven't interrupted her. "During the Permian period, Earth experienced its greatest mass extinction event. Ninety percent of all our planet's species died off. Ninety percent."

I shoot a thumbs-up to Donna: mission accomplished.

She shoots a thumbs-up back to me and mouths, *Thank you.*

Behind me, I hear Max snicker-shout, "Hey, Dessie."

What now? I know better than to turn around. So I ignore him and busily rewrap my scarf, tossing the ends energetically over my shoulder, hoping they will thwack him. Accidentally.

"That would have been you," Max continues as he snorts like a pig rooting around a pile of meanness. "The great dodo of Lunar New Year."

What a traitor. I should have left Max to sulk alone at Donna's party. Even though Grammy could make friends with practically everybody, she also used to say, Do not throw pearls at swine. I have never understood that until this very moment when Lucas guffaws, which makes Max grunt louder. Pigs do not appreciate pearls, just as Max did not appreciate an act of kindness. Rude or not, Max can forget all about my invitation to come over and listen to my mom play the theme song to *The Eight Banners*. Max does not deserve the pearl of a private performance.

But then I think about what Grammy told me last week: *Mean people are hurt people who hurt other people.* So I take a deep breath, and on my exhale, I forgive Max.

Mrs. Pinero, my new-favorite teacher, lifts one thin

eyebrow above her aqua blue glasses. That eyebrow is a spacecraft shooting straight up her forehead, and her eye is a laser beam blasting Max. She tells him, "Max, if you have something to say, please share it with the entire class."

All my good intentions about forgiving Max fly straight out of my head. I spin around in my chair with a spaceship lift of my own eyebrows: *Yeah, share it. Share it out loud.* But Max hunches over like a turtle who finds himself in the middle of a busy intersection. He scowls at me like it is my fault he got in trouble.

"So let's talk about surviving species. Survivors like us. How is it that humanity has survived?" Mrs. Pinero asks somberly as if she knows that middle school truly is a matter of survival with Max and his minions snarking about. She scribbles on the whiteboard and taps her pen underneath each word: nature or nurture. "Is it nature that makes us who we are and what we have the potential to be? Or is it nurture that helps us thrive? Our DNA or our home life?"

DNA.

Donna pivots around to smile meaningfully at me. I smile meaningfully back. Our DNA is on its way to be tested.

Mrs. Pinero continues, swinging her arms wide. "Decades and decades of studies on identical twins who've been separated at an early age and reared apart have helped us understand this very concept: nature or nurture."

Donna whirls to look at me. I look at her. These studies could have been about us: separated and reared apart.

"Genes might determine our potential, but our environment—our home life, our school life, our friend life—determines whether that potential gets to be expressed," Mrs. Pinero says. "Like perfect pitch. That runs in families, but without lessons, you may never know you have it, much less use it."

Perfect pitch, the way it runs in the Breedlove family. Except for me.

But maybe, just maybe, there are parts of me that only Donna and I share. It is thrilling, that thought that I might be connected to someone I know on this very earth.

In social studies, Mr. Guevara has written in large letters, all capitals, on the whiteboard: WHO ARE YOU?

Donna and I look at each other as we take our seats: Who are we? Sister-twins!

"So, class, ready to share the meaning of your last name?" Mr. Guevara booms in his deep voice. "Mine means prominent." He flexes his arms, but if that was supposed to display major muscles, I am sorry to say that I do not see any. "Which goes to show, there's always something interesting about names."

Jacqueline of the big words raises her hand and announces, "I would like to share the provenance of my name."

Provenance? What does that even mean? It's irritating because it feels like Jacqueline is using big words just to sound smart. But as Grammy used to say, You'll never know anything unless you ask. So I ask, "What does that even mean?"

"Provenance," Jacqueline explains, "means the place

where something comes from. Like our last names." She pronounces hers, "Muir. It is an old Scottish name that means the sea." As she now informs us, Jacqueline can trace her family back eight entire generations: names, dates, accomplishments. Three streets in Seattle are named after her great-grandfather. Even a city park is named after her family.

"Max," says Mr. Guevara, "why don't you tell us about your last name?"

Max mumbles, "Morrison is Scottish for son of Morris."

"Who's Morris?" Lucas asks.

"How should I know?" Max scowls. His left hand tightens into a fist like he does not want to be anyone's son. Weirdly, Lucas looks hurt like he wishes he were someone's son.

Class is over before I can take my turn, but Max looks straight at me and snickers. Ever since I was little, Mom's made me listen for that warning rattle because rattlesnakes live in the foothills behind our forever home. Hear that rattle and you stand still; the only thing moving is your eyes as you try to locate that poisonous snake.

I know exactly where Max is.

Max stands up and rattles, "Breeeed-love. Like bunnies. Oh, wait, you *are* a rabbit."

My face grows hot. Of course, now Lucas rattles, "She doesn't look like a Breeeed-love."

My cheeks grow even hotter, and my scarf the size of a blanket is not helping at all. I mean, it's obvious when I look at a picture of myself with my family that one of us doesn't look like the others. But most of the time, I forget that I don't look like Ben and Jacob, who are the perfect blend of my parents right down to their lopsided grins. Every so often, I see Gramps in their dreamy expressions when they're playing music, and Grammy when they smile with their eyes.

A horrible thought infests my mind.

Maybe Lucas is right: I am an impostor Breedlove, the only one in my family missing a lopsided grin and blond hair and perfect pitch.

So who in my family am I like?

"Breedlove is her last name. And I happen to love that name," says Donna loyally.

My heart rate slows because I do look like someone. Someone like my maybe-twin. I glare at Max and his sidekick, daring either of them to breathe a single word. I straighten my shoulders and say, "I happen to love my last name, too."

What I love even more than looking like Donna is that she is sticking up for me the way Ben and Jacob would: Immediate. Loud. Like real family even if we may not share a single speck of DNA.

In a booming voice, I tell Donna, "My mom can't wait to play the theme song to *The Eight Banners* for you again today."

That shuts Max right up.

# Chapter 21

Miracle of miracles. Donna is allowed to walk the three minutes to bubble tea to wait for her mom, who's running late, so long as Donna carries her personal security device and goes with a friend. I am that friend because, second miracle of miracles, Mom says no problem to accompanying Donna. The problem comes when Mom asks before we hang up, "What's bubble tea?"

I have no idea, not that I am going to admit that out loud.

Donna clutches her red alarm in one hand and presses it to her side like she's trying to hide it. If I had mine, I'd hold it, too, so she wouldn't feel so singled out. But my alarm is at home somewhere.

"The wait is killing me," Donna says once we leave the school grounds.

"Me too!" I say.

"We're both impatient." Donna gasps. "Nature!" We beam at each other. Alike, so alike. She gazes at me, wide-eyed. "Do you think the swabs are already on their way?"

It's been over six hours since I dropped off the package. "They better be."

"Optimism!" Donna cries and punches the air.

"Nature!" I yell and punch the air, too, before we sing at the same time: *"Alike! So alike!"*

When we stop laughing, Donna says in a rush, "No matter what we find out, I'm so glad you're here."

"So much ditto."

Donna stops abruptly on the sidewalk with a dramatic "ta-da!" We have arrived at Bubble & Sip, and I hadn't realized it. The window is covered in large illustrations of huge cups filled with black bubbles and topped with striped straws. Her hand rests on the door handle, and she asks, "Ready for your life to change?"

It already has.

The bubble tea shop is layered in pinks upon pinks with frothy white pom-pom lights dangling from the ceiling. A lush wall of flowers lines one side along with a hot-pink neon sign: It's Bubble Tea Time!

The menu is long and bewildering with flavors I don't know: black sesame, taro, ube. And some I do: mango, strawberry, watermelon. I confess, "I've never had bubble tea."

"Never?" Donna asks, astonished.

"You came to the right place," says the young woman with—you guessed it—pink hair behind the counter. A black dragon tattoo spirals down her entire arm, billowing flames on the back of her hand.

I want to be her when I grow up.

But after we order with Donna helping me—strawberry, full sugar, less ice—she angles her head at the pink-haired woman and whispers, "My mom would never let me get a tattoo."

"Mine will. When I'm eighteen," I say.

"Nurture!" we cry out together.

As if she were trained by my dad, Donna pulls out her phone to document my first official sip of bubble tea.

"Make sure you suck up one of those boba things," she says, pointing to the large black pearls pooling at the bottom of the pink drink.

So I do. And swallow one boba. Whole.

"Ack! Don't choke! You're supposed to chew it!" Donna protests.

I flush. And try again with a more tentative slurp. These pearls are . . . chewy. I was not expecting chewy.

"Well? Has your life changed?" Donna asks eagerly.

The right answer is yes, I know. I wish I could say yes. But the best I can manage is, "It's different."

Donna cries, "Nurture!"

"Definitely nurture," I agree, but what if it is nature? What if I don't like bubble tea ever?

"You've been missing out, right?" the tattooed woman calls out to me.

She has no idea. It hits me then, a deep, sharp pain for everything that Donna and I have missed out on together. Not just hanging out with bubble teas. But singing and dancing. And laughing. So much laughing. With Donna in my life, I'd never have felt alone in the world with secret worries and sad wonderings about our birth parents. Our birth family. Our birth home.

I refuse to lose out on a single moment. Not even when Donna's mom breezes into Bubble & Sip, ready to drive me home before taking Donna to her piano lesson. Not even when Auntie Susie invites me over to hang out tomorrow after ballet. I take sip after sip of my bubble tea, committing all these moments to my memory.

"Now that we've found you, we want every second with you," says Auntie Susie, smiling at me warmly.

That's what Mom is afraid of.

Still, as their car pulls away from our driveway, I take the biggest slurp yet of that questionable bubble tea. I chew on the boba bubbles.

And when I swallow—miracles. The bubble tea is starting to taste like home sweet home.

# Chapter 22

The next day after school. I check for the billionth time: still no DNA results. Frustrated, I fling back against the kitchen chair, glare at the DNA website, and return to the last thing I want to work on: my homework.

*What does your family stand for?* One Breedlove who shall not be named stands for "obstacle" because she made a (fake) excuse for why I couldn't go over to the Lees today. Since when in the entire life of our dog has it been imperative for me to take Owen for a walk immediately after school? But I did. And instead, Donna is coming over as soon as she's done with ballet class.

Now I am wondering if that is such a good idea.

Breedloves may stand for merciless teasing, but Mom did not like Dad's joking about her "bugle-like notes" in his new song. Piano notes are now trumpeting from upstairs while downstairs, electronic music is sizzling, as my parents fight with each other, using their music instead of their words. I am left alone in the kitchen with a tray of untouched bittersweet chocolate chip cookies cooling from the oven, Owen snoring blissfully on top of my feet, and worries banging around in my head.

What if they get divorced?

Forget today's homework. I jump ahead to tomorrow's and research Marian Anderson, who just so happens to be my new number one hero. Even the lure of Dad's freshly baked cookies on the counter doesn't stop me from reading about our school's namesake. I am too engrossed to leave my chair. One of Dad's favorite all-time conductors, Arturo Toscanini, said that Marian Anderson had the voice of the century, one people only heard once in a hundred years. No wonder her fans loved her as much as I love A2Z. Yet when Marian wanted to sing at the Constitution Hall in Washington, DC, the Daughters of the American Revolution told her there were no dates available.

That was a big lie.

What they meant was: there were no dates available for a Black singer even if people thought she was the best singer the world had ever heard.

So my second new hero, Eleanor Roosevelt, the First Lady, not only resigned her membership with the Daughters of the American Revolution in protest, but she invited Marian to perform at the Lincoln Memorial. Now *that* is a power move.

On Easter Sunday in 1939, Marian sang her heart out on the front steps of America.

She sang like she belonged on every stage.

I have to hear her voice again, this Marian Anderson, and find a recording—the same one Mr. Guevara shared with us in class. As soon as her soaring voice fills my heart and the kitchen, Grammy bustles in like she is very late.

"Have you seen my sign?" Grammy demands, opening first the fridge, then the oven.

"What sign?" I ask, wishing Mom or Dad were here in the kitchen with us, but when I stop the video of Marian Anderson, the piano notes are still storming upstairs, and downstairs, a guitar plinks a mournful note here, a viola plonks a doleful note there.

That leaves me with Grammy, who is now so frantic she looks like she might burst into broken-hearted tears. Or have a heart attack.

I do not want my Grammy's heart to ache in any way.

"What sign, Grammy?" I ask again.

"My sign for the march," she snaps, upending the neat stack of papers on the kitchen counter. Grammy looks around wildly. "Hurry, I don't want to be late."

"How about I make you a new sign?" I ask, seizing a Sharpie from the junk drawer. "Besides, I need a sign, too, right?"

That calms Grammy. She nods. "You definitely need a sign."

I grab some blank paper from the kitchen desk and slide a chair out for Grammy. Then I sit next to her. "So what's the march for?" I ask.

That stumps Grammy. She waves impatiently. "The march! No more nicey-nice words. We have to march! Make our voices heard!"

Before she can get too worked up, I ask, "Okay, what do you want your sign to say?"

She taps a gnarled finger on the blank page, one rap for every syllable: "Get in good trouble."

It would be better if we had stiff poster board, but I make do with flimsy paper, carefully writing out the words. This is harder than it sounds with Grammy watching Mom-like over every single letter.

I have no idea how Donna thinks lettering is dancing on paper. My words are crooked like they are marching to their own beat. "What does this really mean? Good trouble?"

"It means, get into trouble that can help people. That's what John Lewis, civil rights icon, used to say," answers Grammy, now gazing at me with blazing eyes. "It's what Eddie and I would remind each other. Keep getting in good trouble so hatred has no place to roost in our community."

I think about Marian Anderson as I write the same words on my sign. Who knew singing itself could be good trouble?

"Ready to march?" I ask Grammy, helping her out of her chair.

Outside, it is cold and cloudy. The backyard looks like a soggy swamp. It would be less muddy and messy to pretend-march on the cement sidewalk in front of the house, but the last thing I want is for anyone—say, Donna—to witness our pretend-march with Amah, who already seems to dislike me. Or Max. I groan. If Max saw me, I would be the snicker-snorted laughingstock of sixth grade for the rest of the year. He would make sure of that.

No front yard.

By the back door is a rack of raincoats and candy-colored

galoshes, but not a single umbrella since no one in Seattle ever uses one. Gramps used to say, We laugh in the face of rain. And Grammy used to say, We laugh in the face of opposition.

Grammy complains, "Where is my rally-going sweater? What did you do with my rally-going sneakers? I need the arch support."

I have never even heard about Grammy's rally-going sweater. And I do not know where her beat-up, arch-supporting, rally-going sneakers are. But I have an idea. "Grammy, we can laugh in the face of rain and opposition better in rainboots today."

"Now, that's an excellent idea," she says approvingly.

So I help Grammy into purple knee-high rainboots and a yellow raincoat, then stuff my feet into green boots of my own and get ready to laugh in the face of rain and opposition. We have at least twenty minutes before Donna will arrive. No one will see me. Besides, how long can Grammy march?

As it turns out, Grammy has incredible marching stamina. Remarkable marching stamina. Around and around the soggy yard we go, her chanting, "What do we want?"

What do I want?

Family, my heart screams.

My parents to stop fighting, my head shrieks.

A twin sister, my soul aches.

I used to want to return to my forever home, but now? Now I want to stay here with my forever sister.

When I don't respond fast enough, Grammy commands me, "Say, 'To be heard!'" She chants. "To be seen!" She shouts, "To belong!"

I ask, "To belong?"

"Yes! With our families. Our friends. Our community." Grammy stomps around me. "Shout it like you mean it."

"But, Grammy," I say, catching up to her, "does this really make a difference? Marching? Shouting?"

"When someone is sick, we show up with soup. When someone is grieving, we show up and cry. When someone is silenced, we show up and shout. We show up because an attack on one of us is an attack on all of us. So, yes, we keep marching."

Is that what Mr. Guevara and Mrs. Banerjee and Ms. Lauchengco have been trying to tell us with the Make Our Mark project? That community is work: it is love and action, words and presence. It is work to make it what we want it to be.

"But then why don't you ever talk about all your marches?" I ask.

"Because," Grammy says, finally stopping. "Because it's not about me. It's about us." She waves her sign. "So, what do we want?"

"To be us!" I shout.

Grammy nods like she can hear everything unspoken in my head, heart, and soul just as I can hear the back gate creak open and Donna asking, "Hey, what're you doing?"

I blush bright red. Before I can explain, Grammy does: "We are marching."

Donna grins and says eagerly, "Ooh, can I join?"

Grammy says impatiently, "Well, what are you waiting for?"

I hand Donna my sign, and she holds it up approvingly. "Nice poster."

We end up sharing the sign back and forth as we march with Grammy.

"Guess what?" Donna whispers, eyes gleaming, after we've gotten Grammy dry and warm inside and maneuvered her safely into her bedroom.

"What?" I whisper back and lead us to the staircase.

"My mom is going to talk to your mom about us taking the DNA tests."

"What? When?"

"Today. When she picks me up."

Today? When the piano notes are storming today? "But we've already taken them."

"Yeah, and we can take them again." Donna shimmies on the landing before following me up to my room.

I know why Donna is celebrating: we won't get in trouble now.

Here we are, both of us whispering about the most import- ant thing we have ever done. I do not think Grammy would be whispering about something this important. Not when she shouted the truth to the world for years, as she marched in streets for miles. It makes me uneasy now, even if I know what we did was right.

Donna pulls her computer from her backpack. "Did you

know there was a study where twins and triplets were supposedly separated on purpose at adoption just for research? To figure out how much nurture plays in who we turn out to be?"

What if we were separated on purpose? Anger swells in me. "That's sick."

"Totally sick." Donna slams her hand on the rug. "They changed people's lives."

"Without their permission."

"No consent!" Donna fumes. "It makes me so mad."

That makes the two of us.

"I did some research last night, too." I meet her gaze. "In this Minnesota Twin Study? Identical twins raised apart were just as much alike as twins raised together."

Together, we breathe, "Nature."

Alike, so alike.

We have to be, I think, when I hear the doorbell ring downstairs, then Auntie Susie's voice, warm like she and Mom are longtime friends. And Mom, sounding cool like they are perfect strangers. Like she wants to keep it that way.

I look at Donna, and she looks at me—and it is as if we both understand the assignment: we must eavesdrop. We nod at each other because there is no other choice. Both of us creep to the end of the hallway. Both of us perch on the top step, hugging our knees to our chests. Both of us hold our breath as Auntie Susie says, "I was telling Carl last night, what are the chances of them being sisters, right?"

Mom agrees enthusiastically, "Right!"

"But I can't stop thinking that the girls really do look alike, right down to that wave in their hair. So, what if it's somehow true? That they were separated at the orphanage?"

Mom corrects her, "By the orphanage."

A heavy, heartbreaking sigh. "At or by the orphanage, if it's true, it all results in the same thing. They were separated. I can't stop thinking . . ." A catch in her voice, as Auntie Susie continues, "I can't stop thinking, what if I had a part in inadvertently separating the girls?"

There is a long, painful silence, and I can't look at Donna because an awful thought swirls in my mind. What if our parents are the reason why she and I have lived apart for almost all of our lives? Donna's arm wraps around me like she knows each and every one of the emotions swarming inside me—horror, anger, sadness, loss. So much loss. She leans into me, and I lean back into her. Our heads rest together. This feels familiar, so achingly familiar, us automatically pressing into each other for comfort. I can almost imagine us, wrapped up in our matching baby blankets like little twin burritos, hers lucky red, mine precious green. Somehow, some way, the two of us always finding each other in our crib.

I can almost see Baby Me being lifted out of the crib, leaving Baby Donna behind.

I sniff as quietly as I can. So does Donna.

Below us, Mom finally says softly, heavily, "I know what you mean."

# Chapter 23

**Wednesday**: still no test results.

Instead, after school, a large bronze envelope arrives in snail mail for me. Every single letter of my name on the shimmery envelope is shaped with elaborate swoops and curlicues. I trace my full name, lingering on the ornate initials with all their detailed flourishes. My name has never looked so fancy. So beautiful.

So important, like I am special.

I know the calligrapher: Donna.

Inside, the invitation glimmers on iridescent paper like pixie wings in the kitchen light.

*Rise and Shine! It's Bubble Waffle Time to celebrate Donna's 12th birthday!*

Three illustrations decorate the front of the thick card, each featuring a bubble waffle cone. The waffles aren't traditional waffle cones. And they aren't the square Belgian waffles that Dad fixes every Sunday morning. These waffles have large round bubbles like plastic bubble wrap, the kind that pops in a satisfying way beneath your feet when you stomp on them. One bubble waffle cone bulges with chocolate ice cream and rainbow sprinkles. Another with strawberries and whipped cream. The last with banana slices drizzled with chocolate syrup. I'm starving just admiring the card.

"What's that, sugarplum?" Mom asks as she shuffles into the kitchen with her slightly groggy post-piano look.

I show her the invitation and ask, "What's a bubble waffle?"

She shakes her head slowly: *I don't know either.*

So I search on my phone. "Oh, it's a street snack from Hong Kong back in the fifties. I guess it's super popular now. I've never had one."

"Had what?" Dad says at the fridge, where he's filling a glass with ice. He glances over the invitation that Mom shows him. "Well, that looks delicious. Do you think the Lees would mind if we came, too?"

"Dad."

"But we're already celebrating your birthday by ourselves," Mom protests.

"We're just having a family dinner this year, just us and Grammy," I remind her. "We can do that the next night."

"But you'll be wiped out after the slumber party," Mom grumbles.

Yes, I'll be grumpy from staying up all night with Donna and her friends so we can rise-and-shine for bubble waffle time together, but I'm not admitting that. "I'll be fine."

My parents exchange a look, the one they share when my brothers talk back: *teenagers!* Instead of glowering with irritation, Dad glows with excitement. He says, "Your mom has an important pre-birthday announcement."

"We've thought about it," Mom says somberly, "and you can take the DNA test with Donna."

Her pause is expectant, like I'm supposed to scream and shout. I have. Four days ago. Guilt puts a damper on any glee now. I choke out, "Thanks, Mom. That means so much to me." That, at least, is true.

When I head to my bedroom, there's no mistaking how hurt Mom sounds when she tells Dad, "I thought she'd be a lot more excited."

"She *is* excited," Dad says, but he sounds confused, too.

Even when I check online for the test results—still nothing—I am stuck on the bubble waffles. Not because I want to eat one right now, but because I wonder, what other food from Asia do I not know about? No way am I going to give Amah another reason to dislike me because I don't know my culture. I decide it is time to inform myself. So I start by researching birthday traditions in Taiwan. Did you know that on your birthday, you're supposed to eat long life noodles, the longer the better to symbolize your own long life?

My phone pings.

DONNA: Did you get the invitation?

ME: The invitation with the most beautiful lettering?

DONNA: That is my all-new, extra-special Dessie Mei font.

ME: You made me a font?

DONNA: I made you a font. Mini yet mighty!

ME: I love the curlicues!

DONNA: That's for all your big ideas swirling in your head.

ME: Whoa! What's the Donna font?

Donna sends me a picture of her full name: Donna Yi-Shen Lee. Instead of script, all the letters are printed, short and chubby. Different, yet the same in the most important way: it is mini and mighty, too. Our fonts look good together, one whimsical, the other practical. They would look fabulous on a poster together, and I tell her so.

DONNA: That's how I designed them! Sister fonts!

ME: What does Yi-Shen mean?

DONNA: It means devoting my life to something.

ME: Devoted to calligraphy?

DONNA: I wish! Devoted to A2Z!

DONNA: Lewis and I share the Yi part of our middle name like all siblings do.

That I didn't know either. If we are sister-twins, should my middle name begin with an Yi? Should my brothers and

I share a common part of our middle names, too? I bite my lip and text back.

> *ME:* That's so cool.
> *DONNA:* I know, right?
> *ME:* Yi-A2Z!
> *DONNA:* Yi-Sistas!
> *DONNA:* You can come to my party, right?
> *ME:* Yes!!
> *DONNA:* Yay!!

I like how we match exclamation point for exclamation point.

My phone pings again. This time, it's Sophie, who wants me to text a picture of Owen because he is like her dog, too, since the three of us used to play almost every day after school. But when I tell Sophie about the bubble waffle birthday party, she goes quiet for a long time.

So long that I have corralled Owen.

So long that Owen sits still for one and exactly one picture.

Which I send. And Sophie does not answer.

When my phone alerts again, it is not Sophie.

> *DONNA:* When do you think we'll find out about the DNA tests?

Sophie or no Sophie, I text the truth.

*ME:* Not soon enough.

*DONNA:* I wish we heard today. Boo!!!

*ME:* Double boo!!!

Even the exclamation points don't drown out the silence from Sophie.

# Chapter 24

"Happy birthday to you!" my dad croons from my bedroom door on Friday morning, strumming his guitar.

Mom joins in, harmonizing, "Happy birthday to you!"

Owen howls along with The Twins, who join the traditional early morning birthday serenade by FaceTime. Usually I ask for an encore, but today? Today, all I want is to get to school. And to surprise Donna with the news. I checked as soon as I woke up. Guess what? The DNA results are ready.

And I am saving them to open with Donna.

"Twelve big ones," says Ben, shaking his head in disbelief.

"It's going to be the best one yet," promises Jacob, "with the best birthday present of all time from yours truly. Hey, what'd you get her?" he asks Ben.

Ben flushes a guilty red and mumbles that he'll talk to me later today before hanging up.

From downstairs, the scent of Dad's famous Birthday Brioche French Toast wafts up to me. This french toast is meant to be savored: The extra-thick wedges of bread. The extra-big mounds of whipped cream. The extra-large pud-dles of maple syrup. After all, Dad only serves it four times a year. But there is no time to savor when results must be read with your hopefully yes sister-twin. So I wolf down the french toast ravenously like I am one of The Twins. Which, now that I think about it, I could be.

"Wow," says Dad at my clean plate. "You must be grow-ing."

Growing impatient, yes. I grab my backpack and yell, "I'm going!"

At school, Donna is waiting for me at the steps, and we run into each other's arms, squealing happy birthday to one another.

My words blur, I'm speaking so fast: "They're ready! The results are ready!"

Donna's eyes grow wide, and she breathes, "Whoa." Then Donna, my rule-following maybe-twin, urges as if she does not care about breaking the no-phone-use-on-campus rule, "Check it. We've got to check it now."

So there on the steps of Marian Anderson Middle School, my maybe-twin and I bend our heads over my phone as I click the link to our online test results. And there they are.

I gasp. Donna gasps.

I start to cry. Donna is crying, too. Then I bawl. And she bawls.

Lucas slow-walks toward us as if our emotions are scaring

him. He cannot hide his concern even when he mutters sarcastically, "Sheesh, who died?"

No one has died. Far from it. In fact, it feels like something new has been born.

Donna and I are not maybe-twins. Or even maybe-yes-twins.

We are not alike, so alike.

We are exactly identical with exactly identical DNA.

"We're twins!" I shout for everyone to hear.

"Identical twins!" Donna bellows for the world to know.

"Sisters!" we scream together. "Twin sisters!"


Max Morrison did not get that best-one-yet birthday memo, because in class, he snicker-whispers, "Breeding-bunny-love, your nose is Rudolph red."

According to Max, I am an impostor rabbit. Good, because I am not a mild-mannered bunny who scampers away at the first hint of danger. Honestly, knowing what I know now, I feel like a dragon, the most powerful animal on the Chinese zodiac. So I glare at Max and breathe out as if I am breathing fire. Incinerating his snide little whispers. I glare at him like I am Mom during The Incident when I was five and a grown man asked if I could speak English, and Mom tore into him that of course her daughter could speak English. But perhaps he himself had a problem understanding simple English: mind your own business. (Mom chalks it up to my unreliable five-year-old's memory that I remember her adding a couple of choice curse words. But I know what I heard.)

"What are you doing?" Norman mutters when he turns around to hand me our homework.

Which reminds me that I'm not alone with Max, and everyone in the classroom can see my fire-breathing expressions. Everyone except Mr. Guevara, who sighs heavily. It is just my luck that he calls on me.

Even though I've already explained a couple days ago that Breedlove means someone popular, I share its second meaning now: "catching a wolf" from the Old English *breedle* for catching and *louvre* for wolf. I aim a meaningful look at Max. If my last name means wolf catcher, then just imagine what I can do to a boring, predictable rabbit.

But then Norman Freeland-Boogaard (whose first last name means exactly what it says: free land, and the second stands for orchard) chimes in that according to the Urban Dictionary, breedlove also means "an alcoholic drink before noon."

Mr. Guevara says quickly, "Okay, Norman, thanks for that fun piece of trivia. Let's refocus on what we've learned about our families. Dessie, can you share one thing your family stands for?"

"Breedloves believe in showing up," I say, aiming a meaningful look at Donna, "especially for their family."

Akshaya hastily adds, "And the Sarabhais believe in being true to their friends."

"Good, good," Mr. Guevara says, back to bouncing. "Who else?"

Jacqueline says, "The Muirs believe that words matter."

Norman says, "Mine believes that everyone should be free to be who they are and to love whoever they love."

"Max," says Mr. Guevara, "how about your family?"

Max mumbles like he doesn't want anyone to hear, "My dad believes in beer."

We all laugh, but Max scowls. His eyebrows draw down like a visor on a knight's helmet, and his left hand tightens like he is holding a sword, hunting down the magical weaver of hopes and dreams in *The Eight Banners*. He ducks his head, but not before I notice his cheeks have bloomed the same furious red as when he stomped away from the Lunar New Year dinner table celebrating families.

Even though I've already gone, I add, "Breedloves believe in the power of a good cookie."

Max—Max!—snickers and says, "You are not a real Breed-love."

Mr. Guevara protests, "Max!"

Before Mr. Guevara can say anything more to Max, Donna blurts out without raising her hand, "And Lees believe that our friends are family. All of our friends, no matter what is happening to their family."

As soon as Mr. Guevara turns his back to write on the board, Max lobs a wad of paper. It hits Donna smack in the back of her head with a loud and distinct whack! Donna spins around, holding her hand to her head, shocked speechless. Donna who was just trying to remind Max that he still belonged no matter where his dad was—and that I belonged, too. I cannot believe Max threw something at Donna, his campfire friend since they were toddlers.

As Lucas is about to copy Max, crumpling a piece of paper, my dragon-eyes see red. No one is picking on my sister. I seethe, "Oh no you don't." My dragon-voice roars out as I stand up and point at Max. "You despicable little worm of a traitor."

Donna snorts, then laughs. She laughs so hard, tears stream down her cheeks. We both belly laugh until Mr. Guevara sends the three of us—me, Donna, and Max—to the principal's office, where we all get in trouble.

No one is laughing when Mrs. Banerjee writes us up for disrupting our class.

# Chapter 25

Donna won't stand with anyone in the parking circle after school. Not even Akshaya. Certainly not me. Every time I approach her, she veers away like I am contagious. Like I am the vexatious troublemaker who has ruined her life. Her last panicked words outside Mrs. Banerjee's office still echo in my ears: "It's fine for you to get in trouble. Your family believes in getting in trouble. Mine doesn't!"

But we're family, too, I wanted to remind her. Instead, I said, "Didn't you hear me when I told Mrs. Banerjee this wasn't your fault at all?"

Donna shook her head, back and forth, her eyes on her chunky sneakers. "That won't matter."

"It was Max's fault," I insisted.

She scoffed. "No one in my family is going to believe that."

"Fine, then blame me."

"They already do," she hissed, staring hard at me, then clamped her lips tight.

I demanded, "What do you mean by that?"

But Donna refused to say another word.

Unexpectedly, Dad is waiting in the parking lot for me when I wanted—needed—to walk home alone to think. He pops out of the driver's seat with his lopsided grin. The lopsided Breedlove grin that I do not have no matter how many times I try to grin lopsidedly in the mirror.

"Your birthday chauffeur awaits," Dad says, waving me to the station wagon.

A million emotions are marching up and down my body from my frantic heart to my furious feet that are both pounding toward Dad and his lopsided grin. The loudest emotion is anger at the injustice buried in the bottom of my backpack: the letter from Mrs. Banerjee to my parents.

As I lower the backpack, the straps thwap in the wind like they are spirit banners stolen from Peridot in *The Eight Banners*. Like my backpack wants to jerk free and soar away from the wild storm gathering inside me.

Maybe I will let my backpack with its unfair letter go.

"What do you call a baker with a cold?" Dad jokes. Pause. "A cough-ee cake," he coughs triumphantly.

I don't even groan.

"Bye, Donna," I call from the passenger door.

Donna ignores me.

Shrugging, Dad grabs my backpack right out of my hand. He takes it away from me without asking.

I growl at Dad, my words biting. "Give. Me. Back. My. Backpack."

Dad looks hurt, and he instantly releases his grip. "I was just trying to help."

"I don't need your help!" That roars out of me. Loud. Ferocious. I am a word-breathing dragon. "You can be so pushy sometimes!"

My words don't incinerate. They freeze. Dad's face stiffens. He becomes a marble version of himself. He averts his hurt gaze, and then his eyes widen before he gives a slight wave. An "it's okay, nothing to see here" wave and a half-hearted smile, the reassurance he might send me when he and Mom are arguing and I barge into the room.

I glance over my shoulder to see who is watching us.

It is Donna. And Amah.

They both look word-frozen, too. Donna's eyes are wide with shock. But Amah's—Amah's eyes are narrowing. Spitting fire right back at me. Her mouth twitches like she's about to say something, and I don't think any of it will be good. Amah's powerful glower cuts straight through the blustery wind and pierces straight into me. Disapproval.

No, worse: dislike.

Maybe even: disgust.

That glare whips me into silence. I shove my backpack into the back seat and climb inside our car.

Once the doors are closed, Dad says in a hollow voice, "We all have bad days, but you don't have to take it out on other people." Then he leans over the driver's seat to straighten the backpack with its treacherous cargo.

Tears prick at my eyes. I blink hard, blink them away, and

stare out my window, ignoring Dad. Ignoring Amah's glare that stings even more sharply as a memory.

As we pull out of the parking lot, Dad says, "When you want to talk, I'm always here, kiddo."

*Always.*

The word tastes like bitter melon in my mouth. It tastes like a forever home, ripped away. Forever sisters, ripped apart.

But always and forever, those are promises that I have to believe in.

Finally, I tell Dad the truth. "Donna and I are twins, Dad. We already took the test. The DNA test."

Dad, the one person I can count on to support me no matter what, only sighs my name. "Dessie." My name, two flat notes of disappointment.

I didn't think it was possible to feel worse than a slug on hot pavement on the hottest day of the year. But there, on the middle of my bed, are two sets of brand-new mooncake molds. One mold contains six different flower shapes, each intricate as a snowflake. The other is the shape of a rabbit with tiny circle eyes and two long ears.

A guilty lump clogs my throat. I truly am the meanest person on the planet because here is Dad, yet again trying to help me.

Dad, who convinced Mom to let me take the DNA test.

Dad, who is celebrating that I am a rabbit on the Chinese zodiac.

From downstairs, I hear my parents, playing their different tunes at each other.

Mom's voice is a clatter of discordant chords: "I told you that digging this all up would have consequences. This stupid family heritage assignment. Make Our Mark. Why do we need to Make Our Mark?"

"This must be so confusing for her." Dad's voice is a calm melody.

"She yelled at a boy in her class."

They know, they know, they know.

I sink on my bed, the mooncake molds sliding toward me. This means Mrs. Banerjee emailed the letter to my parents. And Donna's parents.

Dad says, "Dessie did more than that." I don't need to strain to hear Dad telling Mom about the DNA test. Her screech—"She did what?"—makes that clear. Then Mom says, "We need to let Donna's parents know."

"Definitely. Maybe we can talk to them before the party."

But they clearly want to scold me now. Their footsteps clatter in perfect unison up the staircase. I pull my knees tight to my chest until I am a ball. I cannot forget Donna sidling away from me any more than I can forget Amah's glare, chasing me down. Accusing me of being a horrible person. No lecture from my parents can make me feel worse than I already do.

At the foot of my bed, Dad gazes down at me. In a mezzo forte voice that is three times fainter than his usual boisterous tone, he says, "Finding a sister, figuring out who you are, all of this is a lot to process. You know you can tell me anything."

"Us," Mom corrects him.

"You can tell us anything," Dad says, then sits next to me. "I just wish you had worked with us on that DNA test."

"I tried!" I snarl. "You wouldn't let me take the test."

Mom clears her throat and says firmly, "Sometimes we need time to think things through, especially when there are so many implications. But even then, you can always tell us anything, no matter what. We're adults. We can handle anything. I promise."

How can I believe them? I blink back my tears, but I can still see Donna's accusatory expression. Mom sits down on my other side, both of my parents bookending me.

"Hey, we're here to help you on your adoption journey," Mom says softly.

"You're not alone." Dad mentions Donna and her family. "They can help. Especially now that they're your family, too."

That's right. The Lees are my family, too. And families forgive each other.

My heart lifts. It will be a relief to escape to Donna's birthday party tonight. To feast on a homemade bubble waffle filled with chocolate and whipped cream.

To ignore the Make Our Mark project.

To forget Mrs. Banerjee's letter.

Half an hour later, since the invitation said to wear pajamas, I'm changing when my phone pings and pings. And pings.

*DONNA:* I don't know how to say this so I'll just say it.

*DONNA:* Amah says that you can't come to my birthday party tonight.

*DONNA:* I can't be friends with you anymore.

*ME:* But we're sisters.

The pit in my stomach grows so large, so deep, I fall in. My heart is wheeling in wild, chaotic circles. I'm afraid to ask why.

I'm afraid to know why.

I think of Grammy and her scowl because she doesn't remember why. So I ask. I have to.

For the longest time, Donna doesn't answer.

I stare at my phone. At the three dots that appear and disappear. Just like her friendship.

Finally, Donna texts: Because she thinks you're a bad influence. The DNA test and the letter from the principal were the last straws.

Me, Dessie Mei Breedlove, a bad influence? As if Donna understands, as if she can picture me sitting on my bed, halfway into my flannel pajamas, arms hugging my knees tight as I try not to howl and rage and weep, clenching all my messy emotions tight inside myself so I don't implode, she texts one last time.

*DONNA:* I know you're not, even if you are kinda rude to your parents.

There are no more dots on my phone after that. Just silence.

Deep under my shock, deep beneath my anger, is a crushing cold. The cold, bleak ground of truth.

I am being left again. Abandoned again.

Maybe there is something worse than the mystery of why.

It is understanding perfectly, painfully well why.

# Chapter 26

Donna Lee is—was—my newest friend, but she is not my only friend. I call my brothers, first Ben, then Jacob. Neither answer. I text Sophie, who should be brushing her leopard-spotted horse, Dancy, like she always does after school. No response.

I do not like making phone calls, not even to my oldest friend. It is awkward and uncomfortable in a way that texting is not. But today is not every day. With a deep breath, I work up my courage to call Sophie. She answers, and I immediately see that she is not brushing her horse. She is getting ready for what should have been our first middle school dance together, the dance I have forgotten about. Her straight blond hair bounces in fat curls, and she holds her phone close to her mouth, asking me to choose between lip glosses, the barely-there-berry on her top lip or the save-the-coral peachier one on her bottom.

"They both look good," I say because the glosses look practically the same to me.

"That's no help." Sophie launches into an entire mono-logue about which color will better match her outfit and make her lips look kissable and pouts expectantly at me. Which I take is my cue to demand, Who exactly does she want to kiss?

Instead, I say, "I was supposed to go to Donna's birthday party tonight."

"Oh my gosh, it's your birthday!"

It stings, that Sophie forgot my birthday. But I can't afford to lose her as a friend, so I don't say anything.

Sophie frowns. "Why aren't you there?"

I admit softly, "I was kind of disinvited."

"What?"

"And I just found out we really are sisters. Twin sisters."

"I knew she was awful."

"Donna's not awful!"

"Oh yeah?" Sophie's eyes narrow paper-thin, so thin they could cut. "What kind of person disinvites someone an hour before their party? Someone awful."

"It's not like that," I protest.

"And what's worse is that she's your sister. Sisters don't do that to each other."

"She didn't have a choice!"

"We always have a choice," Sophie snaps back, her cheeks flushing angrily. "You could have told your parents that you were going to live with me. My parents said it was okay." Then Sophie, my best friend since we were toddlers, says sharply, "I've got to go. Amara and London are here!"

My screen goes dark.

I feel lonelier than ever.

At six o'clock sharp, Mom knocks on my door. I don't answer.
I am balled up on my bed like I am Owen, shivering after a
long walk in the icy rain. I do not want to talk to anyone,
especially not my parents. Especially not when I am always
rude to my parents, according to Donna. And Amah.

Mom is nothing if not persistent. She raps at the door
again. "Dessie? You ready to go?"

I don't answer. But is not answering rude? It feels rude, so
I mutter, "I'm not going." As soon as the words are out of my
mouth, I wonder, Is muttering rude?

But how can I be rude when this is exactly how Jacob and
Ben talk to our parents? Are the three of us rude?

Mom opens the door without my permission. Isn't barg-
ing in uninvited rude? Did I learn rudeness from my parents?
After all, there was The Other Incident that we never talk
about, the one where Mom and I had slipped off to the Children's Museum while visiting Grammy and Gramps. There,
a bunch of teenagers circled around me when Mom was
distracted, reading a placard for one of the exhibits. They
repeated over and over, "Hong twong wong!"

"What language are they speaking?" I asked Mom, confused.

She had stared coldly at the circling teens and spat out
in a voice so vicious, it reverberated throughout the entire
exhibit, "The language of all racists: Stupidese."

I remember feeling embarrassed, because everyone stared at Mom, especially the teenagers who scattered. Fast. But which was ruder: them for taunting or Mom for snapping?

"Dessie!" Mom cries out, stopping at the foot of my bed, me in my pajama top and jeans. "Why aren't you ready? We agreed to leave at six fifteen sharp."

"I'm not going," I say.

"Are you feeling okay? Are you sick?"

I clamp my mouth shut. Is staying silent rude?

"Dessie." Mom perches on the edge of my bed. "What's wrong? Is this about the mean kid at school? Is he going to be at the party?" Then worried: "Are you afraid to go to the party?"

Silence.

"I can't help you if you don't tell me what's wrong," she prompts.

All of a sudden, I am angry. Furious. Rage is bullying my other feelings away, so sadness and loneliness are afraid to make an appearance. I don't know why I am feeling so mad. Worse, I think I do, but I don't want to look too closely. I'm afraid of what I will discover.

I'm afraid of what will come thundering out of me: the unfairness of life. Max. The birthday party. Donna torn from me yet again. Our parents maybe possibly being the reason why we were torn from each other in the first place.

Is this possibly why my first family gave me up? Is this why Amah is rejecting me? Did they somehow sniff out that I am a terrible, mean person to my core?

So vexatious I'm not worth keeping?

"Dessie Mei Breedlove, what is going on?" Dad demands, joining us in my bedroom. For once, his voice is no-nonsense businesslike with me, exactly how he sounded when he wasn't getting straight answers from Grammy's doctor. How he sounded the night when Ben lied outright about where he was (not at a study group, but at a party). "Who is bullying you at school? Is that why you yelled at that boy?"

Ben may have lied to our parents, but he also earned back enough trust to stay behind when we moved five hours and four hundred miles away. Maybe, just maybe, I can confide one tiny bit of the truth to them.

"It's not because Max is going to be there," I say, then wish I hadn't because Mom and Dad exchange a meaningful look: Max.

Max. I can practically hear them thinking—*The bully has a name!*

"Then why aren't you going to Donna's party?" Mom asks, her voice gentle.

"I can't," I finally admit.

"Of course you can. Your day at school may have been terrible, but you can rally!" Dad says. It is a miracle, really, that Dad was not a cheerleader in school. "It's your birthday! And this is your sister!"

Before Dad can rah-rah-rah one more encouraging word at me, I shake my head.

The head cheerleader of Team Breedlove now lifts to his feet and hollers—I kid you not: "L. E. T. S. G. O. Let's go, let's go!"

"No!" I snap. "You're not listening! I'm not invited anymore."

Is snapping rude? It sure feels like it is. So I snap my mouth shut to trap my rudeness inside. Every time I speak, I am becoming an even worse person.

Mom guesses, "Wait, did something happen between you and Donna?"

My sigh cracks me open so I almost admit, Yes! Yes, something awful happened and I have no clue what to do. But all I tell them is: "I don't want to talk about it."

"Why not?" Dad asks, perplexed.

I think about his depressed face in the parking lot after my word-breathing dragon-self incinerated him and his good mood. I burrow under my thick comforter and cover my face with my pillow as if I can hide from the memory. But Amah's scandalized look, that disgusted look—that is burned into my brain so deeply, I know that dementia and Alzheimer's and even amnesia will never erase it.

I am too afraid—too ashamed—to confess that Amah is right: I am a bad influence.

"Well, I'll just call Donna's mom. We'll work it out," Mom says confidently, standing up as if this is a done deal.

Panicking, I fling the pillow off my face and say firmly, "No."

But is firmness rude?

Firmness seems to make an impression, because Dad places a gentle hand on Mom's arm like he is finally listening to me. He says just as firmly, "We love you, kiddo. When you're ready to talk, we are here."

That pierces me right through my comforter of protection,

my armor of anger. Grammy said there is one sure way to tell the difference between a mean-to-the-core person and a hurt person: by the company they keep.

I must be mean all the way through to my core. Just look at my best friends.

I have none.

When the door closes behind them at last and I am alone again, I finally cry.

# Chapter 27

I am suffocating. death by throw pillow. I knock the downy weight off my face, and in the watery morning light, I make out its message embroidered in pink thread: *Where there is an idea, there is a way.*

It is as if Grammy is talking to me, because that—that is a Breedlove-ism I believe.

Somehow, some way, I will win back Donna and win over Amah. An idea occurs to me. A brilliant idea. I sit straight up in bed. Goodbye, vexatious girl. I will be the model of respectfulness. The picture of politeness. Project Perfect Girl starts with a vow of silence. That way, my words won't land me in future trouble with anyone.

Even so, I am relieved that today is Saturday, so I don't have to face Donna and our non-friendship at school. I don't have to overhear stories about the deliciousness of bubble waffles or listen to replays of the late-night ghost stories, so spooky no one could sleep.

From downstairs, Mom storms, "I am so mad at that

adoption agency. Why didn't they tell us she was a twin? What if we caused this situation somehow? Separated them?" A cabinet door slams. "We would have taken in Donna. I would have said, that child is mine, too."

No, Mom would not have. She can't even look Donna in the eye. Part of me wants to stomp downstairs and tell Mom that, but I remember Project Perfect Girl. Slowly, I breathe out. It is time to think about how I can change Amah's mind about me. It is time to research how I can be more polite.

So I don't get out of bed, not even for Dad's extra-special old-fashioned peanut butter cookies for extra-sad days.

At noon, I don't leave my bedroom for Mom's famous thick ooey-gooey grilled cheese sandwiches or for Dad's attempt to lure me out. "Hey, kiddo, don't you want to open your birthday present?" He hums a tune that I think is supposed to be my favorite A2Z song, it's hard to tell. But all it does is make my heart pang for Donna. And for everything I'm finding out.

Did you know that it's polite in Asian cultures to take your shoes off at home? I think about the way Amah stared at me in my dirty sneakers the first time she dropped me off. Ack.

Did you know that it's polite to offer guests food? I think about Donna and Amah standing in our entry, foodless, even though we were all salivating at the scent of Dad's freshly baked sourdough bread. Ack.

Do you know what's not polite? Piling the choicest bits of food on your plate. I cringe at my helping of the biggest, fattest shrimp at the Lunar New Year feast. Worse, I didn't even eat those shrimp. Double ack.

No wonder Amah thought I was rude.

Finally, on my third hour researching different customs in both Chinese and Taiwanese cultures, I rouse to let in Owen, who is scratching insistently on my bedroom door. His tail wags frantically like he wants me to know that I am still loved. Like I have been missing in action for weeks, not hours.

Despite my intentions, I glance at the clock. Right now, the bubble waffles and pajama partygoers are probably crashing at home, conked out from staying up all night, talking.

I hope they weren't talking about how terrible and mean I am.

How I am a bad influence on them all.

How my rudeness is why Donna had to disinvite me.

It is embarrassing to think about everyone talking about me.

Owen huffs like he does not approve of Project Perfect Girl. So I whisper in a barely there voice that is the closest sound to silence, "Good boy," and as if he agrees that he is a good boy, Owen curls into my lap. How can a dog's snuggle make everything almost bearable in the world? I burrow my head into his thick fur and inhale his dog smell of pine needles and Cheetos and brioche toast with extra cinnamon mixed in with old wet towels. My nose wrinkles.

*You stink*, I think, even as I keep my face cuddled close to Owen's. Then I wonder if even private thoughts can be rude.

But Owen licks me like he knows that I love him so much, I can overlook his doggy smell. He licks me again like he can overlook my rudeness.

Before I can think a silent apology just in case Owen can

detect that, his ears prick up. His furry face tilts to one side, then the other, and he swivels to stare at my closed door. Like he senses a ghost outside. Or an intruder. Owen bounds off my bed and scratches at the door, whining until I leave my cocoon bed to let him out.

Even before the doorbell rings, Owen races downstairs in tiny little thuds. There's a scuffle. Muffled yelps. Owen must be mauling whoever is at the door with slobbery kisses. Is it Donna, here to say that all is forgiven? That everything was a huge misunderstanding that she and her family can overlook?

That her bubble waffle birthday party wasn't a party without me there?

"Double Trouble!" comes a bellow. It is echoed by a different but same-ish voice, "Yo, kiddo!"

My brothers are here! Which is weird because according to the family calendar, they're visiting next weekend.

I can't help but be drawn out of my bedroom to peer down the stairs. At the landing, Ben and Jacob are having a happy family reunion with our parents. Mom is fussing over them, shaking her head. "I wasn't expecting you guys until dinner."

"Yeah, well, we can leave again," Jacob says.

Ben sniffs the air. His nose wrinkles and he says warily, "Mom, you must be cooking."

She sounds offended. "Lentil soup."

"That's our welcome home dinner?" Jacob complains.

I think to myself, *That's my family birthday dinner?*

Ben adds in a disbelieving, disgusted tone that I echo in my head, "Lentil soup?"

"It's meatless Saturday," Dad explains.

Mom tries hard, but as Dad says, her skills lie at the piano keyboard, not the kitchen. Except for her grilled cheese. And her cheesy popcorn.

"That is the stupidest thing I have ever heard. Birthdays are for stuffing yourself with whatever you want," Ben shoots back. "Are you punishing us?"

Mom says, "I should be. Look, it was not cool to get the DNA kit for Dessie and her sister."

"You mean, her twin sister," Ben snaps. "She had a right to know."

"Yes, she has a right to know. But this was—is— momentous. We"—Mom points to herself and Dad—"we should have been involved."

"Hey, Switzerland here," says Jacob, spreading his hands in front of himself. "I wasn't part of this."

"But we all are," Dad says, as he places a hand on Mom's shoulder and closes the gap between them. "We're family and we all need to trust each other. Your mom and I, we appreciate you guys always being there for your little sister, even for this. In the future, though, whenever there's something big that has real-life consequences, let us know. Deal?"

"Yeah, fine, deal," Ben mutters.

"Yeah, whatever," Jacob says, shrugging. I wonder if maybe me not asking him for help has hurt his feelings.

"Hey, where's the birthday girl?" Ben shouts up the stairs. "How about a big fat juicy birthday burger with extra waffle fries? Now, doesn't that sound good? I know you're listening."

Mom retorts with a faint smile, "What sounds good are homemade meals you don't have to cook yourself."

Dad says, "No, what sounds good is you guys grilling us burgers tonight."

I realize, this snappish back-and-forth is the way my family speaks to each other. Is it rude?

I think about all the children's books about adoption that line the bookshelves back in our forever home: *God Gave You Me*. I've always secretly hated those books because they make me feel like God wanted me in the orphanage. But even if that can't possibly be right, I know what is: I have missed my brothers who share my kind of loving rudeness.

I race down the stairs and hug The Twins. Just because I hug them, just because I'm happy to see them, just because I may be a true Breedlove after all does not mean I will risk saying one rude word. The conversation flows so rapidly between the four of them, there is no space for any of mine anyway. The Twins decided to tack on a tour of the University of Washington on Monday instead of next week, then they'll get up early to drive back Tuesday morning to make it to school on time.

Suddenly, Ben turns serious even as he fake-punches me in the arm and says, "Hey, totally uncool that you got uninvited to the party."

"College," says Jacob meaningfully to me, "college is approximately one hundred billion times better than middle school. You'll go to a lot more parties there."

Their words singe: Mom and Dad blabbed to The Twins

about how I got disinvited to Donna's birthday party! There's nothing I can do to stop myself from blushing any more than I can stop Grammy from creeping out of her bedroom cautiously, like strangers have broken into her home. No strangers. Her face breaks into an ecstatic smile: "Ben! Jacob!"

Would Grammy remember me so easily if I were a real Breedlove?

I thud back up the stairs and slam my door shut.

# Chapter 28

Even if I want to stay burrowed in my for-now bedroom, I head downstairs when Mom calls me to help purge the dreaded basement storage. At our current pace of a box a day, I will be eighty-five before the storage is completely cleared out. Then it occurs to me: not only would a Perfect Girl happily help, but she would not call attention to herself with a vexatiously colorful scarf. So I race back upstairs to grab that eye-catching scarf, and hoping no one notices, I stuff it into one of Gramps's keepsake boxes and bury it in the back of the most cobwebby shelf.

"Whatcha doing there, Double Trouble?" asks Ben, watching me carefully.

Who, me? I shrug, silent.

"What really happened with Donna's birthday party?" he asks.

Thank goodness for Project Perfect Girl! Even if I were speaking, which I am not, I may never be ready to talk about being disinvited. Worse, de-sistered. Grief stabs me in my chest. Who knew there really is such a thing as heartbreak? Because my heart has cracked into two identical and separate parts.

Behind me, I can feel The Twins exchanging bewildered looks before they fight to be the first to escape spider central.

Alone in the storage room, my eyes zero in on three large and dusty blue shoeboxes at the very top of today's designated column of shelves. As I rise to my tiptoes to grab them, something skitters down my spine. I scream and swat at my neck. As it turns out, I am not alone. Dad screams. Even Mom yelps a little.

"Dessie!" Mom says, sounding mad when it turns out to be nothing. "I thought you were hurt."

"I thought I felt a spider," I tell her. Death by spider seems like a valid reason for breaking a vow of silence.

"I de-spidered this entire place yesterday," Dad says, which is such a Dad thing to do. It's easy to imagine him ferrying each and every spider gently cupped in his palm and kneeling down in the wet grass to free them outside.

A piece of my heart softens.

"Hey, so how's everything going with your second sixth grade?" asks Ben, clearly procrastinating outside the storage room because, whether he admits it or not, his arachnophobia is even worse than mine.

"She has a bully there," Mom answers for me, then demands, "so the important question is: Do we need to de-bully your school?"

"Wait, who's being mean to you?" asks Jacob, shoving

past Ben, who was blocking the storage door. "Who do we need to take care of?"

I shake my head, wanting to avoid talking about Max and his minion-in-meanness, Lucas. And most important, my own meanness at retaliating against Max. Without a word, I point to the boxes I was trying to reach. Jacob lifts them easily from the top shelf.

Dad grins. "Hey, look, more pictures!"

Mom sighs softly because this means one thing: a detour from our task. But she doesn't complain when we gather around the battered coffee table. Inside the first shoebox is a pile of baby photos, all unmarked. Even so, it's easy to tell which are Dad because in a weird way, he looks exactly the same as he did as a baby: Same lopsided smile. Same twinkly eyes. Same cowlick that arches over his forehead like a puppy's tail.

Mom plucks out a photo and coos, "Look how chubby you were! Even your toes!" She actually kisses the photo of Dad's naked baby butt.

Jacob groans. "Mom."

Ben moans like he can't even manage a real word. "Eww."

I grimace and cover my eyes.

"This one definitely goes in Grammy's Best Of album," Mom says, ignoring all of us.

Dad one-ups my grimace with a deep blush. "Honey. That's not going to help her remember anything."

"Then the kids will keep this for when *you* need a Best Of

photo album," Mom says, grinning. She sets the photo down next to herself. "I'll start another box."

It is a little sad to think that when it's time for me to have a Best Of photo album, there will be no baby photos of me. Not as a newborn. Not as a five-month-old. I only have one tiny, faded snapshot from the orphanage of when I was maybe a year old.

The problem is: my life before the Breedloves may have been short, but I did have a life. It was mine.

I just don't remember it.

Just like Grammy who lived her life, too—even if she can't remember it.

It's a relief when Dad stretches and asks The Twins to jam with him and Mom before dinner. Back in the old days when Gramps was still alive and could remember all the notes to hundreds of songs, he would jump into our family ensemble with his violin. Grammy and I would sit and sway together. She would tell me, "In this world, there are music players and there are music swayers. Both are important when it comes to music."

Yawning, Ben hauls Owen off my lap and says, "Fair's fair, if we have to play, then you need to dance or something."

Back in the old days, I would glower at Ben and tell him that I'd dance on his grave if he said one more word. But today, I am silent.

Ben frowns and says, "Stop being so weird."

Today, when I sit next to Grammy on the orange sherbet

sofa in the living room, listening to my family jam, she does not sway with me. Her eyebrows lower as Pachelbel plays on and on. As if she has no memory of her wedding day. Or Mom and Dad's. Her eyebrows lower like she is resisting the music. Resisting being swept away to the past, to the land of memories. Her body is stiff like she does not want to be here with this family she cannot remember well.

My heart aches. I want to tell Grammy that it is okay. She doesn't have to try so hard to remember what she can't. We can make new memories together. So I reach over and squeeze her frail hand. Grammy squeezes back like she understands.

Maybe this is what I have to do with my memory of our forever family and our forever home: leave it be. I can't retrieve our old family—Grammy is forever changed. Gramps forever gone. Next year, when The Twins are off to college, my family will be forever different.

Yet when I needed them the most this weekend, my brothers came. As if they were bringing my forever home to me, wherever I was.

Just as they had promised.

# Chapter 29

My vow of silence breaks yet again at dinner when I accidentally ask for another serving of Dad's famous focaccia bread that he baked as a peace offering after the lentil soup rejection. A single bite—a single taste—of that chewy yet crisp, salty, and still-warm bread can make everything else taste good. Even lentil soup.

That is how it is with The Twins, too. A single night with them here, right here under this roof, almost makes up for being disinvited to Donna's party. Almost. While The Twins usually slink off to their bedrooms after dinner, they always stay for Family Movie Night, especially for Family Horror Movie Night. Tonight, before the zombie apocalypse starts, Dad surprises me with an ice cream bar with twelve different toppings in celebration of my twelfth birthday: sprinkles, mini chocolate chips, crushed graham crackers, baby marshmallows, and, for the first time, boba balls.

Mom surprises us with her announcement. "We need a Family Meeting first."

That is how I broke my vow of silence for a third time: I groan along with The Twins. Dad looks like he wants to groan, too, but he knows better. Silently, he pops the vanilla ice cream back into the freezer.

In the living room without our ice cream sundaes, Mom clears her throat. "I think that it would be good for us to talk about our new family dynamics."

New family dynamics like Mom and Dad fighting all the time? Or new family dynamics like they are thinking of getting divorced? I am not the only one worried. The Twins exchange anxious glances with each other like they are having a silent conversation in double time.

Watching them have a whole conversation without a single word hurts.

Mom continues, "With Dessie finding her long-lost twin . . ." She clasps her hands tight together on her lap and glances at Dad for help.

He jumps in. "We have always wanted to support Dessie on her adoption journey, wherever that takes her. We just didn't realize that that journey would be so soon. Or in our backyard."

My cheeks are blazing hot because my adoption journey has hit a dead end. No, my adoption journey had a head-on collision with a No Trespassing sign. I blurt out, "What does this matter if I'm not even allowed to see Donna anymore?"

"Because things change," Dad says firmly. "Things always change."

"Yeah, I always thought I'd be scrawny, but then I hit the

gym," says Jacob, flexing his bicep, then gesturing at me to ooh and aah.

I do not.

"I always thought I'd be covered in pimples, but then I went to a dermatologist," says Ben, waving to his clear complexion like he's expecting me to coo.

I do not.

"And I never thought I'd ever have a daughter," Mom says, "not after my gynecologist told me my uterus had petered out."

*Thank you for this moment of family oversharing*, I want to tell everyone.

"My point is, that even when things seem hopeless, things can change for the better," Mom says. "You are never really stuck, not really."

Dad chimes in. "Just like in a game, you always have another move you can make."

Not if you have ever personally experienced Amah's permanent frown—which I have. That's when you know deep down in your every bone that some things will never, ever change. That it is game over, no matter what you do.

"Great, and on that note," Ben says for me, jerking his chin toward the abandoned ice cream bar, "please tell me it's time to return to our regularly scheduled programming of ice cream, zombies, and gore."

At the creepiest part of the movie, I check my phone, because even though I am pretending that I am not scared, it is freaking out my head that dead people can reanimate as zombies who'd consider my arms as tasty as fried chicken wings. And also because I'm hoping that maybe, just maybe, Donna or Sophie has texted me.

They have not.

Reanimating, I decide, is what my family is trying to tell me, and it may not be such a horrible idea. Maybe I ought to reanimate since staying silent isn't working for me, especially when Ben sticks his huge hand into my popcorn bowl and helps himself to my extra-cheesy popcorn.

"Hey!" I swat his hand, but then I think, *Is hoarding your own food rude?*

Maybe I should reanimate into Kind Dessie. Generous Dessie. A non-vexatious Dessie would share her popcorn even though she was secretly dreaming about extra-cheesy movie night popcorn during her hunger strike that began and ended in a single day.

So I very kindly and very generously and oh-so-non-vexatiously tell The Twins, "You can have the rest of mine. I'm full."

Ben says, "You're being weird."

But what if, actually, I'm being normal? That's what I'm counting on.

The kind and generous and non-vexatious Dessie is going to win back Donna and convince Amah I'm a great influence by being Lee-family normal.

"Before you guys go to bed, remember to bring your bowls to the kitchen," Mom reminds us at the end of the movie when all of us are too petrified to move.

I spring to my feet and collect our empty bowls. See how kind and generous, polite and helpful I am?

"Weird," says Jacob, even though he hands me his.

Ben agrees. "Definitely weird."

On Monday morning, my family wakes up especially early so The Twins can have a huge and hearty breakfast before they tour the University of Washington, then drive back to our forever home. For Ben and Jacob, huge and hearty means inhaling three plate-sized pancakes and five turkey sausages dipped in maple syrup each. Even though we'll see them again tonight on FaceTime, Mom looks teary as if she knows how much fracturing our family is costing every single one of us.

The Twins suddenly wear an expression I know well: the We're Having a Big Idea look. Then again, it could be the We're Having a Big Idea for Mortifying Dessie look. They are often the same, this look.

Ben whispers to me, "Hey, do you need us to 'say' anything to anyone at school?"

Jacob grins. "Anyone like a kid named Max."

"Anyone like a kid who needs to be annihilated named Max," Ben adds.

"Anyone—"

"No!" I interrupt The Twins. Then I glare at my parents accusingly. I don't care if it is rude or not; I say, "You blabbermouths."

"Hallelujah! She talks back," Jacob says, messing my hair.

I poke him in the arm.

Mom overhears and stares straight into my eyes. "Is that why you're not talking? Is that why you got in trouble at school? Did Max try to silence you?"

"Who is this Max bully guy?" Ben demands.

"No one important," I say huffily.

"You know when a middle school guy likes someone, he teases them," Jacob explains. Then he grins. "So who's this Max guy who likes you?"

"Eww, gross!" I make vomiting sounds even as I can vividly picture Max and his constellation of freckles.

Ben whispers, "She's ba-aack."

I realize: teasing is the Breedlove way of saying I love you.

Jacob says, "We better drive you to school on our way to UW."

"Drive to school" means "talk to Max." The Twins confronting Max would be a fate worse than being disinvited to a bubble waffle party, even Donna's. Confession is better. I say, "Max did not try to silence me. I tried to silence him. I mean, I got into trouble at school because he threw something at Donna, and I yelled at him."

Instead of glaring at me like I'm a terrible person, Mom says sternly, "Good for you."

Dad nods approvingly. "That's my girl."

Except that's not what the principal thought. Or Amah.

Out of nowhere, Grammy appears in the kitchen and says, "Troublemakers are my kind of people."

She is grinning at me, maybe not recognizing me from the past but respecting me in the present, which is different. Bittersweet.

But bittersweet is still good.

# Chapter 30

**Tragedy**: Max Morrison is my partner for the next part of the Make Our Mark project. At least I also have Norman who knows everything and Jacqueline of the big words.

The big words I want to fling at Max are "Begone!" and "Skedaddle!"

Especially when he sings out, "I love me some bubble waffles." As usual, Max's legs are splayed in front of him as he leans all the way back in his seat, his hands behind his head. "Bubble waffles with extra hot fudge and fresh mochi bites."

Maybe The Twins should have driven me to school after all. Thwacking a boy on the head with my pencil is not only rude but against the rules. Donna is shifting around in her chair like she wants to thwack Max with her pencil, too. It hurts, our sameness. I glare at Max as if he is the reason for all my problems. Isn't he, though? I wouldn't have been so upset the other day if he hadn't thrown a wad of paper at Donna. I wouldn't have yelled at Dad. Amah wouldn't have seen me yelling at Dad. And Donna wouldn't have had to shoo me out of her life.

I sneak a peek at Donna right as she is sneaking a peek at me. Just as fast, she yanks her gaze away because she is not vexatious. She is the good twin, the one who listens to her amah. We are no longer twin magnets. I repel her.

"We have a very special surprise guest who is going to teach you all how to create a family mark of your own, and when we're ready, to create the logo for our school," says Ms. Lauchengco.

You will never guess who sweeps into our classroom: Max's mom.

Max looks shocked. Instantly, his legs retract under his chair, his hands pull back from his head and fall to his lap. It is like watching a human turtle.

No, it is like watching a miracle.

Mrs. Morrison lugs a large black art portfolio in one arm and balances books in her other. Her brown curls are a storm system of their own, blowing in every direction whenever she moves. I think Grammy would love her.

"I'm an architect by day, a graphic designer by night, and Max's mom around the clock," Mrs. Morrison says. "Do not ever let anyone tell you that you are too much."

Max looks like he is dying. His cheeks are the ruby red of Donna's baby blanket. Automatically, I lift my eyebrows at Donna: Do you see Max's face? Instead, my eyes catch on Lucas, who is listening to Max's mom closely in a way he doesn't listen to our teachers. He wears the wistful expression of Peridot in *The Eight Banners* when her head tilts to the clouds and she longs for her mother.

It makes me feel itchy and uncomfortable seeing that longing on Lucas's face because it echoes mine for my lost twin.

And it makes me feel out of sorts and unbearably jealous when it is Akshaya who arches one eyebrow at Donna, and Donna lifts both of hers back. The two of them sharing in silent double time.

Swiveling forward, I return my attention to Mrs. Morrison, as she shows us the Nike swoosh. The windows logo for Microsoft. The FedEx logo with the arrow nested inside the white space between the "E" and the "x." How have I never noticed that hidden arrow before?

Max's mom then shares different family marks from around the world, similar to the ones Ms. Lauchengco showed us earlier: The tartan. The kamon. The coat of arms. Symbols carved into a totem pole.

"The easiest way for us to design your family's mark is to choose a container shape: a square, circle, triangle, or rectangle," Mrs. Morrison advises. "Sketch small, fast, loose. Don't erase. Just try out ideas. Anything that represents your family. Books. Movies. Sports. Inject something new every time."

I am no artist. Even preschoolers could do better than this clumsy family logo I'm creating. As Dad says, it is exceedingly rare to create anything new and novel in the first try.

Just like that, another Breedlove belief that I didn't realize I lived: Breedloves believe in playing with ideas.

After art class, since I do not want to watch Donna and her birthday squad eat lunch together or hear Max reminisce about the deliciousness that is birthday bubble waffles, I skip lunch and head to our school library where I can pretend to be very busy designing my logo.

Music, color, and ideas: those are the backbones of the Breedloves.

I begin fresh with a bar of music, turning that into the double E's in Breedlove. Then I sketch a musical sign, a treble clef. Treble reminds me of trouble, which leads to Amah's frown. So I abandon that for the shape of a poster sign, the kind that Grammy might have held at a march. I am so engrossed in badly sketching my family logo that I don't notice Jacqueline until she asks over my shoulder, "What are you attempting to draw?"

I jump, startled. And embarrassed.

"Jacqueline," I say hotly, hiding my logos with my arm, "spying is rude." I ignore that I am supposed to be a Kind and Generous Dessie of the kind and generous words.

"You are not an especially gifted artist," Jacqueline observes as she sits beside me.

"Excuse me?"

"No need to be offended. I am an especially abysmal artist."

I laugh because Jacqueline says it so honestly. Honesty is the prerequisite of a good friendship. See? Jacqueline is not the only one who can use big words. Maybe she doesn't use big words to act big. But I won't know unless I ask. So I do.

"Jacqueline, why do you use big words?" I set down my pink coloring pencil.

"Because in my family, we do not believe in waste: Wasted food. Wasted time. Wasted words. We say what we mean and we mean what we say—that is our family motto. And we say, It is a waste of perfectly wonderful multisyllabic words if no one uses them. So we do." She shrugs, then grins. Jacqueline Muir is grinning mischievously. "Plus, complex words are fun to say."

"Multisyllabic." I taste the word—*multisyllabic*—and see Jacqueline's point. It is fun to say. Much more fun to say than "multiple syllables."

"Besides, my dad teaches English and Mom is an attorney. We are lovers of big words. So my family logo will feature a tome," she tells me. "As my hero, Anne of Green Gables, would say, 'If you have big ideas, you have to use big words to express them, haven't you?' And as my grandfather says, Compliments are best delivered with specificity. Would you rather be told you are good with color or that you have an exquisite eye for unusual hues? Which you do."

Jacqueline makes an exceedingly good point.

Until she corrects herself. "Which you did. What happened to your scarf?"

The scarf that I entombed in spider central? I blush. Then, I have an idea: maybe using multisyllabic words is like using unexpected color combinations in Grammy's old outfits and in her weavings and in my scarf. Creating an unusual palette isn't just to make a statement, but to show the world something new. Like the way Dad's compositions make you feel the world differently.

Maybe I just need to listen to Jacqueline more carefully to hear what she is trying to say with her unexpected word combinations. Maybe I will see something new in her world. And mine.

Maybe I already have.

"Wait, who's Anne of Green Gables?" I ask.

Jacqueline's green eyes grow wide, shocked. She gasps. "You haven't read *Anne of Green Gables*?"

I shake my head.

Horrified, her mouth drops open. "You haven't watched *Anne of Green Gables*?"

I shake my head again.

Jacqueline flies up to her feet like she is the heroine of *The Eight Banners* and soars to a bookshelf. From the top shelf, she plucks a hardback book, hugs it close before banging it down on the library table. She jabs one finger onto the redheaded girl with two braids on the cornflower blue cover and orders me, "You must read this so we can talk about kindred spirits." Then she sighs. A heavy, chest-heaving, shoulder-drooping sigh that comes from deep in her soul the exact way people sigh after hearing my mom play. "I have always wanted a kindred spirit, but I'm afraid they are challenging to come by in Marian Anderson Middle School."

I think about finally finding my identical twin here and still being disinvited to her birthday party. I nod and say,

"Kindred spirits are tricky to come by in Marian Anderson Middle School in Seattle, Washington."

"They are difficult to come by in sixth grade in Marian Anderson Middle School in Seattle, Washington."

"They are impossible to come by in a sixth grade populated with boys like Max and Lucas at Marian Anderson Middle School in Seattle, Washington."

We beam at each other, maybe not kindred spirits exactly. But much more than strangers who are irritated because one of them uses big words.

Then Jacqueline admits in a voice so soft, it is the barest of whispers that doesn't waste any words, "I wasn't invited to Donna's birthday party either."

*Either. Either* means people know I was disinvited to the bubble waffle birthday party. *Either* means people might even be talking about me being disinvited to the bubble waffle birthday party. My cheeks flame. But Jacqueline doesn't notice. She is focused on twirling a coloring pencil—smoky gray like burned hopes. "I was deeply wounded." She slams the gray pencil down. "But not mortally wounded. Still. My birthday parties are the epitome of boring. My mom only invites adults." Her snub nose wrinkles. "And she serves beluga caviar. Caviar! I would much, much prefer a bubble waffle party."

Caviar at a birthday party is very different from my family's idea of celebrating with a do-it-yourself ice cream bar including every possible delicious topping. Even if our families are different—hers caviar-loving, mine ice-cream addicted; hers big words, mine big ideas—Jacqueline and I are surprisingly similar, both of us wishing for the bubble waffle birthday party that neither of us was invited to attend.

Both of us with the same hurt feelings, even if we express them differently.

Jacqueline looks closely at my abysmal logo and says, "I am going to be a fashion designer one day. With my own line of formal wear for women." She leans even closer to my logo that looks like a protest poster. "This has potential."

So, possibly, do we. I smile at Jacqueline. She smiles back at me.

Yet at the end of the school day, it is Akshaya who slips into Amah's SUV and squeals out of the parking lot race car fast with Donna.

And me? I feel mortally wounded.

The funny thing is, Max Morrison is also standing outside, looking mortally wounded for me, too.

# Chapter 31

Just as I'm about to head upstairs with Owen after dinner, Dad calls out to me, "Hey, kiddo, what do you think about making the golden syrup for the mooncakes right now?"

Even though I want to zone out listening to A2Z, I know what a kind and generous, polite and helpful person would do. Especially a kind and generous, polite and helpful person who knows delicious, authentic mooncakes could win herself into Amah's good graces. Besides, I am not used to all this wide-open free time I have without constantly texting and talking to Donna. So I nod, and Owen flops down in the middle of the kitchen floor. "Sure, why not?"

Soon, we clatter around the kitchen, Dad placing a thick saucepan on the stovetop, me gathering all the ingredients, and Owen snoring. Golden syrup, as it turns out, requires only three ingredients: sugar, water, and lemon juice. I am an expert sugar measurer. There is something highly satisfying about leveling off the extra sugar in a measuring cup with the back of a knife to create a perfectly flat edge.

"Whoa, it says here you can't stir or even touch the sauce for a good forty-five minutes after it boils," Dad says, consulting the recipe, then motioning to me to pour the perfectly leveled sugar into the water. As soon as I do, he gives the saucepan a vigorous swirl. "You can't just leave it either. Kind of like when you got croup right after we brought you home, and Mom slept on the nursery floor for two nights straight just to keep watch over you."

"Yeah," I say as if I remember, but what I remember are all the times Dad has shared this very story with me. "Mom booted you off nighttime duty after you picked me up, wailing, from my toddler bed and then fell asleep in the rocking chair."

"Allegedly fell asleep."

"And I fell to the ground."

"Well, technically, we don't know how you ended up on the ground."

"Except Mom found me there at four in the morning," I say, then laugh as I mimic Mom: "Drew, unacceptable!"

"Totally unacceptable," Dad agrees easily. "But your mom also found me sleeping next to her on your bedroom floor for those two nights even though I was banned from nighttime nurse duty."

"Yeah, snoring so loudly, she yelled at you in her sleep."

We both snarl, "Can you be any louder?" We laugh, me the loudest since it is one of my all-time favorite stories. We are so loud that Owen lifts his head off the kitchen floor and Mom barks to us from the TV room, "Hey, you guys okay?"

"We Breedloves take our promises seriously even if it means making other people mad, and when I became your dad, I promised to be here for you," Dad says in a somewhat softer voice while carefully wiping off the sugar crystallizing on the inside of the steaming pot. He turns to me like he has a particularly bad dad joke he's been saving for this very moment, but instead he says seriously, "Just like Grammy used to say, Breedloves don't just keep our promises, we work our promises."

"Aren't they the same thing?" I ask, as I pick the seeds out of the lemon halves and squeeze the juice into a tiny bowl.

"Not even close. The biggest promises aren't just kept once; they're honored for an entire lifetime. Aunt Cindy told me yesterday that Grammy didn't just go to one rally and call that good. She marched until her hips wore out. Then she wrote letters to Congress and volunteered to register voters. She wove so many blankets for refugees. She worked her promise to make the world a better place. Mom, your mom, she wrote to the orphanage, demanding to know how this could possibly have happened to you and Donna."

"She did?"

"She did."

"As if that's going to help anything now."

"It might give you information. Maybe even closure. Not now maybe. But maybe when you're older." Dad wipes down the counter. "What I'm trying to say is that we Breedloves work our promises even when you don't see anything happening. So when I say I'll always work my promise to be here for you, I mean I'm going to work it Grammy-level."

The water and sugar begin to boil. I know what Dad is really saying: he is here for me right now if I want to tell him what's been clawing at my heart.

But I can't. Donna's texts disinviting me to her party are tight in my throat, and Amah's revolted expression in the parking lot is trapped in my mind. Even so, an accusation springs out of my head, barreling past the rocks in my throat. It is sorrowful, my wail. "But you broke your promise to me!"

Dad looks confused. "What promise?"

"You took me from my forever home!"

Deep, deep down, I know that that promise wasn't actually broken. Deep, deep down, I know that we moved here to take care of Grammy who needs us. It's as if Dad knows that I know, too, because he doesn't say anything. Instead, he places his hands on my shoulders like he's enclosing us in a safe bubble that is just him and me and Owen, who creeps over to lean against my leg.

"Life changes," Dad finally says, his gaze boring right into my eyes. When I look away, he cups his hands feather-soft around my cheeks. I meet his unwavering stare. Only then does he continue, "Life is always changing. Now and forever, life will always change. Someone we love loses their memory. Someone else gets sick and dies. An earthquake might hit. A forest might burn. We might have to move houses. But my heart? Your mom's heart? Your brothers' hearts? Those are your real forever home. And big promises, the promises that matter? Those are the ones we will always honor, no matter what. No matter how hard they are to keep. No matter how long it takes. No matter how many times we want to give up. We Breedloves always work the important promises. And that—that relentless working—that I will always promise you."

I want to trust my dad so badly. I want to trust his promise. Yet it is so, so hard because it means allowing myself to believe deep in my soul that I—the baby who was not worthy of a photo—am worthy of a home. The forever home of my family's big, beating hearts.

My own heart feels like it is going to burst with panic and sorrow. How can I truly count on forever when I can't even count on being remembered? Or on a newfound sister?

As if Dad knows I'm about to splinter, he steps back and says, "Time for the lemon juice, kiddo."

I carefully pour the tart juice into the saucepan. Immediately, Dad lowers the temperature on the stovetop. All we can do now is wait for the mooncake syrup to thicken on its own. While he washes the measuring cups and cutting board, and I dry them, Dad nudges me with his shoulder. "Hey, did you hear about the restaurant on the moon?"

I sigh. "No."

"Great food, but no atmosphere."

Not even my groan stops his next dad joke. Or the next one. Approximately a million and one (bad) dad jokes later, the syrup finally turns golden brown.

"It's supposed to be amber," I tell Dad, eyeing the thin sauce, then double-checking the recipe.

He frowns and asks, "Is that amber?"

"I don't know, maybe? But it looks really runny. Is it supposed to be this runny?"

"I don't know, maybe?" Dad says, then promises me, "But if it's not, we'll keep making batches until it's right, deal?"

"Deal." I nod. That, at least, is one promise I can trust. My heart gives another wistful twist.

If only there was one promise I could make—a billion promises I could work—to bring Donna and me back together, trust me, I would.

# Chapter 32

Not that I will ever admit it. but there are times when I miss my baby blanket, frayed and barfed on as it was. Sleep is so impossible with all my stress about sharing my Breedlove family logo tomorrow I could use my blanket's cozy comfort now. But it is long gone. So I finally pick up *Anne of Green Gables*, the book Jacqueline pushed on me at the school library. Who knew I'd get so into the story because Anne lived in an orphanage like me and Donna? That Anne and her best friend, her kindred spirit, aren't allowed to be friends anymore. (Like me.) Anne-isms are almost as powerful as Grammy-isms. Anne-isms like: "I am in the depths of despair." (I am!) And "My life is a perfect graveyard of buried hopes." (It is!)

Sometime after midnight I must have fallen asleep, because when I wake up, there is a book-shaped dent on my cheek. As it turns out, I am not so worried about sharing my family logo that I forget that A2Z have dropped their latest song. The one that I've been dying for weeks and weeks to hear.

And yet for the first time in my whole entire fandom of A2Z, I do not listen to their new song. On repeat. For a thousand times in a row.

I can't. It is not the same without Donna.

Downstairs, Dad's not making breakfast. He is typing at the kitchen table, his fingers flying over his keyboard like Peridot beating her way through storms and arrows to get home. He is frowning in deep concentration.

"Can I hear it?" I ask him.

"Hear what?" Dad asks, startled. He slams his computer shut.

Weird. Usually, Dad shares snippets of his compositions with me, a few haunting notes here, a spooky melody there. Before I can ask him why he's being so secretive, Dad asks if I want pancakes this morning.

I'm so anxious, I cannot even fathom eating. Not even Dad's extra-fluffy, survive-the-school-week pancakes.

But I manage. Because A2Z can heal all hearts. And Dad's extra-fluffy pancakes can work miracles. On my fifth bite, I perk up. Maybe, just maybe, Donna will want to listen to the new A2Z song together, surreptitiously after school before Dad picks me up and Amah picks her up.

But Donna is not at the paint-stained art tables when the bell rings. She's not there when Ms. Lauchengco starts art class. Or when Ms. Lauchengco calls on Max, the freckles on his face standing out especially bright against his paler than normal skin. Even more weird, Max is not sprawled like usual, snicker ready for action.

Weirdest of all, Max Morrison is silent. Hands twisted into a knot.

"Max, if you're not ready to share your family logo, just say so," Ms. Lauchengco prompts him.

Max's lips press even tighter together. So tight they disappear.

"Okay, then, who is ready to share?" Ms. Lauchengco asks our class.

Just as Norman raises his hand, Max blurts out, "Donna's grandmother was attacked this morning."

Amah was attacked? Attacked as in still alive? Or attacked as in dead? Is this why Donna is not at school? Alarmed, I demand, "What happened? Is Amah okay? Is Donna?"

In words that are spit out like nails, hard and sharp, Max tells us that Amah was punched in the face at the Pike Place Market.

Someone yelled racial slurs at her and stomped on her.

And slammed her head onto the pavement.

She was taken to the emergency room at Harborview Medical Center, where she is being treated. One eye is bleeding. The last Max heard, Amah was unconscious.

All Amah was doing, Max tells us, was taking her morning walk, smelling the flowers at the market. Looking at the fresh fish. Eyeing the colorful vegetables. Watching the market come alive for the day.

Until a man attacked her.

It fills me with anger, this attack on Amah, an old lady who was just enjoying her morning.

Max shows us footage on his phone of a TV crew descending on Pike Place Market. A small crowd is gathered, some people placing flowers around Rachel the Piggy Bank. Lit candles surround the bronze statue that sits in front of the market stall famous for its fish throwers. Yet not one witness saw the attack.

For once, Ms. Lauchengco doesn't utter a single chastising word when the rest of us peek at our phones. I check mine in case Donna has texted. She hasn't. I wonder if Max has heard from Donna. As if he hears my silent question, Max meets my eyes and shakes his head.

"I got a message from Donna." Holding her phone, Akshaya reads, "*We're still at the hospital. Amah is still unconscious.*"

Our principal barges into our classroom to check on us. Mrs. Banerjee says, "This is a terrible thing to happen to our community."

When she asks if anyone has questions, Lucas raises his hand. "Maybe Donna's grandmother shouldn't have been walking by herself?"

"It could have been any of our grandparents out for their morning constitutional," Jacqueline snaps, crossing her arms like she is Anne Shirley come to life.

Max's eyebrows knit together as he stares at his sidekick and corrects Lucas. "This is not Amah's fault. She's a cute, harmless old lady. She has the right to walk around without getting beaten."

I myself would not describe Amah as cute or harmless. Fierce is more like it. But fierce old ladies do not deserve to be attacked any more than cute old ladies. No one does, for that matter.

Lucas's face turns red. "I didn't say this was her fault."

Mrs. Banerjee intervenes. "One of the hallmarks of Marian Anderson Middle School is our ability to communicate with each other with respect. We might not agree on everything, but one, we should be able to express ourselves. And two, we should be able to listen to each other."

Mom says that power is being armed with information. Hard facts. So even though I should be listening to Mrs. Banerjee and Ms. Lauchengco talk about the meaning of community, I research instead. What I find out is terrible: There has been a surge of hate crimes against Asian Americans over the last several years. A lot of those crimes have targeted the elders in different communities around the country. No wonder the Lees thought they needed those personal safety devices from Lunar New Year.

I think about how Donna treated her grandmother: with so much affection. And respect. How it must hurt to have the ones who are treated with the most reverence be the exact ones who are punched and shoved. Attacked.

Mrs. Banerjee says that she'll drop off get-well cards to Amah after school for anyone who wants to make one.

Since I'm not a welcome part of Donna's life anymore, maybe I shouldn't write a card? My fingers clench my pencil. Anyway, if all we are doing is creating a bunch of get-well cards for Amah, each of us writing that we are thinking of her, some of us writing that we are praying for her, it is not enough.

Not nearly enough.

I think about what Grammy said during our backyard march: *We will not let hatred roost in our community.* A get-well card—twenty-five get-well cards, a thousand get-well cards—are not enough to stop hatred from roosting. Whoever hurt Amah did this because she's Asian. They thought they could get away with it because she's old. Cards are not going to make our community safer or stronger.

Miracles: Max Morrison and I have an entire conversation in silence and in double time.

He shoots a look at me: *Cards?*

Me, shooting a look at him: *As if get-well cards from the sixth graders at Marian Anderson Middle School are going to change anything.*

We nod: he and I are going to do something to show Donna and Amah our support.

That settled, we should look away from each other.

We should, but we do not.

"Words are a good start," Mrs. Banerjee says with a sad smile and that snaps my attention back to her. "Our words are a way of showing up when we can't be there in person yet."

That, too, is true. I think about how my boisterous dad did not have the energy to even text his closest college friends after Gramps died. They reached out to him. They showed up to sit in silence with him. Is this how Dad learned to hear music in silence with his friends? When he was mourning Gramps, he must have been listening to the sound of pure love. Love isn't happiness all the time. Sometimes love is rimmed with sadness.

So even though phones are not allowed in school and Donna is not allowed to be my friend and even though she has not responded to my last text, I reach out to her. I write: I am thinking of you.

And then I text: I can just sit with you.

Even though thoughts and prayers, words and gestures, may not stop hatred from roosting here, I am hoping it helps Donna to know that her friends will sit with her through sadness. And fear.

Including me, her twin from afar.

# Chapter 33

The words that have been elbowing each other all day long in my head storm out of me as soon as I open the passenger door. It's not Dad who answered my SOS text to please, please, please come get me. It's Mom.

She takes one look at me and demands, "What's wrong?"

I cry to her, "Amah was attacked at Pike Place Market, and now she's in the hospital!"

Mom's mouth opens and closes without a sound, she is so stunned.

"I didn't hear about this on the news," she says faintly. Her hands grip the steering wheel so tightly, I know what she's thinking: only a coward would attack an elderly woman. "Let's go visit them in the hospital. A show of support."

But what if Donna and her family will think it's rude of me to burst in on them in the hospital? What if they only want family around them, real family? That clearly does not include me, whatever the DNA test said. I stare down at my fist, clamped around my silent phone. Donna has not replied, and that feels like an answer: I am not wanted.

"No," I tell Mom. "They wouldn't like that."

Her eyebrows shoot up fast. If this were Dad, he'd pull out a Grammy quote: "Showing up makes a difference." Maybe: "When someone is sick, we show up with soup."

But Mom insists. "We'll hug them and leave."

"Why aren't you listening to me?" I demand so loudly, Mom startles. That doesn't stop me from charging ahead, gesturing wide. "This is what you wanted! For me not to be part of Donna's life, right? So why are you telling me to show up and hug them? You didn't even want me to know them!"

"No, Dessie, no." Mom jerks our car over to the curb and brakes so abruptly, my head whips back into my headrest. She spins to me and looks me dead in the eye. I wait for her lecture. But instead, Mom sighs. "That's not what I wanted at all."

"Yes, it is!"

"Yes, it is hard for me to know that you don't just have one family. You have three: us, your birth family, and now Donna's. And yes, it's even harder that Donna is right here in Seattle, what, ten minutes away?" Mom sighs and sweeps her hand through her hair so she can see me clearly. Or maybe so I can see her. All of her. "I was so sure you'd want to leave our family. Me. That I was going to lose you."

"That doesn't make any sense," I choke out. "I'd never leave anyone in our family."

"I know it doesn't make sense, but feelings don't always

212

make sense!" Even though the car's not moving, Mom grasps the steering wheel like we are driving into a deep, dark tunnel, and she has no idea where it is leading us. "And that's not even getting into the guilt I feel. I mean, what if us wanting to adopt you somehow caused the orphanage to split the two of you up?"

"I know you wrote to the orphanage to find out what happened."

"I did, and I promise I'll let you know as soon as I hear anything."

"You ignored Donna."

"I did!" Mom groans. "I just imagined the two of you, holding hands and walking out our door and never coming back."

"Mom, you're being ridiculous."

"Not really. You, Dessie, are my daughter," Mom says fiercely. "And if any little bit of you wants to go to your sister, I will take you there right this minute."

Still, it's not what she thinks is right or what every little bit of me wants that matters.

It's what Donna and her family want.

But then the greeting that Donna and her family use with each other and their friends in Taiwanese floats in my head: *Have you eaten rice yet?* I think about the time Donna and Amah came over and I did not offer them a single polite bite to eat.

Grammy's saying rings in my ears: "Nice words are never enough."

I have to do something. So I text Donna: Have you eaten yet?

She texts back: The cafeteria food here is disgusting.

I ask her about Amah.

She answers: Still unconscious.

I think about Dad, who spends so much of his free time cooking and baking because there are so many more ways to care for people than through words, and I ask Mom, "Can we bring them something Dad's made to eat?"

"You got it," Mom says, racing down the street at Amah speed. I know exactly where we're heading: straight to our kitchen.

My parents are stymied about what comfort food to bring to Donna's family in the hospital when we don't know them well. Is their comfort food fried chicken like Mom or grilled cheese like me? Do they have Dad's sweet tooth that craves oatmeal cookies and ooey-gooey brownies when he's stressed? Or do they crave sticky rice with dried baby shrimp like at Lunar New Year?

In the end, we decide you can't go wrong with a platter of homemade bread and thick wedges of cheese and creamy hummus with crispy chips and Grammy's soul-healing Ranger cookies because bread and salt and sweet covers all the major groups of comfort food. Working together, we've miraculously assembled everything—platter, plates, and napkins—in under thirty minutes and race with the fixings to Harborview.

I don't think it really mattered what we brought.

Donna tears up the second she sees me, not the big box of food.

Auntie Susie and Uncle Carl tear up when Mom and Dad promise to do whatever they can to help.

"Just name it," says Mom, her hand on Auntie Susie's. "Do you need fresh clothes from home? Toiletries? Do you want us to take Donna and Lewis home with us?"

"We're here for you," Dad echoes. "Whenever, however you need us."

In a real and terrible way, Donna and her family remind me of Grammy, shrunken and frightened. Before Auntie Susie returns to Amah's room, she glances over her shoulder, then peers uneasily down the hall as if the attacker is lurking around. Or worse, the attacker's returning to finish off Amah. Most of all, the Lees look devastated, the same way Grammy looked when Gramps passed away. Like a vital piece of themselves has gone missing. Like they now have a ghost heart.

"So what's the prognosis?" Dad asks Uncle Carl.

Donna's dad swipes a hand tiredly down his cheek. "The doctors won't tell us anything except that they're monitoring her closely."

"Yeah, the receptionist was a little rude when we checked in," Donna says, glaring over at the middle-aged woman with salt-and-pepper curls at the front desk.

"A little?" Lewis snorts and rolls his eyes. He mimics in a snippy voice, "No, I have no information."

"Excuse me?" Mom asks, her tone sharp.

Oh no. My stomach clenches. Mom's predatorial eyes zero in on the receptionist.

"Pardon me while I go full Karen," Mom mutters, shoving up her sleeves, as she marches with a purposeful clack of her flats to the front desk. I want answers, too. But I trail safely behind Mom and so does Donna, like we are pilot fish swimming close to a shark for our protection.

The receptionist looks down her thin nose at us, which makes me wonder why she would choose this profession. Shouldn't receptionists, especially at a hospital, be receptive to people? Especially people who are scared that their grandmother is going to die? She sniffs, "Information is strictly for family."

Mom scoops me close to her with one arm, then Donna with her other. Firmly, loudly, fiercely Mom states, "We are family."

Of course, Mom does not stop there. She adds something about "families are more than DNA" and "today's families defy labels and traditional structures" and much (much) more, but I am so focused on Mom—Mom!—clutching Donna tight to her like she is daring a single human being, a single twist of fate, to wrench my sister away again.

Donna blinks, not at me, but at Mom. Awestruck.

The receptionist blinks, too. Horrorstruck. Within two minutes, someone in blue scrubs from the medical team hurries out to update Uncle Carl.

Donna pulls me aside while the adults are talking and says, "Nurture!"

I say, "What?"

"You and your mom are the same! Scary amazing! Nurture!"

I have never once thought that I could be scary amazing, but maybe The Wad of Paper Incident was no different from this Hospital Incident?

Donna hisses, "Do you want to see what else makes me mad?" Without waiting for my answer, Donna whips out her phone and shows me a video clip of Amah inside the hospital room, her head wrapped in bandages, her eyes closed. Every so often, her grandmother moans like she is in pain. Or reliving her attack. She looks so tiny: a palm-sized elf owl bandaged in the hospital bed. This is Amah, who included me in the red envelope tradition even though she was already worried that I was a bad influence.

It is not sorrow or grief that fills me.

It is rage.

Donna's jaw tightens. "When Amah was awake for a little bit in the ambulance, she refused to press charges! She didn't want to make a fuss."

"What? She has to press charges!"

"I bet she's scared her attacker will come after us." Donna shoves her phone back into her pocket. "So the police aren't even looking for him."

I am so beyond being simply mad. I want to scream at the person who did this to Amah.

Perhaps I am a bad influence on Donna after all.

I refuse to be a bad influence who is banished forever

from Donna's life, though. I ask, "How about if we organize a fundraiser for Amah?"

Donna says, "Max and his mom have already done that."

"Max did?"

"Yeah, they've set up the page and everything. And Mom's church friends have organized a meal train for us for the next week."

So what can I do? We sit in silence in the waiting room when I remember that A2Z's song dropped this morning. In all the hoopla, I've totally forgotten. And this is the ultimate, perfect distraction. So I ask, "Hey, did you hear the new song?"

Donna uses her hands to show me the dance moves. "You mean this one?"

"Wait, how do you know it already?" I demand, staring at her hands fluttering and snapping.

Donna flushes and casts a cautious glance at the beige doors separating the waiting area from the hospital ward as if Amah and her supersonic ears can hear us all the way down in her room. She whispers her confession, "I joined TikTok."

"You did what?"

Her eyes narrow. "And I wish I hadn't, because the song is awful."

"No way!"

"It's so racist!"

"A2Z?"

"Yes!" Donna pulls up the song on TikTok and thrusts her phone at me.

Our favorite singer struts onscreen. The group snaps to their left. They swing to their right. They bust out one of their signature dance moves: a back run with a leg kick. And then I hear it, a line that boils my blood: *"Asian driver / no survivor!"*

I lower Donna's phone to my lap and stare at her. "Hello, Amah drives like a race car driver."

"I know, right?" Then Donna rants, "It's stereotypes like these that make it okay to mock Asian people—and maybe even attack our elders. I'm glad my parents wouldn't get me a ticket to the A2Z concert." She grabs my hand, her eyes bright and fierce.

I know that expression. It is the expression of a Breedlove exploding with a big idea. It is the expression of inspiration sweeping through my twin.

# Chapter 34

"We have to boycott the band!" Donna announces.

"Boycott A2Z?" I repeat faintly.

"Yeah, until they apologize for the lyrics."

Boycotting feels like breaking up. The worst fear in my life is my forever family breaking up and leaving me. Now I add one more fear: a twin sister doing the same.

I refuse to lose Donna for a third time when I have already lost her once at the orphanage and again after The Wad of Paper Incident.

So I say, "Okay, but how?"

"You have great ideas," she says confidently. "You'll figure out the best way to get people to reject their lyrics and join our boycott."

It's midnight now, and we've been home for a few hours, and I'm still fretting. Boycott A2Z? Since there is zero hope for sleep, I grab my idea journal off my bedside table. I have not written in days.

I sit up against my pillows, hide under my covers, and turn on my flashlight. Clutching the especially chubby seventh-birthday bunny from Ben, I start to doodle. I find myself sketching a logo for Donna and me, the lost-and-found, forever-and-always twins. We have to stay together, forever and always. But boycott A2Z? I try to copy the Dessie Mei font and the Donna font. As it turns out, I am not a natural-born calligrapher.

Or a natural-born A2Z boycotter.

At one, my phone buzzes. It's Donna, finally home. Even though she's clutching a bunny stuffy, too, she still looks upset. And excited. And nervous. She is under her covers like me.

"Hey, guess what?" Donna whisper-asks.

I'm afraid to guess.

Even more, I'm afraid to be on the phone with Donna in case she gets in trouble because of me again. What if her parents agree with Amah that I'm a bad influence and we never talk ever again?

Donna says, "Our former governor, Velma Maeda, wants to rally for Amah and the Asian American community this weekend."

"Whoa," I say.

Donna looks sheepish. "She said I would be a powerful voice to speak out against racism and speak up for the Asian American community."

"You would be," I tell her, nodding enthusiastically.

"I'm kind of scared to get onstage, though. So you'll come up with me and say something, too, right? I mean, Amah is like your honorary grandmother," Donna says hopefully.

Is she, though? It's hard to forget Amah's furrowed eyebrows of disapproval, her look of disgust in the parking lot. Plus, Amah is so afraid, she doesn't even want to report her attack to the police. What if Amah blames me for convincing Donna to speak out? Besides, how can I go onstage to represent the Asian American community when I don't even know how to hold chopsticks properly? Or that you say hello by asking people if they've eaten yet? Or that you're supposed to take shoes off at home?

What if I say something wrong onstage and I'm not just boycotted from the Lees forever, but I'm banned forever? Not just from the Lees, but from the entire community?

"We can announce our boycott of A2Z at the same time," Donna says, her eyes intense. "I mean, what could be more perfect?"

When I stay quiet, Donna offers, "You can just stand next to me if you're nervous. We'll channel your mom."

Hastily, I say, "I need to ask my parents."

It's not exactly a lie, but it's certainly not the truth. I don't need to ask my parents. I've already made up my mind: I am not standing on that stage with Donna.

# Chapter 35

The best ideas need resting time the way bread dough needs resting time to rise. That's what Dad says. Guess what? He is right.

My eyes spring open the next morning. An idea has risen to the very top of my brain.

I will attend the rally.

Instead of standing like a pretender onstage, I will cheer Donna from the mosh pit in front of the stage. I will be spitting distance from Donna. I will hold up a poster in support of Donna. An enormous poster with the Dessie Mei and Donna Lee sister fonts. An enormous poster that calls out A2Z: *"I Like Alike" except your new lyrics!* All I need is for my parents to let me go. So I dash downstairs, where Dad is sipping his morning coffee and Mom is fixing her morning tea.

I tell them, "There's a rally at Pike Place Market and Donna was invited to speak."

"Oh," Mom says, setting down the kettle.

Dad slurps from his mug that reads DAD JOKE PRO. "That's an honor."

"She wants me to come," I say. I don't tell them that Donna wants me onstage with her, not when Dad thinks it's an honor to be asked to speak.

Mom gives Dad a meaningful look. A look I know well: it's Mom's Danger-Danger Warning look that she shot Dad the second she caught him stringing up Christmas lights on the forbidden roofline because the year before, he toppled off the ladder. Mom asks, "And her parents are letting her?"

I nod.

Mom, who is the rain on every Dessie Mei parade, frowns like the world is ending. Dad shoots her a look of his own—the Let's This One Time Say Yes look—but Mom shakes her head. Firmly.

Suddenly, Mom needs to refresh her mug while Dad needs to tend the golden syrup for the mooncakes as if both are national emergencies. It is irritating how focused Dad is on the golden syrup and Mom is on her tea. Neither of them looks me in the eye. Mom takes deep thoughtful sips. Dad shakes the mason jars like they are maracas.

They are not.

"Your dad and I need to discuss this. I know this sounds ludicrous, but honestly, I never thought you could be a target, Dessie. I mean, aside from random guys catcalling you or maybe slipping something into your drink when you're in college or—"

"Okay, Mom," I say, hoping to stop her spiraling.

She clears her throat. "So starting today, one of us will drive you to and from school when we can't walk with you."

"Mom."

"I'm going to talk to the school about making an exception for you and Donna to carry pepper spray. And I've researched a bunch of self-defense workshops that I thought we could take with Donna and her mom," Mom says, as her gaze skitters over to Dad for support. Dad who is now shaking the mason jars like he is a paint-mixing machine at Home Depot. He is not.

"Dad!" I cry out. "You're going to ruin the syrup!"

Dad freezes like my words have lashed him, and immediately I feel guilty. My tone is a whip. My tone belts out, *You're stupid*. Maybe the way we shape our words is no different from a violinist shaping a note: our feelings vibrate in our voices.

And on our faces.

I think about Amah's disapproval in the school parking lot. The look of disgust because she thought I was mean and terrible. But maybe I only *sounded* mean and terrible because I haven't learned to use kinder words and control my tone. Maybe it takes practice, the same as singing. And playing the violin. It takes practice to tame your tone so people can hear what you are trying to say when you're angry.

So I take a deep breath and soften my tone and say, "I'm

sorry, Dad." I think about what I want to say so Dad can hear what I mean. "I don't think we're supposed to shake the syrup hard." Then I talk about what truly matters, which isn't the syrup at all but attending the rally to support Donna.

Mom worries her bottom lip and says, "I'm really, really afraid that it'd be easy for you to be targeted if you go to this rally. I mean, what if the attacker's in the audience? What if he brings reinforcements? What if they bring guns? Or a bomb?"

Dad tells her, "Now, honey, that's not going to happen."

"How do you know?" Mom shoots back.

I hadn't even considered that: that someone might hurt me just because I'm at a rally with a girl who is simply saying that attacking senior citizens is wrong. That someone might attack Donna afterward. Or her family. Or the entire audience.

"How about I stand in the back of the rally?" I ask. "Easy escape."

Mom shakes her head and says, "Oh, honey, I just don't think the rally is a good idea."

Dad harmonizes with her. "Sorry, kiddo, not this time."

"What rally?" Grammy wobbles into the kitchen. Her face is glowing. "When's the rally?"

"No rally," Dad tells Grammy, shepherding her to the kitchen table. "It's not safe."

Grammy shrugs off his helping hand. "Love isn't safe, but we still love. Rallies aren't safe, but we still rally."

"Dessie Mei Breedlove's life is not going to be at risk," Mom says firmly. "Not now, not ever."

That is the end of that.

I am a tiny bit relieved that Mom made the decision for me.

# Chapter 36

Awareness prickles my entire body. I jerk my eyes from my idea journal and there she is: Donna hovering in the doorway of Mr. Guevara's class. Our teacher waves her in with a warm but concerned smile, but even so, Donna looks anxious like she is afraid to be at school. That breaks my heart. Even though class has already started, I run up to Donna and hug her.

She hugs me back.

My heart sings when Donna trades places with Max, slipping into his chair and sitting next to me even though this is breaking the rule of assigned seats. Max doesn't say anything. Neither does Mr. Guevara. He just nods at us as he continues class. "Today, we're going to talk about our community. Our Marian Anderson Middle School community. Dessie, what do you think our community stands for?"

"One where we feel like we belong," I say, surprising myself with my passionate tone.

Norman raises his hand. "A community where we are honest with each other and can tell each other the truth."

A twinge of worry ripples through me. I have to tell Donna the truth about the rally, but I don't want to upset her. Not when we're finally, finally back together.

"I want a community that supports each other, too," Norman adds. "My great-grandparents always said we feel alone until we have community support. That's why the Black church didn't feel alone in speaking up for civil rights. They had community support." He straightens the tall stack of books on his desk. "So I want a community that comes together to use our voices when something is wrong."

"That's exactly right! Support," Mr. Guevara says enthusiastically, writing our community principles on the whiteboard. "Communication."

I look down at my desk guiltily instead of at Donna. I am not communicating with my identical twin.

"I have a few clarifying questions," Jacqueline says, toying with her two Anne of Green Gables braids. "We belong to more than the community here at Anderson. What about our sixth-grade community? Or our neighborhood community?"

Norman raises his hand again. "Or our friends and family community? Church community? The Marian Anderson Middle School choir community? Or all of them combined, because all of those are my community?"

For the first time since I started at this school, Mr. Guevara smiles a real smile that dazzles his eyes. He tugs off his wedding band and holds the ring briefly before pocketing it. "You're right, all of you. I might be getting a divorce I don't want, but I still belong to multiple communities. We all do. Even if one of our communities is falling apart, we have others that we can rely on and new ones we can form."

Donna shoots me a thrilled look, and I shoot one back at her. Are we and our families forming a new community? My stomach wobbles with excitement. And fear. No way am I ruining our new Lee-Breedlove community.

"A2Z is the best," Lucas says so forcefully at lunch, I can hear him from two tables away.

I am so shocked, I nearly fall off my chair. Lucas is an A2Z fan? Lucas McMorrow?

Donna lifts her eyebrows at me. "Good thing we're boycotting A2Z if Lucas likes them. We're announcing that at the rally, right, Dessie?"

Flushing, I take a big bite of my hummus-and-sprouts sandwich on fresh sourdough bread that Dad baked late last night. It tastes like lies: sawdust.

I mumble, "I can't go."

Donna's face grows grim. She demands, "But, Dessie, if we don't say something, who will?"

"My parents won't let me," I tell her.

"But you always talk back to your parents." Her eyes narrow. "So is it you *can't* go to the rally or you *won't* go?"

"I—"

"How terrible will you feel if another one of our elders gets beat up?" Donna asks, staring straight at me.

That's just the thing. These are her elders, not mine. The Asian American community is hers, not mine. The sixth grade of Marian Anderson Middle School has more Asian people in it than I have ever seen before in my whole entire life. I had never even celebrated Lunar New Year before her. I didn't even know bitter melon and dried baby shrimp existed until her party. I will be a fraud if I stand up there. A community fraud.

"And how terrible will you feel if nobody does anything about any of this?" Donna asks, waving her arms. "Nothing at all?"

"Okay, really terrible," I mumble as I stuff my mouth with another huge bite of my sandwich. More sawdust.

"Or another band comes out with another racist song?"

More chewing. More sawdust.

"And you still won't come to the rally?" When I say nothing, Donna shakes her head. "But we're sisters. Twin sisters. Identical twin sisters." Donna glares at me like she wishes this wasn't the truth. Like being my identical twin is the most distasteful thought she has ever had. The new song from A2Z blares from Lucas's table, filling the silence. But nothing, nothing can fill the distance gaping between the two of us.

"Ugh!" Grimacing, Donna screeches her chair back and grabs her lunch tray. "I hate this song."

"Wait!" I call to her, but Donna is already marching out of the cafeteria as if what she's really saying is: I hate you.

# Chapter 37

Even though it has been forever and a day since Sophie has texted me, I ping her right after dinner.

> *SOPHIE:* What? Your new sister too busy for you?

Her words sting. Even if I could convince my mom to let me go onstage with Donna—let alone the rally, I highly doubt that Donna would want me to stand next to her anymore. It is too late. I shudder again. It is a grievous thing to lose your twin right when you find her.

> *SOPHIE:* Well, guess what, she's not the only one too
> busy for you.

I think about what Grammy told me: *Mean people are hurt people.* Underneath Sophie's prickling words, I can feel her hurt. I have been so focused on Donna that I have ignored my oldest friend in the world. My oldest friend who has had to make new friends with girls we've known since we were five. Girls we have snubbed because we had each other.

*ME:* I haven't been fair to you.

Sophie doesn't respond for a long time. Such a long time that I give up on hearing from her tonight. Maybe, like Donna, it is too late to fix this friendship. With one last regretful look at my phone, I pull out my computer even though the last thing I want to work on is the final segment of my Make Our Mark project: creating the logo for Marian Anderson Middle School. My phone pings. Is it a hopeful ping or a get-lost ping? There's only way to know. I have to read the text.

With shaking hands, I pick up my phone.

*SOPHIE:* That makes two of us.

Two of us. My heart lifts at those olive-branch words like it is winging through the clouds, searching for Donna. Soaring through the bleak sky, calling out for my lost-and-found and lost-again twin.

Yet Sophie is my friend, too. Maybe there are more than one "two of us-es" in our lives. More than the twin I have always wanted to have, like Ben and Jacob have always had each other. I turn on FaceTime. There is Sophie, the girl I've known since before I could even run. The minute she sees my crumpled face, Sophie asks, "What's wrong?"

Even with her sticky lip gloss and clashing eyeshadows,

Sophie is my history. So I tell her everything: Amah and her attack. Donna and her parting "I hate you."

"First of all, poor Amah!" Sophie tells me, her eyes wide with horror. "What kind of jerk would attack an old lady? And second of all, I would feel worse than a horse with a billion burrs in its hooves if my own sister—my new identical twin sister—did not even show up at the rally for me."

"But she hates me now," I protest.

"Donna did not say she hated you. She said she hated the song."

Sometimes, it is easier to hide behind a miscommunication than it is to face the hard truth. Or to do the hard work of understanding each other.

I have not been trying to understand how Sophie has been doing with me gone. So I ask her, "What's going on with you? Tell me everything."

And I mean it.

Especially when Sophie sighs the most sorrowful of sorrowful sighs. If Jacqueline were here, she would say it sounded woebegone. And if Sophie were at Marian Anderson Middle School, I think she and Jacqueline might have been a "two of us." Sophie admits, "It is really, really, really hard to make new friends."

"That's exactly what Jacqueline says!" I tell her. "She says she's always wanted a kindred spirit, but they are hard to come by here in Seattle."

"And here in Chewuch."

"You would love her if you met her."

*This,* I think, after we have said our goodbyes and I am back to the blank page in my idea journal. *This is how we build community: we try to understand each other.* And when we don't, we listen. We support. We try again.

# Chapter 38

Swooshing around the art room. Ms. Lauchengco announces. "It is time for the Marian Anderson Middle School logo. How are you going to show that we believe in respect and communication? And belonging?"

"And showing up for each other, no matter what," Donna blurts out without raising her hand. For the first time in what feels like days, Donna makes eye contact with me. It is scorching, her glare.

For the first time ever, I break eye contact with her.

"Dessie and I are both abysmal artists," Jacqueline warns our group, even though she's placing her perfectly sharpened colored pencils in a tidy row at our art table.

"We are," I agree, because it is true. "And we are both lovers of big words."

Beaming, Jacqueline asks, "You read *Anne of Green Gables*?"

"It saved me," I tell her, because I have to believe that if Anne could make up with her best friend, then somehow,

I will, too, with my twin sister. "And don't worry. We have Max, who is an excellent artist."

I turn around. And there is Max, listening.

Instead of mocking me, Max meets my eyes even when I scowl at him. He does not look away even though his face is fiery red. Not the angry kind of blush. But the embarrassed-pleased kind of blush.

My own cheeks flush. The heartbroken-and-irritated-I-am-a-ghost-sister-thanks-to-you kind of flush.

My pod leans toward each other, even Max, the official sprawler-in-chief of our school. Norman suggests, "How about a microphone? The kind Marian Anderson used?"

"How about binoculars?" I offer loudly, hoping Donna will hear. "So we can see each other clearly."

From Donna's table, I hear a snort. It's not Donna, but Lucas, who is eavesdropping.

"As if you can see anything." Lucas squints at me, then sings, "*Asian driver / no survivor.*"

My cheeks flame. I burn with fury. Lucas McMorrow squinted at me. He actually squinted at me. Maybe this is the problem with hatred: Mean people may be hurt people who hurt others. But those hurt people then become mean people, because I want to spit out hot words. So hot they'll torch Lucas and scorch his voice.

Hatred grows and swells, a tidal wave, building power in my heart.

I open my mouth, but Max cuts in. "Hey, uncool."

His every word is a punch, aimed not at me, but at Lucas. He glowers at his best friend, daring him to say one more mean word.

Lucas mutters, "Geez, I was just singing. It's in the song."

"But you didn't just sing. You squinted on purpose, and no one thinks that's funny," Max says softly.

"My dad would," Lucas shoots back.

"Would your mom have?" Max holds Lucas's gaze and does not let go.

That shuts Lucas up.

*Wow*, I think. Donna nods like she is thinking the same. Wow.

"Whoa," Norman whispers.

"Wonderful," says Jacqueline simply.

*Ha*, I'm about to snark at that Lucas. A hot burst of lava anger. *Ha. Ha. Ha.*

But it is as if I hear Grammy: *Mean people are hurt people.*

It is difficult and somewhat annoying to hear a tiny, almost Max-ian voice in my head: *So stop hurting people yourself.*

It is as if my own ears open and I wonder for the first time: *What on earth is hurting Lucas McMorrow? Could missing his mom maybe, possibly be hurting him? Or something else?*

"Dessie, can you stay for a second?" Mr. Guevara asks at the end of his class, his voice somber like he has bad news. Like I'm in trouble again.

All I can say is this: Max Morrison better not be the reason that I do another walk of shame to the principal's office.

But when it is just me, Mr. Guevara says the absolute last words anyone wants to hear coming out of a teacher's mouth: "I received an email from your dad."

I blink at him. "What?"

A flush darts up Mr. Guevara's neck, then pools behind his scraggly beard. This cannot be good. Even though he looks embarrassed, he meets my eye. "Dessie, I'm sorry for sending you to Mrs. Banerjee's office when you were speaking up for Donna."

*Dad!* I'm too embarrassed to think of anything to say.

Mr. Guevara happens to have much, much more to say. "While I agree with your dad that I was punishing an advocate for justice equally with the perpetrator of injustice, I wish you had told me yourself directly." He stoops as if that will bring him to my eye level, which is impossible because Mr. Guevara is beanstalk tall. "Being able to confront each other respectfully is one of the principles of Marian Anderson Middle School. Communication builds community. I let you down."

I nod as if I understand, but I don't. What is Mr. Guevara saying?

He must practice yoga, Mr. Guevara. He bends so low that I can't help but meet his eyes.

"You were confronting Max when he was harassing your friend, and I made a mistake of punishing you and Donna. Of silencing your voices," he says. "I am so sorry."

I nod at Mr. Guevara like all is forgiven. But inside—inside all I want to do is confront Dad who broke the sacred vow of secrecy when a daughter divulges something private to her father.

Which is exactly what I plan to tell Dad, except Mom picks me up from school. At home, I find Dad in the kitchen, puttering around while attempting to sing. And what he is singing—could it be? Could it possibly be? It is A2Z, the Asian driver song.

"Dad!" I roar, hands on my hips.

That startles Dad into dropping the rolling pin. It clatters on the countertop. He recovers quickly, grinning at me. "Kiddo! I thought we could do a trial run—"

"Dad! You tattled on me," I say, interrupting him.

"Excuse me?" Dad asks, confused, then seeks out Mom's help from behind me, but she doesn't know what I'm so heated about either.

So I tell them. "You told Mr. Guevara about Max."

"Yes, because your punishment wasn't fair," Dad says easily. "We all agreed that it wasn't right."

"But I didn't give you permission to email him!"

A still, small voice in my head whispers, *But Donna gave you permission to go onstage with her.*

"Your dad was just trying to help," Mom offers.

I snap, "But I didn't ask for help!"

The still, small voice in my head whispers again, *But Donna asked for help. She said she was scared to be onstage by herself. She said she needed you.*

"You're right," Dad says, frowning. "I guess in my head, I still see you as my little girl."

"I'm not!"

"If it would help, you can read my letter."

Nothing will help when I keep hearing that still, small voice insistently pointing out the truth: Donna asked for my help. And I said no.

My sister—my twin sister—needed me. And I said no.

I, a Breedlove, did not show up.

# Chapter 39

**My pencil rolls off my desk and hits the floor with a tiny** *plunk*. Max's head jerks up. He is too surprised and too slow to cover his work. Max isn't taking notes in Mrs. Pinero's class. He's not even sneak-working on our group's dismal school logo.

Max Morrison is drawing the magical weaver from *The Eight Banners*! He is drawing Peridot, the fairy who lived in the clouds and could weave people's wishes into reality. Except his Peridot is all bold, swooping lines, like graffiti art. The colors are vivid like you'd see in a mural. Or one of Grammy's weavings.

If I saw any other person drawing a graffitied Peridot, I would think they were cool. But even if he stood up for me yesterday, it is difficult to move Max from the bully column and into the cool column. Not even when Max shoves the Peridot drawing at me after class with a gruff, "Here." Then he ruins the moment with his "Since you keep staring at me."

"I am not staring at you!" I deny fast. Too fast. "I was staring at the drawing."

That Max grins at me: yeah, right.

This is the moment to talk to Max about our logo, how it's just not working. But I had no idea that his eyes were quite so green. A mesmerizing peridot green.

Wait, mesmerizing?

Horrified at myself, I rip my gaze off Max and drop my eyes to his drawing. Even graffitied, Peridot doesn't look like the one in the game. "Hang on, is this Donna?"

Max flushes and mutters, "I'm worried about her."

Max, admitting he's worried? I reach out my hand—to what? To touch Max Morrison on the arm? To hold his hand? We retract at the same time. And he flies out of the class as if he has sprouted wings.

"That is one heavy sigh," Dad says after school, as he sets a slice of freshly baked bread slathered with peanut butter and honey in front of me as soon as I'm home.

"Our school logo is a disaster," I say, sighing again.

"When my composition isn't working, I go back to the drawing board." He sets his hand on my shoulder. "Never be afraid to start over."

Easy for him to say, Mr. Video Game Music Composer. The empty page is scary with so much wide-open space to get lost in.

But I crack my notebook open. Out falls Max's drawing of Peridot.

"Hey, is that your scarf?" Mom asks, peering over my shoulder at Max's drawing.

"My what?" I ask.

"Your scarf," she says, tapping the sheet of paper. "Who drew this?"

"Max," I say faintly and look closely. Really closely. And I cannot believe my eyes because—

Because Max Morrison's graffiti-version Peridot is wearing my scarf. My enormous, eye-popping, screaming-loud scarf.

Which means that this is not Donna he has drawn.

Max Morrison has drawn me.

"Hmm," Mom says with a secret smile.

"Hmm," Dad says with a not-so-secret smile. It is the imminent dad joke smile.

I flee the kitchen but not before I hear my parents laughing. It is a good sound, my parents laughing together. Even if they are laughing about me. And Max. In the privacy of my own room, I have to admit: Max's illustration has so much energy, I can almost feel Peridot in flight. And I can definitely hear *The Eight Banners* theme song, since Mom is playing it downstairs on the keyboard. At full volume.

*Mom!*

A peal of deep laughter floats up to me.

*Dad!*

It is possible I feel a tiny bit guilty that I broke my promise and did not invite Max over to hear Mom perform that very song.

I reach for my phone to text this shock-of-the-century scarf revelation to Donna.

And then I remember.

It is not always such a wonderful thing to remember.

Maybe the empty page is not such a bad idea. I open my idea journal. I think about the first question Mr. Guevara asked when we started the Make Our Mark project: Who are you? I have spent so much time not offending people because I've always been stomachache worried that they will up and leave me. And guess what? They still left: Donna and Sophie. The Twins. Gramps.

Grammy even though she is still here.

So why am I afraid to consider, *Who am I?*

I find myself studying the scarf on that graffitied Peridot.

The loud scarf that I had hidden away because it made too much of a statement.

Because it singled me out when I wanted to blend in and belong. But how can I truly belong when I am not truly being me?

If Grammy could muster the courage to march and if Donna can gather her courage to return to school, then I can risk spider central downstairs to reclaim my scarf. Still, there is nothing wrong with a little extra protection. So I shrug into the thickest sweatshirt I can find in my closet and grab the widest-brimmed sun hat from the mudroom. Nothing is going to squirm in my hair or skitter down my back if I can help it.

Once armored, I slip downstairs. Dad is not at his bank of computers, capturing all the snippets of ideas he's had over the day.

I am alone.

I open the creaky storage room door and quickly snap on the light. Gramps's keepsake box is where I shoved it: banished to the very back of a bottom shelf. The storage light blinks out, and I jump-scare myself. There is no way I am sticking my hand into a dusty old box in the pitch black to scavenge my scarf. Even holding that box a safe distance from my body as I carry it to the sofas, it feels thick with grime. And sticky with spiderwebs.

I set the box down on the coffee table with a shudder. Holding my breath, I lift the dusty lid, sneeze, and rescue my scarf. Underneath are a bunch of postcards, all from Gramps. Then I spot it: a faded photo I didn't even know I was looking for. Grammy. Except she's not marching but standing at the back of a rally. Holding a sign: Oppose All Racial Attacks. Other people around her are holding signs, too: Justice for Vincent Chin. It's Not Fair. Chin Up for Justice.

The colors may be muted with age, but the old photo is clear. Along with a police officer, Grammy is one of the few white people among hundreds of Asian people. Hundreds and hundreds. Throughout the crowd, Black supporters are carrying signs in solidarity, too.

"Where was this?" I ask, holding up the photo as my parents thud down the stairs, Dad humming tunelessly, Mom groaning about the spiders.

Dad takes the photo from me and tilts his head, thinking. "I don't remember this either."

Memories, I've decided, are not a very reliable source of information, and I'm going to tell Mr. Guevara that tomorrow. I wriggle my phone out of my back pocket and search for Vincent Chin. What I read horrifies me. Back in 1982, Vincent was out celebrating at his bachelor party, until he was beaten in the head with a baseball bat by two white men. He died, but the men didn't go to prison, not for a single day. Instead, they paid three thousand dollars and were set free.

Vincent Chin was twenty-seven. That's ten years older than The Twins.

My eyes burn. Vincent didn't get to have a fifty-year marriage with the love of his life like Grammy and Gramps. He didn't get to make memories that lasted until his old age.

Was it really possible he was killed just because of how he looked?

Sickened, I tell my parents all this now.

Then I say, "So of course, you don't remember the rally at all, Dad. You might have been inside Grammy!"

"Which wasn't safe for her to attend," Mom mutters.

Dad's eyes tear up and he says, "Go, Mom!"

Then my eyes tear up for a different reason and a different emotion.

"People are beating up elderly grandparents today just because they're Asian." I sniffle. "It's no different from forty years ago! How is this even possible?"

No one has an answer for that.

Later after dinner, I continue reading about the rallies and protests and marches that changed the justice system: Vincent's killing helped define hate crimes to mean using or threatening force against anyone based on their race or religion or place of origin. I think about the different responses Mom and Dad had to Grammy attending the rally. Maybe they were both right: that the rally may not have been safe to attend, but because people showed up, the law changed.

Even if hate stayed the same.

# Chapter 40

A copy of Dad's email to Mr. Guevara is lying on my pillow after I say good night to Grammy. As if I want to read it.

A tiny part of me does.

Sitting on the edge of my bed, I skim the email fast, then reread the words more slowly. My fingers tighten on the paper. I can hear Dad's voice as he makes it clear that by disciplining me the same as Max, I was being punished for speaking up for my friend and myself. That that is an extremely dangerous lesson to teach girls. He wrote, "How do we expect girls to believe that their no means no when they get punished for saying no more?"

I have to admit: Dad makes a good point.

An excellent one, in fact.

Then as the kicker, Dad quotes Grammy: "An attack on one of us is an attack on all of us."

My still, small voice is no longer quite so still and definitely not so small.

*DESSIE MEI BREEDLOVE*, it yells when I set the email down

on my bedside table next to the photo I found of Grammy at the rally. *GRAMMY SHOWED UP FOR A COMMUNITY THAT WAS NOT HER OWN.*

*JACQUELINE SAYS BIG WORDS ARE SUPPOSED TO BE USED, NOT WASTED IN SILENCE!* it shouts when I click off my bedside lamp.

*MR. GUEVARA SAYS THAT CONFRONTING RESPECT-FULLY IS THE HALLMARK OF MARIAN ANDERSON MIDDLE SCHOOL!* it roars when I stare up at the ceiling.

*EVEN MAX SHUT DOWN LUCAS, WHO IS HIS BEST FRIEND!* it thunders when I cover my head with a stuffed bunny.

*So what am I doing to stand up for all the amahs of every color in my community?* it whispers when I close my eyes. *What? What?*

*What?*


I jolt awake. I was dreaming about my Best Of photo album, except there was nothing in mine. Not one picture. Like I have no past. My chest is heaving when I turn on my light. And there is the photo of Grammy at the Vincent Chin rally where I left it on my bedside table.

Unlike my dream, this will be yet another addition to Grammy's ever-fattening Best Of album. We have been poring through all her photos, hoping each one will be a breadcrumb back to her. Back to the memories that have disappeared. Hoping that the album will stop the mass extinction of Grammy's memories: Childhood. College. Marches. Marriage. Family. Me.

Grammy lived a life that is being taken from her. And I was taken from a life I never got to live.

But I can decide how I want to live this life, starting right here.

I can make my own Best Of album, starting right now.

Maybe my Best Of begins with this old photo carefully cupped in my hands. Norman said the Black church would have felt so alone if other groups hadn't come to their side to speak out for civil rights. Maybe that's why so many Black activists spoke out against Vincent Chin's killing. And maybe that's why Norman believes we need to lift our voices for everyone.

I study Grammy's no-nonsense expression, as she took a stand alongside a community that was not her own to create a bigger community that everyone could call their own. In a weird way, it feels like Grammy was expecting me to join the Breedloves. That she was showing up at the rally for future me. Working to make the world a more welcoming place for today me. A place where I would belong.

Today, I need Grammy to be here, present with me. I have so many questions for her about marching.

Was she scared when she attended the rally for Vincent Chin? When she marched for justice for him and the Asian American community? Was she afraid of being rude? And unwanted?

Did she feel welcome?

Will this same community that is not my own welcome me to take a stand for it?

My throat feels parched like I've spent the last few hours shouting at a rally. I creep downstairs to the kitchen for a glass of cold water. In the dim moonlight, a dark shadow moves at the kitchen table. I nearly scream. Intruder! Maybe even: attacker! Then, I make out Grammy, looking like she has been waiting all her life for me. She is cradling my scarf in her lap.

I pull out the chair beside Grammy's and place the photo of the Vincent Chin rally between us like a bridge, her to me, me to her. Confused, Grammy stares at it. But then she finds herself like she is her own forever magnet and caresses her young Grammy face with a bent finger. For once, her hand isn't shaking. It is steady and sure.

"Someone beat up my friend's—my sister's—grand-mother," I tell her. "Just because she's Asian."

"That's terrible," Grammy says, the weight of history in her words.

"How were you brave enough to get into good trouble?" I ask her. "Grammy, I need to know."

Grammy sighs as her knobby fingers now hold the photo, and she says something so softly, I almost miss it. "Good trouble isn't one person doing everything. It's everyone doing something: marching, voting, speaking, singing, even weaving." Grammy taps the image of herself in the photo and then strokes one of the thickest stripes on my scarf. "So many scarves to keep people warm."

Wait a second. I bend over to study this photo of Grammy showing up for a hurting community, but the kitchen is too dark to see clearly. So I slip out of my seat and flick on the light. The mossy green sweater in the picture and the mossy green stripe in my scarf are the exact same color.

"No way," I breathe.

I peer at her photo, then at my scarf. My scarf, her photo.

"Grammy," I say, staring at my grandmother intently as if I have never seen her before. "Grammy, did you weave your sweater into my scarf?"

"My rally-going sweater," Grammy corrects, rocking herself and my scarf back and forth.

Above that mossy green stripe is a thinner band of a different green. A brighter green. So thin, you could mistake the two for the same color. So thin, I have never noticed it before because, honestly, I have never stopped to study this scarf.

I should have looked closer.

This jade green stripe is the exact color I have searched for everywhere. The exact color I know by heart. The exact color I have held out hope, for as long as I can remember, that I would find again one day.

This jade green stripe is the exact same color as my long-lost baby blanket.

But it has never been lost. Not really.

Grammy has woven my beloved baby blanket directly above her beloved rally-going sweater like she is my foundation. Like she is lifting me up. Supporting me, then, now, forever.

I stare, stare, stare at this jade green that means "brilliant ideas" and "good luck." That means "precious."

"Grammy," I say slowly, lifting my eyes to study this wrinkled face that I love so, so much. "Grammy, did you weave my baby blanket into my scarf?"

Grammy does not answer.

Maybe she doesn't even need to remember because I know. I know she has.

Breedloves show up for each other. Even for me to find that out years later in a scarf.

After I help Grammy back into her bedroom and settle her in bed, she pats me on the hand. I close her door softly, thinking about Amah's little hand patting Max's at the Lunar New Year party like she was claiming him even though they look nothing alike. He wasn't part of the Lee family, but he still showed up when invited. He learned. He tried. He was accepted.

What is worse than feeling like an impostor is feeling like a traitor.

I was supposed to show up for Donna no matter what.

No matter if the Asian American community does not accept me.

No matter if I felt like an impostor onstage.

My sister needed me, and I did not show up.

Now I want to. But how?

Inspiration, as Dad says, comes in the strangest ways. I put on my headphones, listening to music, as I tape Max's drawing of Peridot (me) wearing my good-luck scarf on the wall between two of Grammy's posters. I can hear Mr. Guevara asking us in class: *What kind of community do you want to live in?*

I jerk back from the wall. I finally know.

I, Dessie Mei Breedlove, want to live in a community where people are welcome as they are. I want to live in a community where we all belong. Isn't that what Max was telling me with this drawing? He was welcoming me. He was telling me I belong, flashy-loud scarf and all.

Before I can forget, I jot this down in my idea journal. I know I am making a promise. A promise to Amah and Grammy, Donna and myself.

One song slips into another. And another. My eyes flutter shut. And then there is A2Z, their new song, because I haven't taken the time to delete it from my Midnight Emo playlist.

Too late, the racist lyric blasts in my ear: *"Asian driver / no survivor."*

I switch on my bedside light.

I know exactly how to use my voice.

# Chapter 41

**When inspiration strikes, you grab it.** You cling tight wherever it leads you, even if it is racing a billion miles per hour. Even if it corners wildly one way, then whips around another. You hang on. You trust yourself. That is the Breedlove way.

So that is what I do.

Even though it is well past one in the morning, I grab my words, the angry ones that spit from my gut. The heartfelt ones that spill from my soul. The multisyllabic ones that furl from my head.

Most of all, the healing ones that sing from my heart.

I write for Donna and Amah.

And for myself.

My hand cramps from writing so quickly in my idea journal, filling blank page after blank page.

Finally, I turn to my computer. I type and type. And type some more.

With every sentence, I feel my family coursing all the way

down through my fingertips. It is like I am weaving with my words: Hope and honesty. Truth and encouragement.

When I am done, I read my words again. And again.

Cutting one here. Choosing a different one there.

Finally satisfied, my finger hovers over the post button. What if I offend someone? What if the trolls unleash themselves against me?

I have to stand with my sister. I have to add my voice for my community to be safer. To use my voice for us to become stronger. I tighten my good-luck scarf around myself.

With a deep breath, I hit post.

# Chapter 42

My alarm buzzes. Insistent. Annoying. It cannot possibly be time for school, can it? My teeth feel gritty, my head groggy. A fragment of a song burbles in my mind: *Asian driver / no survivor.* Was it a dream that I posted a comment on A2Z's last Instagram post, calling out my all-time favorite band in the whole wide world?

Telling A2Z that they can do better?

I swipe my phone off my bedside table.

It was not a dream.

There in my hand is proof that I did not imagine my open letter:

> Dear A2Z, I am your biggest fan and probably one of
> your original fans. There is a phrase in your new song
> that is offensive because it stereotypes Asian people.
> That is how a group of people gets turned into a
> target. First comes mocking, then comes assaulting. A
> Taiwanese grandmother in Seattle was just attacked, and

she's too scared to talk to the police because she's afraid the attacker will find her and her family. So he is out there somewhere, free, while she is in the hospital. And, by the way, this grandmother is one who speed races—yes, she's a speed-racing amah. Shatters your stereotype, doesn't it? We all need to keep each other safe with our words and our actions. An attack on one of us is an attack on all of us. So we all need to do better. I do. And you do, too.

With twice the love,
Dessie Mei

I did not imagine commenting on their last post.

I did not imagine reposting my comment on my own Instagram page.

Sophie was the first to like my post. Norman liked it next.

And Max. He even added a comment: "That phrase really is offensive."

*That phrase really is offensive.*

Who knew solidarity would feel so good?

I bound downstairs where Dad grins at me from the griddle. He says, "You're looking sprightly this morning."

"I feel sprightly this morning," I tell him.

He reaches up to jiggle the golden syrup, but I know what I'm watching. I'm watching Dad work his promise to become an expert mooncake baker with all its many steps, including tending the golden syrup daily. Rocking it one way, then another like it is a baby.

If I can trust Dad to work his promise to me, then perhaps I can trust him with the full truth. I clear my throat like I have something to say. I do. "So I didn't go to Donna's birthday party because her grandmother disinvited me." And then I tell him that Amah thinks I'm rude.

"Amah thought what?" Mom asks as she joins us in the kitchen, her sweaty face flushed not because of her morning run, but because of indignation. Thin-lipped indignation.

I start panicking.

I don't want Mom to rant about Amah's disinvitation and rage over "let's talk about what's really rude," especially when Amah might still be in the hospital. Dad places a calming hand on Mom's arm. He asks me, "Why do you think Amah did that?"

"Because I'm rude to you," I tell him. "Because I'm vexatious!"

"Could it be that we have a different way of communicating with each other?" he asks. "Maybe we're more . . . feisty with each other?"

But the way my parents have been arguing with each other, they are one discordant tune against the other. I tell them, "It's like you used to play one song together, left hand and right hand. You guys had different parts, but it was the same song. But now . . . when you fight, it's not feisty. It's more like ferocious."

Dad says slowly, "And that's been hard for you to hear. I'm really sorry, kiddo."

At the same time, Mom says, "That's because we have a healthy relationship!"

Dad clears his throat, and Mom bites her lip. Then she tries to explain. "You know, all those happy-happy, we-never-fight couples? A lot of them are just going along to get along." When I frown, not understanding, Mom continues, "They never have the hard conversations."

"That's right. We argue to resolve the problem, not to cut each other down. Or to win. Big difference," Dad says. "But we can definitely work on our tone."

Mom blushes but nods, too.

"And maybe the way I speak to you guys is hard for Amah to hear," I think aloud. "So I'm sorry, too."

Mom says sharply, "Well, you don't have to apologize to us! Their way doesn't mean it's the right way!"

"Mom."

She clears her throat, and her face flushes again. I know Mom's not upset at Amah so much as she is upset for me. She says, "That must have been so hard for you, being disinvited. Especially since Donna is your sister."

"Well, Amah has a point," I say, thinking about how my cutting tone with my parents made Donna feel uncomfortable. "That's something I can work on."

"Okay, but," Dad says, refilling Mom's tea, "could it be that vexatious people are the ones who don't back down no matter what when something is wrong? That they are the squeaky wheels who change the world?"

Not in a million and one years have I ever considered that. "Vexatious like Grammy?"

"Vexatious like the Breedloves," he answers.

Vexatious like the Breedloves. That thought feels like home.

I grin at my dad, who vexed Mr. Guevara into seeing the truth. "Not that I'll ever admit this again, but your email kind of inspired me."

Dad splutters, spitting out a mouthful of coffee, and says incredulously, "It did?"

So I tell my parents about what I wrote to A2Z, which makes Dad immediately check his phone. And like both my comment on A2Z's page and the post on mine. He holds the phone so Mom can read, too, as he says, "Hey, look at all these comments."

"You started an important conversation," Mom says, beaming at me. "The hard one."

"Let's continue it," says Dad. He clears his throat and reads as he types, "*Talk about speaking truth to power. Care to join the conversation, A2Z?*"

Before I can protest, Dad reposts and shares what I've written with his bajillion followers, mostly fans of *The Eight Banners* who adore his music.

He returns to the fragrant pot simmering on the back burner and reads the question in my eye.

"Congee this morning," he explains, then shrugs sheepishly. "I thought I'd make some for the Lees since Donna's dad said this was Amah's comfort food."

The new aroma of rice porridge fills the kitchen like a

warm embrace. My dad, he is always working to make everyone feel supported. To feel welcome, wherever they are: In this house that is not our forever home. In the hospital where they are scared.

"That's exactly why I want to go to the rally," I tell them.

Mom is already shaking her head slowly no, no. No.

I simply state the truth. "I want Donna and Amah to know they're supported. I have to go."

Dad says, "You do."

For a long moment, Mom is silent. Her face is a sunset, blazing crimson red before fading into a light pink. Dad and I wait. Finally, Mom says, "We all have to go."

I don't need any more encouragement to text Donna the good news immediately.

*ME:* Mom says I can go to the rally with you!

No response.

*ME:* I can stand next to you onstage if you want!

Grammy clomps into the kitchen, wearing her beat-up rally-going, arch-supporting sneakers. She sniffs the congee appreciatively. "Where's my sign?"

On the way to school, I check my phone again and again.

Again and again, no answer from Donna.

# Chapter 43

With my best race car driver moves that I am pretty sure would impress even Amah, I zip around a group of eighth graders, maneuver past seventh graders, and corner over to Donna in the hallway and announce, "We have to talk."

"Wait, did your parents give you permission to talk to me?" she fumes, sounding more like a Breedlove than a Lee.

"I am sorry I didn't want to stand on the stage with you." A lump of regret is lodged in my throat, but I have lost too much time wishing things were different rather than working to make things right. I push on because having Donna in my life is worth the pain of failing. "Max—Max!—can use chopsticks better than me. The only food I recognized at your Lunar New Year party was the rice. And even that didn't taste like what we make at home. We put butter in ours!"

Donna wrinkles her nose. "Butter?"

"I thought I would be a stupid impostor at a rally for Asian Americans. I am a Chinese culture dud!"

Donna's face softens. "Well, I am one, too! I know more about Taiwanese culture than I do Chinese culture. And I'm not sure how I can even learn it without making Amah mad. So you are not an impostor."

"I notice you didn't say that I'm not stupid," I mutter.

"That's because for someone who always has the best ideas, like calling out a certain band, you are being really stupid."

A smile creeps onto my face. "Wait, you saw the post?"

"I loved the post! The boycott is on!"

It would be easier to stay quiet, nod in agreement, go along to get along, but I have to tell Donna another truth. My smile fades. "Actually, I don't want to boycott them. At least, not yet. I wanted to try to, I don't know, maybe have a conversation with them first, which is kind of stupid, I know. Like, are they really going to see my post?"

"But that's even braver," Donna says, nodding vigorously.

"Braver?"

"Yeah, because it makes me wonder what I have to say that adults would even want to hear. Maybe they'll just pat me on the head after the rally like, 'Aww, you're so cute.' Like I'm just some stupid kid they don't need to have a conversation with at all. So, excuse me, who's the real impostor?"

"People want to hear what you have to say," I tell her fiercely.

"And people would want you onstage," she tells me just as fiercely. "And who cares if they don't? I want you there! I just found you."

"I just found you, and I don't want to lose you." I sniffle and brush away my tears.

So does Donna. She heaves a woeful Anne Shirley sigh that would make Jacqueline proud. "Not that it matters. My parents think the rally's too dangerous."

"That makes two of us," I say, loving those magical words: *two of us.* "But mine'll let me go if they go."

"Mine are too afraid to go."

Reluctantly, we head to the art room where we have the entire hour to work on the Marian Anderson Middle School logo. At my table, Max is sketching banners flapping in the wind. Norman is poring over his books about the civil rights movement. Jacqueline is smoothing her braids while studying one of Norman's books on Marian Anderson.

No one is talking at our table.

We need to talk so we can harmonize our ideas.

I sit up straight. *Talk. Harmonize. Ideas.* I say, "Community isn't about one note, all of us sounding the same."

Norman puts down his book. "It's music made of all our notes."

"And we need to get louder," I say slowly as an idea begins to swirl in my head. "Marian Anderson Middle School needs to get louder. A crescendo."

Jacqueline flips her braids over her shoulders. "*Crescendo* comes from the Italian word, *crescere*. To grow."

"Our community is growing. We are the crescendo," Norman says, his huge eyes growing huger.

"Crescendo," Max says confidently, picking up a pen. "I can do something with that."

While he begins to sketch one concept after another, my ears tune in to the conversations around us. People are chattering about the new Marvel movie opening this weekend. I can't believe that everyone has moved on from Amah's attack. Since yesterday, the news hasn't mentioned a single peep about that attack.

It is like it never happened.

But it did.

My words to A2Z have not made one iota of difference, because Amah is still in the hospital and her attacker is still on the loose.

Maybe this is exactly why Grammy said nice words are not enough.

I tap my eraser against the art table. What action can we take? What action? My pink macaron cookie eraser bounces up and down. Up and down. Faster, faster.

"What are you doing?" Max hisses at me, like my eraser and I are giving him a headache. "Why do you look so weird?"

Donna glares at him from the table next to ours. "She is obviously thinking." *Duh.*

I know exactly what expression I'm wearing: the slightly dazed—and, frankly, weird—look. The I'm Having a Big Idea look.

The inspired look of all Breedloves when we are solving a problem or considering a project.

And most especially, when we are working a promise.

I have promised myself to make some noise about Amah's attack. Perhaps we can't attend a rally in downtown Seattle. Or give a speech onstage. But we can still protest somehow. Some way.

But how?

How?

Forty-five minutes later, we file out for lunch. Brainstorming, as it turns out, takes a lot of energy. My stomach growls, then gurgles with dread: Lucas. Of course he is wearing an A2Z T-shirt. Of course he is. Lucas taunts, "How stupid must a person be to think that they can get a band to notice them?"

Donna snaps, "Tell that to the two hundred people who've already liked her post, including me."

I just sigh, a sad little sound, and say, "Plus, your T-shirt really hurts my feelings."

The tops of Lucas's ears grow hot red, but what I notice is how Norman picks up his book about Marian Anderson. A book about a singer who was told: no, she did not belong.

A book about how that same singer belted out loudly, proudly on the steps of the Lincoln Memorial: oh yes, she did.

And I notice Max noticing me.

Inspiration strikes faster than my self-conscious blush. A lightning bolt stops my whirligig brain. It is like I am weaving all the dots of inspiration around me: Norman who knows everything and its place in history. Jacqueline who finds the perfect words to express everything. Donna who designs fonts for every person, every mood, every occasion. And Max who creates art that tugs at people's hearts, even mine.

The idea grows. It spirals inside me, gaining speed. It is like the surprise emergence of a rainbow, sudden and perfect and fully formed, where only dark clouds had scudded a moment before. Donna stares at me as if she can hear the pinging, pinging of my mind at work.

"What?" she asks.

"I know what we can do," I tell her, grab her hand, and tug her away from Lucas, collecting Jacqueline and Max. When we are all gathered around Norman in the library, I ask if they will help me with my idea for Amah. I hope they will say yes.

They do.

# Chapter 44

It is six in the morning, and five hundred people have liked my comment on A2Z's post. Five hundred people who now know the lyrics are offensive. Five hundred people who have heard about Amah's attack, even though it was not reported to the police.

This is a sign that what we have planned is important.

We just need to convince our school.

I arrive at Marian Anderson Middle School especially early on Tuesday morning. Norman and Jacqueline are already waiting outside, shivering in the cold. Donna's mom putt-putts into the parking circle, so slowly she would lose a race with snails. Donna and Max spill out of the minivan and run to us.

Norman says, "You know, the leaders of the civil rights movement were sometimes called the Big Six, which makes us the Mini Five."

Mini Five? Max frowns like I knew he would. He says, "The Mighty Five."

"The Anderson Five," corrects Jacqueline, and it is so indisputably perfect pitch, that name, we all nod.

That is how the Anderson Five meet Mr. Guevara before school starts.

I tell him what we want to do. "Mr. Guevara, after we present our logos to the school, we would like to rally for Amah."

Before I am finished speaking, Mr. Guevara begins to frown. A frown that says, No way. A frown that says, We are not having this conversation.

Firmly but politely, I ask, "What's the worst that could happen?"

I swear, I can hear Mr. Guevara running through an entire inventory of worries: Some parents will complain. People will go to war on social media. He might get in trouble with the principal.

Before he can reject my idea, Norman tells him, "Mr. Guevara, if we aren't able to speak about what it means to be a true community, then we'll never be a healthy community."

I add, "We can't be healthy if we tolerate hatred. That's why we want to have a school rally."

Then Jacqueline says, "Marian Anderson did not stay silent."

Max points out, "She just needed one person to stand up for her. That one person was Eleanor Roosevelt."

Donna finishes for us, "We need our one person to be you, Mr. Guevara."

Mr. Guevara is struck silent like he cannot believe his ears. Then his eyes glimmer like he *can* believe his ears. Like he *can* believe in us. He bounces to his feet. "Yes, let's do it!" Bounce. "But can you get all this organized by Friday?"

"Yes," I say confidently. "Norman"—who knows everything—"is going to make sure that our rally echoes with Marian Anderson and he is working with the choir. Jacqueline"—and her big words—"is helping us figure out the right words for our posters and speeches. Donna"—of the epic calligraphy—"is in charge of writing all the posters." And finally, the words I never thought I would speak, "And Max"—and his magnificent artistry—"is decorating all the posters."

Mr. Guevara's no-longer-sad mouth curves into a knowing grin as he looks between Max and me, me and Max.

Max blushes a brilliant red. I am pretty sure I do, too.

"Our community is already getting healthier, I think," Mr. Guevara says.

I know it is.

"But we better check in with Mrs. Banerjee," says Mr. Guevara. He glances at the clock behind him. Twenty minutes before school starts. He jerks his chin at the door. "We might have time."

"We got it, Mr. Guevara," I tell him, because I have already booked a meeting with our principal.

He nods at me and sits back down. "You definitely do."

Mrs. Banerjee is not convinced.

She picks up a ballpoint pen, then sets it down on her large, tidy desk, only to grab it again as she frets out loud, "Some parents are not going to be happy about a school rally."

"We can't make everybody happy," I tell her because that is what Mom says whenever she and Dad make a hard decision that Ben, Jacob, and I hate. Like fracturing our family to move to Seattle.

"No, not everybody," says Mrs. Banerjee with a knowing smile. She pushes her thick black hair over her shoulder. "Not even one of the hottest groups in the world today. I am very proud of you, Dessie, for using your voice."

Our principal hands me her phone—her phone during school hours.

My eyes widen, stunned. The studio head of *The Eight Banners* herself has added her voice, sharing Dad's repost with her two hundred and seventy-five thousand followers. She wrote that *The Eight Banners* has always lifted up other creators to do their best work. That's why Dad—Dad!—collaborates with so many musicians. He is using their game to launch countless careers and to inspire their best work. A2Z can do its best work now by addressing community concerns.

Below her shared post, at least five different Asian American organizations have also chimed in, all of them agreeing with me.

Me.

I exchange an astonished look with Donna, who says, "See? I told you, you belong."

Mrs. Banerjee laughs at my surprise. "A2Z just issued a statement."

They did?

"They did." Mrs. Banerjee swivels her computer screen around so we can read their response for ourselves: "We are grateful for a young fan who brought to our attention that we inadvertently included an offensive phrase in our latest song. Derogatory language hurts all of us, just like an attack on one community is an attack on our greater community. So we've made a change to the lyrics and are rerecording today. We hope this might help keep all our communities safe. Most of all, we hope that if anyone saw anything, they say something for the speed-racing grandmother in Seattle who was attacked one week ago. Stay tuned for more."

"Whoa," Max says, looking at me, awed. "You did that."

I shake my head. "Amah did that." I look at Mrs. Banerjee expectantly. "So Friday is on?"

Mrs. Banerjee clicks her pen, shaking her head with a slight frown. She says, "As well-intentioned as your plans are, a rally at school will make things even more divisive. I am sorry, but the answer is no."

# Chapter 45

**No? How could Mrs. Banerjee say no?**

Tears well in Donna's eyes. Jacqueline's mouth gapes open, uttering not a single word. Not even a tiny "oh." Norman is shaking his head, arms crossed against his chest. Max tucks his legs under his chair.

The Anderson Five are all shocked silent.

I think about how so many people, even strangers, have added their voices to mine in confronting A2Z. So many people from so many communities—my old school, my new one, gamers, the Asian American community.

I think about Grammy, who marched for a community that was not her own. Most of all, I think of Marian Anderson, who, I have to believe, would be disappointed if we simply took no for an answer.

Not when we are a chorus of change.

So I say, "I think every single person would agree that elderly people should not be punched in their faces until they're bloody and unconscious and have to recuperate for multiple nights in a hospital and are still there because they were injured so—so—" I struggle for the right word.

Jacqueline supplies it: "So grievously."

Perfect. I repeat, "So grievously."

Mrs. Banerjee grimaces. "True."

"And I think most everybody would agree that no one should be attacked just because of the color of their skin," Norman says.

Mrs. Banerjee says, "Also true."

Max—Max!—adds, "And if they don't agree, then maybe we need to show them that our community doesn't accept violence, and we never will."

"But a rally on school grounds?" Mrs. Banerjee asks softly, more to herself than to us.

I have done my research, and I am prepared. I take out the page I have printed from the school district's website last night and read our district's mission statement in a clear voice: "As a learning community that values one another's humanity, we provide courageous support for an equitable and exceptional education for all students."

Mrs. Banerjee murmurs, "Well, then."

Donna adds, "We designed our school logos based on that mission statement."

"A rally would demonstrate what it means to be a real school community," says Jacqueline.

Max says, "And it'll show that we value every single person in our community, amahs included."

Finally, Norman opens his book about Marian Anderson, and reads, "'The minute a person whose word means a great deal dares to take the open-hearted and courageous way, many others follow.' She said that, Marian Anderson."

"This is the open-hearted and courageous way," I say, then hold my breath.

Mrs. Banerjee does not speak. Not for a long time. So long that we exchange worried looks, the Anderson Five. And still, Mrs. Banerjee ponders, her fingers steepled together, her forehead pleating in a frown.

So I move to Plan B: negotiation. Sometimes, as we learned from Marian Anderson, progress is made in baby steps. She may have sung on the steps of the Lincoln Memorial in 1939, but it still took another twenty-five years before Black people could drink from any water fountain and use any bathroom and attend any school they wanted.

I nod at Jacqueline, grateful she helped me with this careful wording last night. I ask, "What if we submit our speeches for approval ahead of time?"

"No," says Mrs. Banerjee with finality, as she presses both hands flat on her desk and stands up.

My heart plummets straight to the tan carpet, burrows under the concrete, and seeps into the dirt.

"No," our principal repeats with a firm nod, "we let you speak or we don't at all." Mrs. Banerjee has the same look that Grammy wore in that photo at that long-ago rally: beautifully determined.

"We speak," I say.

"Oh, Dessie," Mrs. Banerjee says with a warm smile, "I don't think anyone could stop you."

# Chapter 46

**Mooncake Attempt Number Three is going the same way** that Mooncake Attempt Number One and Mooncake Attempt Number Two have gone: dismally. Verging on disastrously. Since there are so many steps to making mooncakes, last night, I called dibs on the red bean filling and began soaking the hard-as-rock adzuki beans. As soon as I got home from school, I placed the red beans in the instant pot to pressure cook for thirty minutes. Finally, they're soft and ready, and I smash them with an immersion blender, which is highly satisfying. I add sugar and butter just the way the recipe instructed and smoosh them again. While I do all that, Dad makes the dough. I roll my red beans into twenty little balls. Dad flattens his dough into twenty palm-sized disks. Together, we wrap my red bean balls with his dough.

At last, it is time for the mooncake molds, what I've been waiting for. There are three parts to the mold: the barrel that holds the mooncake balls, the plunger, and the decorative disk. I know exactly the stamp I'm going to use and select the most intricate flower design. A chrysanthemum, which is a symbol of long life. That's because the Mandarin word for the flower is similar to two other words that mean "to remain" and "long time." I can't think of anything I want more than to remain with Donna and my entire family for the rest of my life.

"Ready?" I ask Dad, as I screw the stamp for the chrysanthemum onto the plunger.

I think Dad is sweating a little bit. Our dough ball is slightly too big for the barrel, but he stuffs it in anyway.

"Ready," he says.

With that, I smoosh the plunger down onto the baking sheet we've prepared for rows of beautiful mooncakes. Exquisite mooncakes. Mooncakes that are little works of art.

Except: our first mooncake sticks inside. As in: it refuses to release from the mold.

"That's unfortunate." Dad frowns and flips back through his three recipes and notes from four YouTube videos.

Meanwhile, I google for help. "Oh, wait, we were supposed to dust the mold with cornstarch first."

With a sigh, I use my finger to dig the ruined mooncake out of the mold while Dad hunts for the cornstarch. Let's just say, even with the cornstarch, our dimpled mooncakes look nothing like the artistic photos posted by a baker in Brooklyn famous for her mooncake designs (not to mention her support of my A2Z post). Hers are delicate and delicious: the lotus green mooncake with green tea filling. The pink peony with red bean. The yellow chrysanthemum with lotus seed.

Ours are blobs. Squishy reddish-black blobs.

Dad pokes the sticky mooncake gingerly. The skin clings to his finger. "Maybe it's because I used store-bought golden syrup for this test run."

He heaves a deep, defeated sigh like he has failed me, my Chinese heritage, and three thousand years of mooncake history.

"Who cares if they look like duds?" I tell him with a side hug while he eyes the mooncakes mournfully. "This was fun, and I bet they'll still taste good." I turn on Dad's playlist of Mongolian throat singing and think about Peridot from *The Eight Banners*, who never gave up, no matter how much she failed. "Dad, we'll try again this weekend," I promise him.

I wouldn't have heard the light knock on the front door except that Owen is barking his head off and racing back and forth between us in the kitchen and the entry. His floofy tail wags with furious joy.

It is Donna. And her parents.

They stand uncertainly at our doorstep. Their shoulders are stooped over as if they are wearing the heaviest back-packs in the world, but they are not.

At first, I think they are afraid, because Owen is so rowdy that Mom clips a leash onto him so he can't leap all over the Lees. But Auntie Susie keeps her body slightly angled toward the street like she is prepared to fend off anyone who dares to pounce on them from behind, and Uncle Carl is holding a walking stick though he walks perfectly fine. They look relieved when Dad invites them inside.

Suddenly, I'm unsure: Are they here because they're mad that Donna and I have conspired to throw a rally for Amah at school? And if they're mad at me, are they still Auntie Susie and Uncle Carl, or are they Mr. and Mrs. Lee? My hands go clammy.

"Dessie," says Auntie Susie / Mrs. Lee. "That was very brave of you to speak up about A2Z. We so much appreciate your support."

"We wanted to thank you," Uncle Carl / Mr. Lee says.

Brave? Thank you? I can hardly believe my ears. I look uncertainly at Donna, but she is beaming like she is thrilled to be at my ultra-colorful home. Like she is proud to be my identical twin sister. Donna says, "Thanks to how you stood up to A2Z, Amah is going to report her assault to the police!"

"She heard about A2Z?" I ask faintly.

"Who hasn't heard about your epic post?" Donna responds. "She says if a girl can be that brave, so can she. The police can look for her attacker now!"

Donna's dad laughs. "Yeah, Amah kept repeating, An attack on one of us is an attack on all of us. So she decided to do her part in keeping the community safe."

Mom, Dad, and I exchange a look. Even though Grammy may not remember all the rallies she's attended or all the marches she's marched in or all the signs she's created, her words—her strong, beautiful, empowering words—continue to make a difference.

Donna glows at me. "So Amah had a change of heart."

Those words warm me. Maybe, just maybe, Amah had a change of heart about me, too.

I remember my manners, not just the Breedlove ones, but my Asian ones. I ask, "Mr. and Mrs. Lee, would you like something to eat?"

But Donna's mom frowns. Her eyebrows lower. She looks like Amah, only younger. Same disapproval, smoother face. What have I done this time? Tears prickle in my eyes. Mrs. Lee says, "Why are you calling me Mrs. Lee? I'm Auntie Susie, remember?"

Donna's dad says, "And I'll always be your uncle Carl."

I do not know why, but I cannot control my tears when Mom chimes in, smiling at Donna, "And I'm Auntie Leisa."

"Call me Uncle Drew," says Dad, grinning down at Donna like he is on the cusp of breaking out a dad joke.

Quickly, I lead everyone to the kitchen. Behind me, Mom murmurs to Auntie Susie, "The orphanage is ghosting me. They won't tell me why they separated our girls!"

"Maybe that's something for the girls to explore when and if they're ever ready," Auntie Susie answers gently.

Surprise, surprise: Mom nods.

Instead of joking, Dad is making hemming and hawing noises. I've forgotten that the kitchen is ground zero of The Great Mooncake Debacle. Dad takes almost as much pride in his baking as he does in his music. He is actually sweating, my dad.

I say proudly, "Dad and I are learning how to make moon-cakes."

"Emphasis on learning," Dad mumbles.

Uncle Carl steps closer to the baking sheets and studies our catastrophe cakes with wide stunned eyes. "Is that what these are?" Then Uncle Carl laughs, a big, booming laugh. Not unkindly like he is mocking us, but like we are all in on a joke. He says confidentially, "Do you want to know the secret to a truly great mooncake?"

Dad nods, his eyes glued hopefully on Uncle Carl.

Uncle Carl says, "You go to Cam Chen Bakery and buy them there. That's what we all do!"

Now Dad guffaws alongside Uncle Carl like they are best friends. Or brothers. Mom and Auntie Susie exchange pained expressions like good sisters. And best of all, Donna and I laugh together like we have known each other our whole entire lives.

It feels like we have.

Our kitchen feels warm and safe.

So does my growing family, until Grammy ventures out of her bedroom, and my stomach knots up: What is Grammy going to say?

She scowls. "What's going on?" But then she sees Donna and me, and she beams. "I told you twins run in our family."

# Chapter 47

"We have until Friday to get all the posters done," I remind Max when the last bell rings on Wednesday.

"I'll start soon," Max says, shrugging easily. Like it will take him no time at all to decorate twenty-seven posters, not to mention finalize our group's school logo.

Max is wrong; we need to start *now*. Friday is the day of the big reveal of our new school logos to the entire Marian Anderson Middle School community: teachers, families, students. Friday is also the day of our school rally. Friday is two short days from now. Two. So I find myself asking him, "Do you want to come over and work on them together?"

Quickly, like all he has been thinking about for weeks and weeks is my promise, Max asks, "Will your mom be there?"

I nod. "And my dad. He composed the music."

Max croaks, "He did?"

Over my shoulder I tell him as I head into the hall, "Yep."

"Whoa, wait for me!" Max cries, grabbing his backpack and following me to the parking circle, where his mom is waiting. So is Lucas, who watches us leave, one after another, almost like he wishes he were the one calling out, "Whoa, wait for me!" Soon, we are caravanning to my home: Dad who is driving me, Max and his mom behind us. And far, far, far in back, Auntie Susie is chugging along with Donna.

Five minutes later, Max barrels through the front door, immediately becoming a tour guide of my home.

"Whoa!" he says, mouth dropping as he walks slowly, reverently to Grammy's loom in the living room. "This looks exactly like the loom in *The Eight Banners*."

"That's because it is," I tell him.

His beautiful green eyes pop out.

Wait, beautiful?

"Hang on, that"—he points to one of Grammy's weavings hanging on the wall—"that's the Tapestry of Fate." He is so shocked, he collapses weakly onto one of the pink armchairs.

I laugh. *He is almost adorable, Max Morrison.*

Wait, adorable?

Donna thankfully arrives and makes herself at home by laying out her calligraphy pens on the kitchen table. Just as Max rouses himself out of his superfan stupor, Dad ambles up from his basement studio. Max freezes, staring awestruck at Dad. If he is surprised to see Max in our home, Dad doesn't show it. He grins like he was expecting my friend.

Is that what Max is becoming? Another new friend?

*Or maybe something more?*

Wait, something more?

I blush.

Max watches me, interested.

So does Dad. He smirks—my dad smirks—but blessedly does not drop a dad joke about crushes, boyfriends, or other mortifying topics. Instead, he asks, "What are you all up to?"

"Our posters for the rally. Max is drawing, Donna is lettering, and I am zhuzhing," I answer because, miracle of miracles, Max remains silent. That seems to be a good enough answer for Dad, since he strolls over to pull cookie dough from the freezer. His famous chocolate chip cookies that power the imagination.

"How many cookies per human today?" Dad asks as he sets a cookie sheet on the counter.

"One," says Donna.

"Two," I say at the same time Max finds his voice. "Three, please."

I can read Dad's expression: *This kid has good manners.* So Dad counters, "How about four?"

I shake my head and remind him of what I had discovered the other day during my Moon Festival research. "Four is bad luck, remember?"

"I guess that means five cookies per human," Dad says as Mom walks down the stairs from her piano studio. Dad quickly amends, "Five small, bite-sized, so tiny they are more like wafers than cookies per human. Plus, chocolate is excellent for creativity."

"One for me, thanks," Mom says approvingly.

After I introduce Max to her, Mom's arms fold over her

chest, and I can see that she is putting two and two together and is highly suspicious of the result. Even if this is Max who drew Peridot wearing my scarf, this is the same Max who chucked a wad of paper at Donna. The same Max who Grammy said was being mean because he was hurt. She watches Max like a lioness ready to pounce if he so much as looks at me funny. Max flushes, clears his throat uncomfortably, and seizes the chrysanthemum mooncake mold like it is a rare piece of art.

Hastily, I say, "Max is a huge *Eight Banners* superfan."

"Is that right?" Dad says, plopping golf ball–sized dough balls on two cookie sheets.

"Ask me anything," Max says, not bragging. But confident.

"Do you all want to try on the leather jacket the studio gave us when the game launched?" Dad asks. "And maybe Dessie's mom can play the theme song for you guys?"

Max grins at me, sets down the mooncake mold, and shouts, "Heck yeah!"

Donna traipses after them, leaving me alone in the kitchen, but I don't mind. Not when I can still feel the warmth of Max's grin and I am not sure I like the one butterfly—maybe two—flitting around my stomach uninvited. But then I hear the oven ping that it is ready, and I slide the chocolate chip dough balls inside.

As the cookies begin to bake, Donna races up the stairs, clutching her phone. She is radiant. "They caught Amah's attacker!"

"What? Really? Already?" I ask, stunned. "How?"

"A2Z! They dropped a new version of their song, and they offered five thousand dollars for a tip. Someone called the police with information."

"They did?" I cannot process all this news. I blink at Donna, who is cuing up the song. Not only have A2Z re-recorded it, they replaced the troubling lyrics with something even better: "*Amah driver / hella survivor.*"

"Amah is famous," I tell Donna.

"You are, too," Donna says.

Famous or not, I know what I have to do: I message A2Z privately first, thanking them for making the change so fast. Telling them that the song is even better than before. And sharing that Amah's attacker has been arrested, thanks to them.

Then in a post, I thank the ultimate best band in the world, along with all our countless supporters.

As I do, Donna plays the song, and when it gets to the "Amah driver" part, we scream along in the kitchen. Then and there, an idea bursts into my brain. I sprint to my bedroom to grab the game controllers that attach to my phone. Panting, I shove them into Donna's hand. "For Amah. You guys can play Dad's race car game together until she can drive again."

Donna says, "That's so nice of you, but she doesn't approve of video games."

"She will after this."

"I don't know."

"Change of heart," I remind her, and after a moment, Donna takes the small controllers.

Max thuds up from Dad's studio, soaring with happiness. I know the feeling.

"Your dad has the sword from the Underworld," Max announces, wonderstruck. His excitement fades into disbelief when I look at him blankly. "Wait, you've gotten to the Underworld, right?"

No. I haven't even made it past the second level. I admit that out loud because there is no sense in hiding it when everything coming out of Max's mouth sounds like a foreign language.

"That's because you are making the two deadly mistakes," he says. "Most people try to outrun the bad guys. Or they waste Peridot's lives by trying to return her home. What they should be doing is increasing her power."

Max is already attaching the controllers I just handed to Donna to either side of his phone. "Here," he says, "let's play."

Now that I know the key to leveling up, it is tempting. It really is. But I say, "This weekend."

There is a promise I need to work first.

# Chapter 48

The day before the rally. Max joins Donna and me at our lunch table. His undereye bags are as big and dark as his enormous art portfolio. Reluctantly, he unzips the black portfolio. Painfully slow. So slow, a sloth could meander through an entire tropical rain forest in the time it takes Max to share his artwork.

It is worth the wait.

Both Donna and I gasp. "Whoa!"

The top drawing is of Peridot, soaring, graffiti style. Her long sleeves double as widespread wings, cupping Donna's beautifully lettered sign: Our Community Loves. A wingspan as large as a rainbow, so colorful the inspiration could only have come from Grammy's home.

The tips of Max's ears turn pink. He mumbles, "She's based on Amah."

Donna's eyes skitter to me and she nudges me hard.

That's what Max might say, but he has drawn the flying

weaver-fairy with wavy black hair so she looks exactly like Donna.

And me.

Jacqueline draws over to us and sighs. "These are lovely."

Lovely. I half expect Max to snicker at that old-fashioned word. But he doesn't, because Max Morrison is mouthing that word silently to himself while he is looking from Donna to me.

Norman nods. "Your posters make me feel."

"All the feels," I say, the words out of my mouth before I even know what I'm saying.

Max's ears are no longer tipped in pink. They are so bright red, they could stop a mile of traffic. I know my cheeks could.

Even though Max tries to shut his portfolio, our astonishment draws the rest of the sixth graders over and keeps his art out in the open.

"These aren't my posters; they're *our* posters," he tells the crowd around our table. "Norman researched what the old civil rights posters said, Jacqueline updated those sayings for today, and Donna did all the lettering." Then he looks at me proudly. "And Dessie had the big idea."

Akshaya taps one of the posters with swoopy letters and says, "I call dibs on this one. But can it say *Make good trouble with us*?"

Even as Donna adds the "with us" in bold lettering, everyone in the sixth grade at Marian Anderson Middle School clamors for their own poster.

That is, almost everyone.

Lucas is glaring at Max like he is a traitor.

Lucas, who does not take a poster.

I remember how Lucas had stared after our caravan of cars yesterday like he wanted to join us.

So I ask him, "What do you want on yours?"

Lucas flinches like I've hit him. Wariness flashes over his face like he's expecting me to turn my invitation into an insult.

Within a blink of an eye, Lucas McMorrow's smirk-faced armor is back in place.

"As if I want a stupid poster," he scoffs before he storms off.

# Chapter 49

I am late to set up for the rally, but I dart back inside our home.

From the driveway, Mom hollers, "Dessie, you don't have time for this."

But I do. I will always have time to do things right. From the back door, hanging alongside the colorful raincoats above the cheery galoshes, I grab the long scarf that Grammy wove for me. Salvaging bits of my precious jade green baby blanket from the orphanage along with the mossy green sweater she wore at a rally on behalf of my community, weaving them both into this Best Of tapestry of love.

This scarf that is so big it could warm two sisters. Maybe even two families. And hopefully, one community. I would not be surprised.

So what if it is loud, my statement-making scarf?

Today, I want all eyes on me when I say what I have to say.

The sixth graders of Marian Anderson Middle School are transforming the cafeteria into a pop-up art gallery: logo designs for our school line three walls. Circles, squares, rectangles, triangles. Images of open books, open minds, microphones, megaphones, cyclones, and one crescendo. Each chair in the front two rows gets one of our custom-designed and custom-lettered posters. It should have taken Max and me all of three minutes to do this together, but I admit, I am dragging it out.

I think Max is, too. You couldn't more perfectly position each poster against the seat backs if you used a ruler.

"Thanks for understanding that I wanted to use one of Grammy's old posters," I tell him softly.

"I like seeing you happy," he says, then blushes.

Even though I swear I can practically see steam coming off his scorching-hot cheeks, Max does not look away. Not for a second. Not for two seconds. As it turns out, two seconds of wordless staring happens to be a long time.

*Make a move, Dessie Mei*, I tell myself firmly at the same time Max must be pumping himself up with a pep talk, too, because we both say, "What do you—" We blush, then laugh. Almost like we are twins.

*Or sixth-grade soulmates.*

Sixth-grade soulmates do run in my family, you know.

And who am I to turn my back on family tradition? So I continue, "What do you think about getting a bubble tea later?"

His mouth opens but not a single word comes out. Max Morrison, Mr. Smirk and Sprawl, can only nod. My smile widens. No one has ever told me what a rush it is to render a boy speechless.

So much for a power rush. The moment grows awkward, and we ignore each other again.

Thankfully, Ms. Lauchengco calls out, "Ten minutes to showtime, everyone."

I scan the cafeteria. Everything looks better than I had imagined. Even the bejeweled voting box in front, next to the stage. The stage. My stomach snaps back into a knotted pretzel. Why did I write my speech on notecards? What if my sweaty hands make the ink bleed?

Even worse, I don't see my parents anywhere.

Jacqueline's large family clusters around her. It's easy to tell they are family since Jacqueline is the perfect blend of her redheaded mom and fedora-hatted dad and her bow-tied grandfather. Norman's moms press kisses on top of his head as they ooh and aah over our logo. Max's mom is walking slowly by herself, visiting each logo in our art gallery like a long-lost friend. She stops in front of ours, so clearly a Max Morrison original.

With a nod to old-time records, our logo sits inside a circle, Max's idea. Norman had researched the most popular fonts from 1939, the same year Marian Anderson sang on the steps of the Lincoln Memorial. While we are no Donna, Jacqueline and I did our best to replicate the Ticket Booth font with its glam square-shaped letters to write our school name. And then Max—Max in his brilliance—dipped a piece of raw broccoli into ink the exact royal purple of our school color and drew two bowl-shaped swooshes as if Marian Anderson herself were singing our school name in a crescendo. As if she were belting out: Here we are.

Max's mom shakes her head in awe.

Just wait until she sees the posters.

Donna races over to her family as they edge into the cafeteria. They are one tight bubble, and I see why: Amah is here. The Lees surround her like she is a precious, endangered baby in their endangered orca pod. Like they are still afraid even though Amah's attacker is in jail. Even though our school cafeteria feels safe with friends and family and their encouraging compliments.

Finally, I spot Mom and Dad. I blink. Then blink again. Between them, like she is yet another daughter, is my oldest friend, Sophie.

"Dessie!" Sophie squeals.

Before I can squeal her name back, I swallow in disbelief. Behind my parents, dressed in an amethyst purple sweatsuit with a teal scarf and her rally-going sneakers is Grammy. She is not marching alone. The Twins bookend her, one on each side like stone lions on guard in front of a Chinese temple. With one hand, Grammy clutches Jacob's arm, and in her other, she holds a sign. It reads: Listen to Our Youth! Her arm falters as if the sign is too heavy. I rush to her, but Ben has already grabbed the sign before it can even graze the floor.

On the back: Make Your Mark!

*I am, everyone. I am.*

# Chapter 50

"We asked our sixth graders to envision a new school logo for our new school name," Mrs. Banerjee says from the stage.

I swear I hear Grammy cry out in a feeble voice, "Less talk, more action!"

Soon, it is my turn to speak. It feels like I am crossing two continents and an ocean to get from my seat to the podium. It is no easier when I stand onstage at the front of the cafeteria, sweating under my scarf. The crowd looks enormous. Expectant.

Will my words be enough to express everything in my heart? Will I sound rude?

My parents are beaming at me, Dad holding up his phone to take pictures of me as usual. Jacob and Ben are chanting my name: "Dess-ie! Dess-ie!" In between them, Grammy is waving her sign. So do the rest of the sixth graders, who have all grabbed their posters from their chairs.

Even Lucas. His face goes statue still when he sees that Max has drawn him as a superhero with his mouth wide open, blaring: *We want you.* On the back of his poster, I've added a tiny note: *You have a voice people listen to, you know.*

As it turns out, I do not need my index cards. I know these words that I have pored over with Jacqueline to make sure each is "precisely perfect." Words I have practiced over and over. And over.

Words that Mrs. Banerjee and Mr. Guevara and my class and mostly Donna have entrusted me to speak. I glance down at Donna, who is grinning at me. Donna who is wearing the exact same A2Z T-shirt as me without us planning it.

I step forward to the microphone.

"Marian Anderson had a beautiful voice. Some called it angelic. But the beauty of her voice is not why our school is named after her. We chose her for the bravery of her voice," I say.

Norman starts clapping. So does the Marian Anderson Middle School choir, surrounding him.

I pause, then continue, "Ballads, sea shanties, Mongolian throat singing, Gregorian chanting, fight songs, lullabies, the theme song in *The Eight Banners*, A2Z's every album"—people scream in the audience—"every kind of music requires more than a single note. They require many notes, harmonizing with each other. Isn't this just like our community? But recently, someone tried to shove one of the notes out of our community song. This is why we are speaking up and speaking out today against violence against our elders. Let's promise never to go off-tune with hate."

A tall man with silver hair standing in the back of the

cafeteria makes an impatient sound that echoes in the room. He is shaking his head like he disagrees with every one of my words. Shaking his head at me like I am a terrible, mean girl who does not know what I am talking about.

Who does not have the right to speak.

"I don't mean to be rude," this grown man says, as he interrupts my speech. There is a shocked rustle in the cafeteria, and I see Lucas sinking down in his seat, sinking like he wants to seep deep into the earth and never be found. The silver-haired man stands and spreads his arms wide like he is an expanding storm cloud in a sweatshirt with our school's old name, SHERIDAN. He continues, "But aren't we here to hear about the logo for a new name that we didn't need in the first place, not get a lesson on racism?" Then he laughs, not a friendly boisterous laugh like Dad's. It is a counterfeit boisterous laugh that mocks me while pretending to be innocent.

Mocks me while whittling me down to a tiny rabbit, too scared to make a sound.

Too bad for Lucas's dad that I am not, and will never be, a quivering rabbit.

"We are here to talk about our community," I correct him calmly, because I am busy working a promise to myself: I will be unafraid to be who I am.

Who I am is: a girl with my mother's courage to stand up for the ones I love and my father's sensitivity about other people's feelings and my brothers' protectiveness. A girl who carries my Grammy's clear sense of justice and my sister's steadfast belief in me. A girl who loves her friends.

Here, on this stage and in the forever home of my own heart, I stand, wholly and unapologetically me.

This time, I know I hear Grammy because she roars, "Let her speak!"

Ben and Jacob leap to their feet and shout as one, "Let her speak!"

People begin applauding. My class waves their posters overhead: Come Together in Peace. Choose Kindness. Hate Has No Place. Images of vibrant rainbows and bold red hearts. Black hands clenched in fists and Chinese zodiac rabbits. Dad is right. If you listen hard enough, you can hear music in almost everything. Like this crescendo of support and respect washing over me.

So I speak.

I speak about what it means to be a community: It means we are welcoming of everyone. It means we are stronger when we are united.

I speak even when the silver-haired man makes an exasperated expression and waves dismissively before settling heavily on his chair, scowling. I ignore the way his arms are crossed over his muscular chest, and I continue speaking because just as he is part of our community, so am I.

I speak because I finally understand that I have spent way too much time trying to get Grammy to remember what she's forgotten and not enough time creating new memories with her. Like this one. Even if Grammy won't remember today, I will carry this memory forward for the two of us.

When I finish, I hand off the mic to Jacqueline, but Lucas—

Lucas!—grabs the mic from her like he wants to silence every other speaker and to steal this moment and to stomp on its significance.

His dad nods proudly.

I am about to take that mic back when Lucas parts his lips. It is as if an angel has descended into the cafeteria of Marian Anderson Middle School: "*My country 'tis of thee.*"

Lucas McMorrow can sing. Beautifully. Even if his first notes wobble.

Norman stands up and harmonizes with Lucas. "*Sweet land of liberty.*"

Akshaya adds her powerful voice. "*Of thee I sing.*"

The rest of the award-winning choir of Marian Anderson Middle School—even the eighth graders—stand up and finish the song with Lucas. "*Let freedom ring!*"

In this musical landscape that sings of hope, I have to believe that Marian Anderson would have been proud. I know I am, especially when Lucas mutters with his eyes cast down at his feet, "I like a community with different people because that's what my mom would have liked, too."

Jacqueline rejoins Lucas on the stage and says decisively, "I know for sure that my great-great-grandfather did not fight for freedom in World War II just so elderly ladies would get assaulted in broad daylight in our city. He would have rejected that notion as utterly repugnant."

*Repugnant.* Jacqueline chose the perfect multisyllabic word.

We all end up speaking, sharing our logos, explaining what it means to stand for community.

Every one of us speaks, including Donna, who is the last to take center stage. She looks at me in my seat below and I know that look: it is a silent plea to stand beside her.

So I do.

And I bring my poster with me: the one I recovered from the storage closet. Grammy's poster from a long-ago march: Make Some Noise and Get into Good Trouble. In a strong voice with me at her side, Donna declares, "All of us should feel safe in our community. Newcomer and old-timer. Visitor and voter. Every. Single. One. Of. Us." Donna tells the audience about what happened to "our" grandmother, pointing at herself and then me.

*Our* grandmother.

That one powerful, perfect-pitch word rings inside me, and my universe expands. My family is birth family, adopted family, chosen family. School community. Asian American community. And, yes, favorite band community.

# Chapter 51

As Mrs. Banerjee predicted, not everyone is happy with the school rally. Alarmed, I watch as Lucas is being shoved outside by his dad. As if Lucas senses my concern, he glances back at me and nods: *Don't worry.* I don't wave at him or give him a thumbs-up. I do something much better: a signature A2Z dance move, the back run with a leg kick. *We want you.*

Lucas gives me a ghost of a smile-smirk, which only goes to show that the A2Z community really is boundary breaking.

From behind me, I hear a familiar voice. A much-missed voice: "Dessie!"

I spin around and close the distance between me and my best friend so fast, I must have set a world record in race-walking. "Sophie, I can't believe you came!"

"Of course I came," Sophie says, adjusting her pink shirt with puffed sleeves. "'Nothing but death can part us two.'"

"Excuse me," says Jacqueline, spinning around to us even though her mom was in midsentence. Her breath comes out fast. "Did you just quote from *Anne of Green Gables*?" Her hand rests on her chest. "Are you wearing Anne of Green Gables puffed sleeves?"

"Yes and yes," says Sophie, shimmying her shoulders to show off those sleeves. "I made this."

Jacqueline looks like she's going to faint. Or ask for Sophie's autograph. "You did?"

"Wait, you know Anne of Green Gables?" I ask Sophie, astonished. "How did I not know this?"

Sophie shrugs and quotes, "'There's such a lot of different Annes in me.'"

Jacqueline continues, "'I sometimes think that is why I'm such a troublesome person.'"

Both of them blink at each other, astonished.

Well, what do you know? I am the Cupid of kindred spirits. Yet. For one very long and one very uncomfortable moment, I feel a sharp, stabby poke of fear. All I want to do is clench Sophie and claim her as mine. To beg her: don't leave me. Poor Sophie—this must have been how she felt when I found Donna. And Akshaya when Donna found me. And Mom, Mom who must have been so, so afraid when I didn't just find Donna but found Donna's family, too. Yet if my heart could expand to hold Donna and her entire family and every one of the Anderson Five—including Max, and maybe even Lucas!—then maybe, just maybe, everyone's heart can also expand. So I introduce them, my two favorite Anne of Green Gables superfans.

Sophie admits, "I hate to say it, but I always kind of thought I was more like Anne's best friend."

"And I always thought I was more like Anne with an E!" Jacqueline says.

Sophie waves an extravagant flourish at Jacqueline. "That makes you Jacquie with a Q."

Jacqueline beams back at Sophie right as her mom tells her they need to go.

Just as Jacqueline is leaving, I call out to her, "Jacquie, you were incredible."

Jacqueline's mom says, "Her name is—"

My friend of the multisyllabic words interrupts and simply says, "I like Jacquie."

"You know your grandfather despises that nickname. It sounds like a boy," her mom protests.

Jacquie shrugs. "Oh well." She holds her mom's gaze until her mother says, "Jacquie, you are a very hyperarticulate changemaker. My heart reverberates with pride."

*Hyperarticulate changemaker.* I like that. And I like the Muir family tradition of using big words, the bigger, the better.

This is a magnificent new family tradition that I can adopt alongside my own family tradition of marching and rallying. Baking and eating. And creating, so much creating: music, tapestries, and community. My own heart reverberates with possibilities.

Above the noise of the crowd, Grammy cries, "This is the best march I've been in."

I can't help but grin at Grammy as she, my parents, and The Twins make their way to me because even though

I've maybe taken all of twenty steps from my chair to the podium, this is the best march I've been in, too. I tell her so.

Grammy beams at me and hefts her sign like she is still marching.

Mom says, "We are so proud of you."

"We're always proud of you, but today, today . . ." Dad's hands raise to his head and his fingers make an explosion gesture.

Ben and Jacob copy him, adding loud sound effects. Which becomes a competition of who can make louder explosions. Until Mom death-glares at them.

Dad continues, "I knew I was right when I imagined you at this very age when I composed *The Eight Banners*."

"Wait, Dessie was the muse for the theme song?" Max asks, astonished and not one bit embarrassed that he was unashamedly eavesdropping. And not one bit intimidated that The Twins are staring him down. I see Ben nudging Jacob: *Is this the bully?* And Jacob waggling his eyebrows: *Nah! It's her boyfriend.*

Thankfully, Dad interrupts their silent but not-so-secret conversation to promise, "Dessie will be the muse again for the next version of the game."

The way Dad's eyes look off dreamily into the distance as he listens to the patter of rain on the cafeteria roof, the chatter of parents, the chiming of the bell to announce that this event has ended, I know exactly what Dad is doing.

He is working his promise even now, composing this new theme song in his head.

I am so glad to be with my family—even fractured as it is—that I don't notice until now that the Lees are sweeping toward us.

And Amah is glowering at me.

# Chapter 52

*Amah, this was all my idea.* I want to confess so Donna doesn't get in trouble. But my throat chokes at the title and name, Amah. She is not my birth family Amah or adopted family Amah. She is Donna's amah, not mine.

Unlike me, Amah is not at a loss for words. Her eyebrows furrow even more as she jabs a finger arrowlike at me. She announces in a loud voice that could have made every leaf on every tree in Seattle tremble: "You will be president one day."

I laugh at those ludicrous but well-meant words, then shake my head. "Amah, I wasn't born here."

Amah tsks impatiently at me, the same way I have heard her tsk at Auntie Susie and Donna. She tsks again and says, "Then you will be governor."

"Or senator. Maybe Speaker of the House," chimes Grammy, waving her poster.

"Yes, those are almost the same," says Amah, exchanging a conspiring look with Grammy like they have just designated themselves as my campaign managers.

But those positions are not almost the same. They are very different.

It is uncomfortably sad knowing there's at least one dream that will never be mine simply because of where I was born.

All the same, this is a wonderful compliment to receive: Amah believes in me as much as Grammy does.

I say, "Donna can be governor one day, too."

"No," says Donna softly. She straightens her shoulders and announces in a firm voice that rivals Mom's when a decision has been made, "I want to be a calligrapher by day and dancer by night."

Amah laughs and says the very thing that makes both me and Donna go incandescent: "You two can be anything."

*Anything.* That word spurs Donna into action. She holds Amah's hands gently in her own.

"Amah, I want to learn what it means to be both Taiwanese and Chinese," Donna says, gazing at her grandmother.

My sister holds her breath; I hold mine. Finally, Amah nods slowly. Then her nods pick up speed, and her eyes brighten. "Okay, we'll watch Chinese soap operas together."

It is not exactly the answer that Donna wants, but it is a start. A good start. Donna pirouettes once, twice, a dance of joy. "Nature," she whispers to me when she stops twirling.

"Nurture," I whisper back.

"Both," we say together.

"You guys are so weird," says Lewis, like a classic little brother.

"Definitely weird," echo The Twins, like classic big brothers.

Then I remember my manners. In the Taiwanese I have practiced for the last two nights, I ask Amah, atrocious accent and all, "Ja ban bae?" Have you eaten rice yet?

"Guai-guai." Amah beams at me like I have just won an election plus a Nobel prize.

She takes my hand in her much smaller one that looks so much like Grammy's and whispers to me, "I like the race car game. It's helping me drive faster. We'll go driving soon, okay?" Then Amah pats the back of my hand gently.

Like I am hers, too.

Later, after everyone has straggled out of the cafeteria, after the chairs have been carefully stacked and stored, all that remains are the school logos. The community voted. As it turns out, they chose Max's design and Donna's font. I cannot wait to see what Max's mom does to combine those into the official, professional design that we will use for years and years and years.

Footsteps tap behind me, and I spin around to find Mr. Guevara looking tired but euphoric. "Dessie," he cries, "just the person I wanted to see. You did an epic job today." He stands beside me, both of us facing all the logos. He is quiet for a moment before he says, "On my parents' apple orchard, do you know why we grafted trees together?"

I shake my head, wondering why my teacher is about to give me a lecture on grafting.

"Grafting doesn't just make the tree stronger, it makes the roots and fruit better." Mr. Guevara nods at me before busying himself with putting away a straggler of a chair.

*Stronger*, I repeat.

*Better*, I promise myself.

# Chapter 53

Convincing our parents to allow us to go to the A2Z concert may not have been the smartest idea Donna and I have ever had in our twelve years on this planet Earth. Not only did A2Z upgrade our tickets, but they sent us two extra ones to the sold-out concert.

Our fathers insisted on chaperoning us.

Now they are "dancing." For a man who makes his living composing music, Dad has no sense of rhythm. Uncle Carl, I hate to say, is not much better. Everybody around us is snicker-snorting at these two grown men twisting and twitching in their matching Marian Anderson Middle School Parent Club T-shirts featuring our brand-new logo. It is beautiful, the crescendo of our school name. A reminder to make some noise. The dads have taken that to heart: they are barking out an unidentifiable tune.

"Wait, are they singing 'I Like Alike'?" Donna asks me, dismayed.

"I think so?" I answer, averting my eyes from our dads. "Aiya," I say, horrified, in Mandarin to Donna.

Donna adds, equally horrified, in Taiwanese, "Aiyo."

We could be watching one of the hair-raising, nightmare-inducing Chinese horror movies we've just discovered. Make it stop. Our eyes and ears are bleeding.

Still: mortification by father is a small price to pay to be at the Concert of All Concerts.

The arena lights go dark. But the stadium glows with pinpoints of light from thousands of upraised phones. A rainbow of laser beams sweeps across the dome, spans the audience, then settles on the stage. Notes burst all around us like sonic fireworks.

Donna grabs me; I grab Donna. We scream and jump. And scream and jump some more.

I think our fathers do, too, but I cannot bear to check on them.

More than that, I cannot believe that I am here. That we are here together, the two of us in our own matching T-shirts care of one Max Morrison(!). Max has silkscreened two mooncakes stamped with chrysanthemums, the flowers of forever and always. Surrounding these mooncakes are the words in the Dessie Mei sister font: *We are the Love-Lees!*

It is the perfect logo and nickname for sister-twins.

That Max.

My eyes spring with tears, and without looking at Donna, I know hers have, too.

*Verklempt*, I can hear Jacqueline whisper in my head.

When you are swept away with emotion.

We are swaying to the music, all of us in this stadium. Me, Donna, our rhythmless fathers. All the A2Z-ers gathered right here, right now, to share this moment.

The first notes of the newly re-recorded A2Z song hits our eardrums, then fade before the song starts. The arena thrums with anticipation. Confusion. Why did the band stop when they only got started?

The lead singer peers into the large stadium like he is seeking someone.

Not someone. But two somebodies.

He points to us in our upgraded seats in the balcony and says, "This next song is for two special girls here and their speed-racing grandmother."

I spin toward Donna just as she spins toward me. Both of us are stunned.

"No way!" Donna screams.

*Yes*, my heart screams back. *Yes way!*

We, the lost twins, have found our way back to each other.

*Verklempt* doesn't even cover how I am feeling here, screaming next to my sister. Our fathers sheltering us with their presence, our mothers plotting a summer trip at a nearby restaurant, our grandmothers having tea together at home. Us surrounded by thousands of fans, all of us belting out every single word to this song. Singing out the new lyrics, words changed because of one voice.

I raise mine now.

Because I belong.

Which is a good thing, because I, the vexatious Dessie Mei Breedlove, am here to stay.

Forever and always, I am at home in this beautiful and confusing and mysterious world. I clasp Donna's hand in mine and feel the most precious squeeze of hers. I return it. I have so much love to give. And so, so much love to receive.

And that—that is a promise worth working.

# Author's Note

Dearest Readers,

What most people don't know is that I am also a story-teller for leaders. Over the past fifteen years, I've helped Team Xbox tell the story about gaming's highest purpose: to create a community of belonging. This mission speaks to me. As a little girl, I never felt like I truly belonged—not at school, not on the playground, and not at home. (Thank goodness for libraries, where I've always felt safe and welcome.) Over this same period, I have watched the rise in hate crimes with horror because belonging is our primal longing, and violence is the ugliest way of othering.

Today's tension between belonging and othering became deeply personal to me. A decade after an unexpected divorce, I found second-chance love. Not just with my beloved new husband, but with two bonus children, my stepdaughters, who were both adopted from China into a white family. My stepdaughters who look like they were born belonging to my family, the Chens.

Creating a blended family is an exercise in creating community, one with delights and challenges. It's like merging two different countries, each with its own traditions, ways of being together, and values. Now layer on sharing the very food, languages, and customs that my bonus girls might have experienced in a different life—and there's an entirely different set of exquisite delights and unique challenges.

This intersection of securely attaching to each other and an evolving cultural identity came at a time when that very Asian American identity could imperil my bonus daughters. Yes, imperil them. I worried as I beheld my beautiful and brave stepdaughters: How are they—and other young Asian Americans—going to claim their identity amid rising anti-Asian sentiment?

My sense of urgency to answer this question grew to such a pitch, I did what I have always done: I learned from smarter people. I consulted experts in transnational and transracial adoption. Experts in community building and blended families; attachment theory and abandonment wounds; forgiveness and intergroup contact theory. I reread the research on belonging and dove deep into othering. I consumed books about adoptee journeys and mothering adoptees. I found mentors for stepmothering adoptees. Importantly, I found a guide in our matchmaker—Shari Leid, the mutual friend who introduced me to the love of my life. Shari was adopted from Korea, and then herself adopted a daughter from China. Mother and daughter with two distinct experiences as adoptees and a mutual desire to belong to the Asian American community that didn't always feel entirely welcoming.

That—that not feeling a belonging in our Asian American community—was a knife in my heart. I am convinced that we can be the healing second-chance love our world desperately needs. How? We meet this moment with our whole selves. We do the countercultural: we welcome each other. So I did what I always do when my heart grows furious: I wrote. What burst out of me is this love letter for my stepdaughters and all young people who are discovering their roots and their heritage, yes. But also their voices.

My hope is that *With Twice the Love, Dessie Mei* can in some small way illuminate the vastness of love, community, and belonging. That it does so through these two irrepressible sister-twins with wildly different adoption journeys who learn what it means to be Asian American at the same time they experience their first crisis as Asian Americans. They learn everything you can overcome when you are able to accept the assurance of love.

I hope that every word resonates deep in your soul: you belong.

You. Belong.

All of you.

As ever, thank you for being the ambassadors of books, these bridges of belonging from author to reader. Thank you for reading my work. And thank you for welcoming me whenever we meet.

♡ Justin Chen

# Resources and Further Reading

## SOME REFERENCE BOOKS ON ACTIVISM

### YOUNG READERS

*When Marian Sang: The True Recital of Marian Anderson* by Pam Muñoz Ryan (New York: Scholastic Press, 2002)

### YOUNG ADULTS

*From a Whisper to a Rallying Cry: The Killing of Vincent Chin and the Trial that Galvanized the Asian American Movement* by Paula Yoo (New York: Norton Young Readers, 2021)

*March: Book One* by John Lewis and Andrew Aydin (Marietta, GA: Top Shelf Production, 2013)

## ADULTS

*Keep Marching: How Every Woman Can Take Action and Change Our World* by Kristin Rowe-Finkbeiner (New York: Legacy Lit, 2018)

# ADDITIONAL RESOURCES FOR AND ABOUT ADOPTEES

## CHILDREN

*I Can Make This Promise* by Christine Day (New York: Heartdrum, 2020)

*Wish* by Barbara O'Connor (New York: Square Fish, 2017)

## YOUNG ADULTS

*Welcome Home: An Anthology on Love and Adoption* edited by Eric Smith (New York: Flux, 2017)

*When We Become Ours: A YA Adoptee Anthology* edited by Shannon Gibney and Nicole Chung (New York: HarperTeen, 2023)

China's Children International, an organization founded by Chinese adoptees for Chinese adoptees

Also Known As, an organization for international adoptees

# ADULTS

*All You Can Ever Know* by Nicole Chung (New York: Catapult, 2019)

*Growing Up Asian American in Young Adult Fiction* edited by Ymitri Mathison (Jackson, MS: University Press of Mississippi, 2019)

*Parenting in the Eye of the Storm: The Adoptive Parent's Guide to Navigating the Teen Years* by Katie Naftzger (Philadelphia, PA: Jessica Kingsley Publishers, 2017)

*The Primal Wound: Understanding the Adopted Child* by Nancy Newton Verrier (Murphys, CA: Gateway Press, 2003)

*Searching for Mom: A Memoir* by Sara Easterly with Linda Easterly (Heart Voices, 2019)

# Acknowledgments

**D**ecades ago, when I didn't feel like I belonged anywhere, ten-year-old me promised myself that one day I would write a book. A middle grade book about belonging everywhere. Finally, here we are—thanks to my community, who helped me work my long-held promise and who made me feel like I, too, belong:

Steven Malk, my forever agent who has cheered me on for nearly twenty years, always insisting that I tell my story, wherever it leads us. Julia Johnson, who picked up Dessie Mei, wanted to time-machine it back to her younger self, and championed this book from page one. Christine Collins, my authenticity reader, who pored over each and every sentence and scene with insight and sensitivity. And Mabel Hsu, whose brilliant story sense and incisive editing leaves me marveling at the vastness of her heart and brain. Few writers are as blessed as I am with this quartet of support.

Much gratitude to the HarperCollins team: Jon D. Howard, Gweneth Morton, Meghan Pettit, Allison Brown, Emily

Mannon, Robby Imfeld, Patty Rosati, Mimi Rankin, Christina Carpino, and Josie Dallam. Copy editor Jill Amack and proofreader Monique Vescia, you are pure wow (try correcting that). Special thanks to designers Kathy H. Lam and Celeste Knudsen, and cover artist Cornelia Li for creating such an exquisite reading experience.

Every teacher, librarian, bookseller, podcaster, reviewer, book clubber, conference coordinator, and reader who has ever reached out to me, shared my books, and invited me to speak: Please know it is an honor to be on your bookshelf. Your emails and posts shore up my soul.

A special shout-out goes to Julie Abe and Jessica Huang, who graciously invited me to write a middle grade short story when I had never written for middle grade or a short story. This book exists because of them. Also a million thanks to Shari Leid, my friend and Cupid, who introduced me to my husband and encouraged me to write this story for her younger self and her daughter, both adoptees. Her blessing upon this story has pillowed every word.

My writing community, who teach me about generosity of word and spirit: The Hi-Yah Sisterhood of Janet Wong and Grace Lin. My life-changing mentor: Meg Lippert. My forever and always touchstones: Janet Lee Carey and Lorie Ann Grover. The Masterminds who cheered on every word on these pages: Bruce Hale, Martha Brockenbrough, Lilliam Rivera, and Tammi Sauer. My three longtime writer-friends who said YES, try middle grade: Debbi Michiko Florence,

Lisa Yee, and Anjali Banerjee. And Paula Yoo, who dropped everything to take my call.

All the friends from every stage in my life, whose love and loyalty reverberate in these pages: Deb Cragen-Larsen, Julie Johnson, Kelly Sheiner, Molly Goudy, Margaret Williams, Melissa Waggener Zorkin, Susan Sullivan (whose Max will live forever in our hearts), and Sayuri "Si" Oyama. (Si, my Donna, you are so deeply missed.)

Generations of Team Xbox who have taught me about the absolute need to build community for belonging: Robbie Bach, Phil Spencer, Toni Philbrick, Catherine Gluckstein, Sarah Bond, Bonnie Ross, Matt Booty, Kenny Birge, David Hufford, Joslyn Main, Jessica Cook, Kari Perez, and so, so many more.

And my beloved family. If you loved Uncle Carl in this book, I wish you had known the real and irreplaceable Carl Lim in life. Sue, thank you for being a staunch supporter of every version of every story I've written. Mama and Baba, you are the best Amah and Agon in the world. My new family— Danny, Nancy, Shannon, Donna, and Aunt Cindy—thank you for snugging me into your fold. My greatest gratitude to Dan—you constantly redefine what it means to be a wonderful husband, life partner, coconspirator of adventures, and keeper of your word. Tyler and Sofia—our eleventh book together! And Alex, Zoe, and Nester—welcome to book one.